High Rise

The Complete Collection

HARPER BLISS

ladylit_ publishing

Also by Harper Bliss

Seasons of Love
Release the Stars
Once in a Lifetime
At the Water's Edge
French Kissing Season Three
French Kissing Season Two
French Kissing Season One

Copyright © 2013 Harper Bliss
Cover picture © Depositphotos / konradbak
Cover design by Caroline Manchoulas
Published by Ladylit Publishing – a division of Q.P.S. Projects Limited - Hong Kong

ISBN-13 978-988-12259–0-0

CONTENTS

FOOL FOR LOVE

MADDIE

"We have to stop doing this." Maddie tucked her blouse in her skirt and leaned against the door. She should have said it before allowing June into her office again—and in her panties. "It can't go anywhere. We both know that."

"Yeah." June avoided Maddie's eyes while she zipped up her pants. They'd had this conversation before, but it wasn't easy for Maddie to resist June, and the delicious molten copper of her skin, when they had to work side by side every day. "I know." Maddie realised June didn't take her seriously anymore when she said it.

"Would you consider transferring to another department?"

This caught June's attention. She fixed her black eyes on Maddie. "Really? You want to get rid of me?"

Maddie felt guilty already. She should never have let it come to this.

"Look, babe." She cursed herself for using the term of endearment she resorted to when approaching orgasm. And June had given her plenty of those. Usually against the closed door of Maddie's office. Their affair didn't have room for beds or sleep-overs, which was exactly what was wrong with it. "I'm not the one who's unavailable."

"You know how I feel about you." June inched closer. Too close. Maddie could smell her perfume and the musky scent of sex clinging to her skin. "Boss."

Maddie sighed and let June kiss her neck before pushing her away. "That's hardly the issue." She held June at arm's length. "When I go home tonight, it's to an empty apartment. And when I wake up tomorrow morning, it'll be in an empty bed. I can't do it anymore."

"So I should just up and move? I don't think so." June shook herself free from Maddie's hold and took a step back. "I'm not ruining my career over this."

This irked Maddie, but she restrained herself. "I'll make sure your new position is better than the one you have now." She took a deep breath. "How does Team Manager of Operations sound?"

"If you don't want to fuck me anymore, you're just going to have to work on your willpower." June pouted her lips and narrowed her eyes. "I didn't do this to get a promotion."

"I know." Maddie threw her hands up in despair. "But you must understand my point of view."

"I do." June's face softened. "And I'm sorry, but I can't just run off with you. We've discussed this and I was always very upfront about it." A sharp pang of jealousy coursed through Maddie's bones as June checked her watch. Hubby must be waiting. Maddie didn't understand how June could lie to herself, and everyone around her, like that. She was born in Australia, for heaven's sake. She didn't need to be so Chinese and repressed about it.

"Fine. Go home to Mark. Snuggle up to him closely tonight." Maddie stepped away from the door and opened it. "I hope you sleep well."

"It doesn't have to be like this." June smoothed out one last wrinkle from her blouse before positioning herself in front of Maddie. "It's not easy for me either." June's voice was soft and sultry. "Give me a little credit."

Maddie wanted to pull June close again and kiss her until day break. She also wanted to run away from this mess. She'd always believed she was smarter than this. What a joke.

"Good night." She pulled her face away from June—the time for meaningless displays of affection had passed. Her eyes followed June's tall, slender form as she walked away. Maddie wondered how long she'd be able to resist this time.

She retreated back into her office and dropped down into her leather chair with a big sigh. Maybe she should be the one to leave. This city wasn't really working out for her anyway. Swivelling around to enjoy the view sprawling out around the windows of her corner office, she reclined and let the city's evening glow surround her.

"Not that jaded yet," she whispered to herself. "This view still kills me." She'd stared into Hong Kong's illuminated skyline countless times while June delved her fingers into her depths. It added romance to the act.

Maddie reached for her phone and called the first number in her speed dial list. Isabella picked up after the second ring.

"Hey neighbour, please don't tell me you're still at work?"

"I've no choice if I ever want to make a bid on your penthouse."

"My time is for sale, but my home will never be. You know that." Isabella chuckled on the other end of the line. "But I do agree that you should become a bona fide home owner."

"Buying here feels too permanent. Anyway, I didn't call to get a lecture on my real estate status. I'm willing to give that body combat class a try tonight."

"At last, she relents. Rough day?"

"Hong Kong has beaten me to a pulp again, I need to fight back."

"Hong Kong or a certain resident of this decadent Special Administrative Region?" Isabella was the only person Maddie had confided in about June. She was a psychiatrist and her body language invited confessions like that.

"I ended it. Again."

"Body combat it is then. Meet me in the lobby at eight."

ALEX

Alex had energy to burn. She always had. Rita always said she was born with way too much of it. Then again, Rita had also looked her in the eyes and told her she loved her. She'd whispered it in her ear before they went to sleep and before she left for Mandarin class and started chatting up her teacher. Rita was a big fat liar.

Scanning the studio for newcomers, Alex shut down the road her thoughts were going. All the familiar faces were present. Her Wednesday evening class was always full. She'd give them a good workout. She'd taught five sessions today already, and still she felt as if she could go on for days. Maybe she didn't have a girlfriend anymore, but at least her lean muscle mass had increased after the break-up.

"Do we have anyone new today?" Two people raised their hands. An older Chinese man with an impressive moustache and a blond lady who'd come in with Isabella.

"Don't overdo it the first time. Let your body get used to the new movements. And don't lock your elbows when you punch." Alex nodded at the newbies and shot them an encouraging smile. "I'm Alex and I'm here to kick your butt." She grinned at the two dozen of people in front of her. "Let's do it."

She searched for the first track on her iPod and began the class with a taxing warm-up. People who attended body combat didn't come to mess around.

During the boxing round she locked eyes with the blond newcomer a few times, impressed with the intensity of her punches. Maybe she had as much frustration to burn as Alex. In all honesty, most people looked quite ridiculous when cleaving their fists through the air—always catching up to the beat, or racing way ahead—but the blonde had a certain elegance to her movements.

After class, she walked up to Isabella, a faithful regular, and her companion. They both had sweat running out of their hair, their faces sporting a healthy pink flush.

"Not bad for a first timer." Alex wiped her brow with a towel. "Will I be seeing you again?"

"I really needed that." The new woman had an Australian accent, just like Rita. "And yes, I might be persuaded." She smiled confidently at Alex.

"Excellent." Another convert always filled Alex with professional pride. "What's your name?"

"Madison, but everyone calls me Maddie."

"Maddie it is then." Alex noticed the peculiar colour of her eyes, not quite blue and not quite grey, but very distinct. "Let me know if you have any questions."

"Thanks." Maddie curled the corners of her mouth into a smirk. "I'm about ready to collapse."

"You've earned it." Alex shifted her attention to Isabella, whose shoulders stood out nicely in her tight lycra tank top. "You're in great shape, Isabella. Keep it up."

"All because of you." Isabella winked at her. She always messed with Alex's gaydar. Then again, most women in sweaty workout clothes did.

"Have a nice evening, ladies. I hope to see you again on Friday."

They both nodded enthusiastically. Alex shot them one last smile and headed out of the studio to make room for the next class. She was done for today. Back home, her new home, she had two more boxes to unpack, and then she'd be done with Rita too.

She'd moved out as soon as she'd found out about Rita's extracurricular activities with her teacher, crashing on Nat's couch the first night. The next day, Nat had made up the spare bed in what had fast become Alex's new room.

"Frankly, I don't need the rent but I could sure do with the company," Nat had said. "I hate living alone."

Without even looking for it, Alex had found a new place to live. In a building she'd never be able to afford on her own. With Nat no less, for whom she'd had a soft spot since meeting her three years ago. A small silver lining to a very dark cloud.

"Did you knock the wind out of them, roomie?" Nat asked as Alex entered the apartment.

"I'm sure some will have difficulty getting up in the morning." Nat sat at the wooden dining table in the silver glow of her flipped open laptop, surrounded by a stack of dishevelled papers. "Where were you, anyway?" Nat took most of Alex's classes, assuring her rock hard abs Alex had, admittedly, glanced at a few more times than strictly necessary among flatmates.

"The muse called… you know how it is." Nat sipped from a glass of whiskey flanking her computer.

Alex rolled her eyes. "We both know you hate the M-word and it's only Wednesday. Go easy on that stuff." She'd probably taken advantage of Alex's absence and brought a girl home for a few hours of no-strings-attached fun.

"Yes, mom." Nat leaned back in her chair and gave Alex her signature cocky smile. The one Alex was such a sucker for. "Did I miss any hotties?"

"No one you'd be interested in." Since her sudden break from Claire, Nat only went for younger women—plenty of them and never for longer than a fortnight. Alex sank down on the sofa and picked up the TV remote. "Has the great Nathalie Orange finished for the day? Can we finally watch *Snow White and the Huntsman*?"

"I told you not to wait for me for your drooling session over Charlize Theron. And you know I prefer my entertainment a bit more intellectually stimulating."

Alex propped her feet up onto the coffee table. "Fine. *Young Adult* it is then."

"You're an excellent negotiator, Pizza. I'll give you that." Nat closed the lid of her laptop and settled next to Alex. "I can live with that compromise."

Alex playfully nudged her in the ribs. "Don't call me that."

"Only if you give me control over the remote."

"Never." Alex dangled the remote in front of Nat's face. "You'll have me watch some pseudo-intellectual indie movie again where no one ever stops talking." She fixed her eyes on Nat's bright blue ones. "I still haven't forgiven you for *Synecdoche, New York*. Two hours of my life I'll never get back."

"May I respectfully remind you that you slept through more than an hour of that unrecognised masterpiece."

"You can hardly blame me for that." Alex used the remote to flick to the iTunes movie channel and sank down into the soft cushions of the couch until her shoulder comfortably rested against Nat's.

MADDIE

Maddie couldn't wait for her morning espresso as she stepped into the elevator at seven thirty. Her muscles ached from last night's workout, especially in the area around her shoulders, which felt as if it had taken a nasty beating. Good thing the instructor was cute, she thought as the elevator stopped on the forty-second floor.

"Morning," a cheerful voice Maddie vaguely recognised chirped. She looked up and stared straight into Alex's eyes.

"Hey." Maddie certainly hadn't expected to share her morning elevator ride with the sexy gym instructor. "What a surprise."

"A welcome one I hope." Alex beamed a broad smile and Maddie wondered how someone could look so fresh and energised at this ungodly hour of the day. "Not too sore today?"

"Yeah, about that…" Maddie shifted her weight to her

other foot. "Do you do massages?" The words just slipped out, surprising Maddie. She wasn't the flirting type anytime before noon.

"There's an idea." Alex stroked her chin pensively. "Break 'em and then fix 'em. A potential gold mine." She grinned at Maddie. "I just moved in so I may need some time to set up."

Maddie snickered at Alex's playful repartee. The elevator chimed twice, indicating they had reached the ground floor.

"Down the escalator I presume?" Maddie had a hard time peeling her gaze away from her companion's pronounced biceps as she held her backpack over her shoulder.

"Just like everyone else on this mountain." Alex exited the building with what seemed like a spring in her step. "But not without fuelling up on coffee first."

"That makes two of us."

They walked the short distance to the escalator in silence and slid down to the street below. Maddie perked up at the sight of her favourite coffee house. And the company she was keeping. Ever the numbers' person, she did wonder how much money gym instructors made to be able to afford rent on the forty-second floor of a prime real estate location like The Ivy.

Alex gallantly held the door of The Bean open for her, sparking the question if she might be of the same sexual persuasion. Maddie made a mental note to ask Isabella, who would surely know. She had a better eye for lesbians in this town. Maddie didn't have a clue, which was probably why she had ended up fumbling with a married woman behind closed doors for the past six months.

"Busy day ahead?" What was that accent? The sexy instructor definitely had Chinese blood running through her veins, but it was mixed with something darker and more exotic.

"Always." They shuffled forward in the line to place their order. "As good as married to the job."

"What do you do?" Alex's dark eyes locked with hers and Maddie felt something flutter in her belly.

"Ah, the most frequently asked question in this city."

Maddie held Alex's gaze. "I'm an investment banker at Crawford & Charles."

"Oh." Maddie couldn't help but notice the disappointment in Alex's eyes. She figured she'd probably heard the words investment and banker one too many times. Half of the expat population in Hong Kong practiced the same profession.

"I do sincerely apologise." Or maybe she was part of the Occupy Movement. Or a communist. Either way, if you lived in The Ivy you had to love money at least a little.

"May I take your order, please?" The girl behind the counter asked in broken English.

"A tall espresso and whatever this lady is having."

"A skinny mochaccino, please," Alex told the barista, then turned to Maddie. "Thanks. I owe you one. I gather I can find you here every morning?"

"Like clockwork." Maddie paid for the beverages and they padded over to the reception counter. She suddenly thought that, despite being the opposite of a morning person, she wouldn't be opposed to having a coffee with this tank topped beauty every morning.

Their drinks didn't take long to arrive and they left the shop together, joining the dozens of other escalator commuters down to Central.

"I swear to you, this is my only vice." Alex shot her a gloriously caffeinated smile. "I'm usually such a good girl." A little bit of froth clung to her upper lip and Maddie was convinced it would be the cutest thing she'd see today.

"Really? That's it?" Maddie raised her eyebrows. "No skeletons in your closet?" She mildly regretted her choice of words, but was curious to see the other woman's reaction.

"I'm half-Chinese and I came out at the tender age of eighteen. I've respectfully buried all the skeletons and the door to my closet is wide open."

In the two years Maddie had lived in Hong Kong she'd never heard a Chinese woman speak so candidly about her sexuality, without obvious qualms or hang-ups. Refreshing, she thought, as her interest in this new addition to her building heightened by the second.

"I was twenty-one, but I believe I'm a generation older than you."

"Don't be fooled by the smoothness of my skin. It's an Asian thing. I'm probably older than you." Alex winked at her. "This is my stop." They stepped onto the platform between two moving parts of escalator together. "See you tomorrow night for combat?"

Oh yeah, Maddie thought, but just nodded before Alex, along with her impressive shoulder line, was swallowed by the crowd. Maddie continued her journey to work with a surprisingly sunny disposition.

When she arrived at the office, her assistant Venus was already present, buzzing like a bee.

"Morning, Maddie." Venus was always around, lurking about, which was basically her job, but still, with Maddie's recent indiscretions she might know more than was good for her. "June called in sick."

The mention of June's name made Maddie stop dead in her tracks. "What do you mean sick? What does she have?" This was Hong Kong. You didn't call in sick unless you were almost dead—and even then it was frowned upon.

"She didn't give me any details."

"When will she be back?" Relief—the guilty kind—washed over Maddie at the prospect of at least not having to avoid June today.

"She said she'd call once she'd seen a doctor."

"All right. Keep me posted." It was too much of a coincidence for June's sick day to not have anything to do with last night's events. Maddie closed the door of her office and wondered if she should call her. Better not when she's at home, she concluded.

ALEX

"Is she blond? A bit uptight looking?" Nat asked. They munched on Thai salads, beef for Nat and pomelo for Alex.

"I wouldn't say uptight. She's a banker though." Alex couldn't help but scoff at the word. She'd slept with her own private banker for six years and was adamant not to repeat that mistake.

"I think I've seen her around with Isabella." Nat bunched her lips together in a pout. "I'd never pegged her as gay though, but you know what bankers are like. Poker face until they die."

Alex puffed out a disdainful snort. "You're preaching to the choir."

Nat dropped her chopsticks and patted Alex's hand. "It's not because Rita was such a bitch that they're all the same."

"I haven't made this assessment lightly, Orange. I've thought long and hard about this. I even suffered for it. And the evidence is glaring. They're all stone cold greedy bastards for whom nothing is ever enough—especially the women." Alex leaned back and held her arms wide. "Look at me. I work out thirty hours per week, if not more. I have a pleasant enough personality. Some people might even call me 'a catch'." Alex curled her fingers into quotation marks. "But not Miss Rita Lowe. Oh no. She had to go and have a bit on the side."

"Rita obviously lost her mind." Nat let her blue eyes glide over Alex's form. "You are a catch, and don't let anyone ever tell you differently." Alex wasn't especially gunning for the compliment, she was more joking—or rather, venting—when she'd said it, but it was a welcome balm to her bruised ego.

"And let's be honest here." Nat caught Alex's gaze. "Our neighbour does sound like your type."

"Nu-uh, I'm done with that type. I don't want another Rita."

"I'm not saying you have to marry her. You can simply have a bit of fun."

Alex sighed. She'd never see eye to eye on this with Nat, who was always pushing her to have more *fun*.

"So fundamentally different, but such good friends." Alex didn't feel like the twelve-hundredth quibble on this topic. She had three more classes to teach that afternoon, of which two back-to-back RPM sessions, and she needed to save her energy.

"If the need ever gets too big, I'm in the next room."

Alex got to her feet and mock-slapped Nat over the head. "You disgusting specimen of a woman." Not that Alex hadn't ever entertained the notion. Nat was certainly pretty, with her big blue eyes and unevenly cut black bangs, but she wouldn't ruin their friendship over a one-night-stand. And a relationship with someone like Nathalie Orange was out of the question.

"That's what friends are for." Nat grinned broadly at her. Alex did love her dearly. She had been the one to pick up the pieces of Alex's broken heart after she found out about Rita and her Mandarin teacher Peggy.

"What about Isabella?" Alex changed the subject. "I've had my suspicions about her."

"She's a tricky one to figure out. I've only had a few short chats with her at The Bean." Nat painted a pensive look on her face. She took matters of determining someone's sexuality extremely seriously. "And everyone in body combat looks gay." With her mouth drawn into a smirk, Nat locked eyes with Alex. "Especially you. You're a beast up there with your little microphone and bumbag. A completely different person than the one sitting in front of me now." She took a sip of her lime soda. "Don't get me wrong. I love your fitness dominatrix persona. And I'm sure I'm not the only one."

"Shut up." Alex dipped a finger into her glass of water and sprinkled some in Nat's direction. "Anyway, I'll have my revenge later. Pump or spin today?"

"I'm not sure I want to take a class with you when you're

in this kind of mood. I fear I may live to regret it." Nat bent over the small formica table. "You need to get some. Trust me, I know the signs," she whispered. "And you may not want to see it that way but, from where I'm sitting, Blondie looks like one hell of a prospect."

Usually, Alex found Nat's ceaseless innuendo amusing, but today it grated her nerves a little. Maybe because there was an inkling of truth to her statements. "Well," she stood up. "We can't all sit around and do nothing all day. I have to get back to work."

"I don't feel spoken to in the least." Without a care in the world, Nat folded one toned leg over the other and fixed her eyes on what looked to Alex like a sixteen-year-old girl who had just walked into the restaurant. "I do a lot of research for my next masterpiece in places like this."

"Good luck, Hemingway. See you in class later." Alex left some bills on the table to pay for her share of lunch and left the diner.

On her way back to the gym, she contemplated seeing Maddie the Banker again. Maybe if she shut off all her emotions—or if she had a lobotomy. Alex wasn't one to make the same mistake twice. The first time around had hurt too much for that. And, unlike her flatmate, she didn't have a problem with staying dry for months. She had other, more sane ways of draining the excess energy from her body. Hell, she used her body all day long. In bed, all she wanted was a good night's sleep—which, due to Rita's antics and the effect they had on Alex—was pretty hard to come by of late.

MADDIE

On Friday morning June was back at work, the pallid complexion of her skin contrasting with the big dark shadows under her eyes. Maddie's first reaction was concern. She figured June had called in sick the day before because of Maddie's umpteenth lousy attempt at a break-up. Now it appeared there really was something wrong with her and, apart from concern, Maddie had to deal with floods of compassion washing over her. She wanted to call June into her office, close the door, take her in her arms and tell her everything would be all right. Except, it wouldn't. It never would.

While squinting at a spreadsheet on her screen, her thoughts kept drifting to her sexy co-worker. Was it love? Maddie didn't have a clue, which was probably a clue in itself.

By eleven she couldn't take it anymore and punched in June's number.

"Hey," she whispered, even though she was hiding behind a closed door. "Could you come and see me for a second, please?"

"Is it business or pleasure?" June's voice sounded measured, her tone clipped, as if, this time, she'd really resigned herself to the fact that they were over.

"I…" Maddie hesitated. "I just need to know you're all right."

"I'm fine." June sighed into the receiver. "I have a lot to catch up on. Is there anything else?"

"No, not—"

"Good." With a cold click, June hung up.

Maddie massaged her temples. Two years in Hong Kong and only some heart break to show for.

Stretching her shoulder muscles, which were still slightly sore from Wednesday's brutal immersion into the world of group fitness classes, she wondered what she'd do this weekend. Probably come into work on Saturday to pick up the slack of the week. There was always slack to pick up. Always an excuse to not take a junk invitation or go hiking with Isabella. Then there was Sunday. How to get through that again?

On impulse, she picked up her phone once more and called Isabella.

"Let's do something this weekend."

"Is that an indecent proposal?"

Maddie chuckled into the receiver. She'd never really thought of Isabella that way. She might as well face it. Maddie had a serious penchant for Asian girls, which was probably the only reason she was still in Hong Kong. But she decided to play along. "It can be if you want it to be."

"Your blatant enthusiasm is really winning me over."

"Don't take it too personally, please."

"No worries. And leave it to me. I have two clients to see Saturday morning, then I'm free. Maybe you should take Monday off."

"Impossible."

"I thought so. See you tonight for another round of combat."

"Can't wait."

Maddie hung up and let her thoughts wander to Alex. She had hoped for an impromptu elevator encounter again this morning, but in a massive building like theirs you hardly ever rode the elevator with the same person twice.

She had the same smoky eyes as June, but her hair was much too wavy to be exclusively Chinese.

A beep from her private phone jerked her out of her reverie. A text message from June. *It's for the best we ended it. Trust me.*

One lunch and two more meetings and then the weekend awaited. She might even be frivolous and have a lie-in on Saturday.

* * *

Body combat hurt like hell. Clearly, Maddie's muscles hadn't recovered yet. If it weren't for Alex's encouraging smiles, she would have given up. She wondered how Alex did it. How many classes did she teach per day? Per week? And what must that body look like underneath that skimpy tank top?

"Left foot in front, please. Maddie?"

While dreaming of Alex's abs, Maddie had missed the

supporting leg switch. Alex nodded at her and, before shifting her focus to the group again, shot Maddie a quick wink. Maddie felt her cheeks flush but didn't know if it was because of the strenuous workout or the special attention from Alex.

"Hey, teacher's pet," Isabella teased, while reaching for her bottle of water. "Did I miss something?"

"Teach likes her," a voice whispered from behind. Stunned, Maddie turned around and stared straight into Nathalie Orange's face. As the week had progressed, the days had gotten stranger and stranger, culminating in a body combat class with one of her favourite writers. Maddie had seen her around the neighbourhood, but, as if victim to a teenage crush, hadn't had the nerve to address her. "She's my roommate, so I know." Nathalie grinned at Maddie. "Although she'll be the last to admit it, so don't press her on it."

"Enough talking, ladies," Alex yelled from the front, her voice so naturally authoritative in front of a group. "This class is not over yet." She clapped her hands. "Save the gossip for happy hour." Did she just wink at Maddie again? "Come on. Front stance. And keep that guard up."

Maddie had even more trouble keeping up now. The instructor lived with Nathalie Orange. Clearly they weren't an item. But still, she couldn't help but look at Alex with whole new eyes. And by god, the hotness level in that flat. And Hong Kong was already so warm and humid.

"Let's ask them for a drink." Isabella stood panting against the studio wall. Maddie had barely made it through class and had trouble catching her breath.

"What?" She rasped.

"It's common knowledge Nathalie Orange can't say no to a fine single malt and I happen to have a bottle of Cadenhead lying around."

Maddie slurped her water as if she hadn't had any fluids in days. For all her shrewd banker brain cells, she was stumped for words.

"I'm the boss of you this weekend. And we're all

neighbours. Why the hell not?" Isabella continued. "Hey, Nathalie."

In two strides, Isabella was by the writer's side. Quick enough for Maddie to wonder if she had ulterior motives of her own.

Nathalie looked up from her iPhone, which she appeared to be glued to. She probably had a hundred messages from admirers.

"Can I interest you and your flatmate in a Friday evening sampling of some of the world's finest Scotch?"

Nathalie's face brightened instantly, as if someone had said the magic word to her well-guarded kingdom.

"There's an offer I can't refuse. Penthouse right?"

"Correct. Let's say in an hour, and don't forget to bring your flatmate."

Alex was just approaching after showing an elderly lady the correct execution of the side kick a few times.

"Good to see you again, Maddie." She smiled with an energy Maddie had seldom, if ever, witnessed. "Good class, Isabella. Keep it up."

"These ladies have invited us for friendly neighbourly drinks. We can't possibly decline. Imagine the awkwardness in the elevator if we did," Nathalie chimed in.

Maddie scanned Alex's face. Her first, purely physical reaction seemed to be cautious, doubtful even.

"Sure, but I have a class tomorrow morning, so don't count on getting me tipsy." She jabbed Nat playfully in the bicep. "This one is a really bad influence."

Maddie was intrigued by the jesting interaction between the two friends.

"Wonderful. See you in a bit." Isabella said her goodbyes and Maddie sheepishly followed. She had trouble determining if it was because of meeting Nathalie Orange or because of Alex's intense bedroom eyes—and the two winks she had been the recipient of during class.

ALEX

Usually, Alex had the place to herself on a Friday night, resulting in a YouTube clip hopping frenzy of interviews with Charlize Theron—to whom Rita bore an uncanny resemblance. She could hardly pretend to have forgotten about Rita altogether, no matter how hard Nat was trying to push her into the arms of another woman. It had only been five weeks and two days.

"Why do I have to change, anyway? We're only going two floors up and I didn't know you were such a stickler for decorum." Alex asked Nat, who stood adjusting the collar of her shirt in the bathroom mirror.

"It's the penthouse, Alessandra. You can't go to the penthouse in sweat pants. It's not right."

"Well, excuse me, Miss Donatella Orange, but if I'm not welcome the way I am, I might as well stay in." Alex slanted against the door frame of the bathroom. "And don't call me Alessandra."

"Donatella is worse." Nat stuck her tongue out and her reflection in the mirror looked ridiculous enough to coax a smile out of Alex. Nat turned towards Alex, an unexpected kindness in her eyes. "It's just a drink. Nothing more. And no funny business on my part, I swear."

"Oh, all right." Alex was getting sick of sulking at home, anyway.

"Now put on those cheap H&M jeans. It shouldn't be said out loud, but your ass looks absurdly good in them." Nat took a step closer and put her hands on Alex's shoulders. "I know you've been hurt. Badly. But you're hot stuff, Pizza. And the world is a better place with your ass in those jeans in it." She quickly pecked Alex on the cheek. "And last I heard, looking good never hurt anyone."

"What am I supposed to say to that?" Alex fought the

urge to draw Nat in for a hug.

"Absolutely nothing. Come on, hurry up. I can taste that Scotch already." Nat combed two fingers through her bangs and straightened her posture.

"You're so easy to get, Orange."

"If only someone could keep me, though."

* * *

Isabella's penthouse was a lavish affair. She'd set up a table on the roof terrace that overlooked all the Mid-Levels buildings below, backdropped by the harbour and another batch of illuminated skyscrapers in Kowloon. Maddie had dressed down in jeans and a plain white t-shirt. Isabella probably didn't understand the concept and wore a loose-fitting but sumptuous purple and turquoise dress.

Maddie got up and kissed Alex and Nat on the cheek. She smelled of coconut soap and expensive banker's perfume.

"I can't handle hard liquor, so I brought this." She pointed at an ice bucket holding a bottle of Veuve Clicquot.

"Please, sit." Isabella gestured to two chairs facing the magnificent skyline. "Enjoy the view while I get the goods."

"I'm surprised you ladies are still standing," Alex tried to break the ice. "I must not have been hard enough on you." She sat down and the thousands of scattered lights in front of her made her blink twice.

"And I'm amazed you're still up and about. You must be exhausted after a week of teaching classes like that." Maddie fixed her greyish eyes on Alex. It was uncanny how much they reminded her of Rita's. Alex had to look away for a moment, before being able to face Maddie and the intensity in her eyes again.

"It's my job." Alex shrugged. "I'm used to it."

"We should go to the beach together some time," Nat said. "Then you'll be able to see Alex's body in full glory." Nat accompanied her statement with a wolf whistle. "I've done some research and I can safely say Alex has the best body in Hong Kong. Period."

Alex sighed. So much for Nat not embarrassing her. "Good grief, Orange. Inappropriate should be your middle name."

Nat smiled her trademark smile and Alex felt the budding anger seep out of her. "She also can't take a compliment. It's a funny combination."

Alex felt Maddie's eyes scan her torso. The feeling wasn't entirely unpleasant.

Isabella returned with the bottle of Scotch. That should keep Nat off her case for at least ten minutes.

"That looks like a bottle only a serious collector would have." Nat addressed Isabella. "Care to show me what else you've got?"

"I'd be delighted." Isabella nodded eagerly as Nat pushed herself out of her chair.

"Excuse us, ladies." Nat followed Isabella into the flat.

Alex couldn't believe how stupid she'd been. She'd walked straight into Nat's trap. She'd made her dress up. She'd plied her with a few false promises of not trying to set her up. And they'd barely arrived and already Alex found herself alone with Maddie, framed by one of the most romantic vistas in the world.

Alex gave Maddie an apologetic look.

"Some friends—" she started, at the same time as Maddie said something.

"Sorry, you first." Maddie smiled warmly at her. Her smile was completely different from Rita's. Much warmer, almost maternal. The smile of someone who'd take care of you forever.

"I wouldn't normally be so forward, but I think it's time you opened that bottle," Alex said. "If we have to wait for Nat to recover from admiring Isabella's liquor cabinet, we'll be here all night." She needed a drink. It only took one sip to take the edge off, anyway. She was a lightweight like that.

"My pleasure." Maddie rose from her chair and Alex couldn't help but notice how her jeans clung to her well-built hips.

"I know you're new to Shape, but you hardly look new to working out."

Maddie had just finished untangling the wire cage from the cork. She looked at Alex with a stunned but amused expression.

"I'm sorry," Alex rushed to say. "Noticing things like that comes with the job, I guess."

"Unlike what I've heard about you," Maddie said, "I'm perfectly able to take a compliment." There was that smile again.

Alex shyly reciprocated. What was she doing? Was she flirting now? And how did that work again?

MADDIE

While pouring two generous glasses of champagne, Maddie cast a glance through the full-length windows. Isabella and Nat appeared to be in the middle of a debate on a bottle Isabella held in her hands. She still couldn't believe Nathalie Orange was here, in Isabella's flat, on a regular Friday night. She'd brought a treat as well. Maddie wasn't stupid. Isabella and Nat seemed to have found a common goal all of a sudden. One Maddie could hardly disagree with. Alex was a real stunner and she could be just what Maddie needed to rebound from June.

Maddie sat back down and held out her glass for a toast. "To the weekend." She looked straight into Alex's dark eyes and a small tingle crept along her spine.

"Yours, anyway," Alex said before clinking the rim of her glass against Maddie's. "Not that I mind. I'm only teaching body balance tomorrow. Which, after twenty-five hours of mostly combat and spin, is a nice end to the week."

"I'm sorry. I wasn't thinking." Maddie brought her hand to her mouth. "But, truth be told, you can usually find me at the office on a Saturday morning as well."

"What about tomorrow?"

"Nope. I promised Isabella I'd be all hers this weekend."

"Oh." Was that a glimmer of disappointment in those bedroom eyes?

Maddie was quick to correct herself. "She's a good friend. And neighbour."

"Maddie has more exotic tastes." Isabella walked back onto the terrace, Nat hot on her heels. "She'd never go for the likes of me." Maddie hadn't seen them coming and was slightly disappointed her little tête-a-tête with Alex was ending already. She'd have to do something about getting Alex alone again soon.

"If the topic of conversation is about to migrate to yellow fever, we have another expert in the house." Alex pointed at Nat and dazzled Maddie with her quick wit. June would never say something like that.

"You know I'm very much for equal opportunities." Nat sank down in a chair opposite them, a tumbler of amber liquid in her hand. "But when in Rome…"

"Our writer friend here is doing all she can to sample as much of the local population as possible."

Maddie witnessed how Alex and Nat exchanged glances, increasing her suspicion that, at least at some point, something must have happened between them.

"Interesting." Maddie knew Isabella could never switch the analytical part of her brain off. "Why do you—" Suppressing a smile, Maddie could see the wheels inside Isabella's head turning.

"I'm in favour of free flowing conversation and a wide range of topics," Nat cut her off. "But, trust me, the state of my love life is not worth your time." Maddie was convinced Isabella would not pass on the challenge Nathalie Orange represented.

"My bad." Isabella brought a hand to her chest. "Once a shrink, always a shrink."

"About that," Nat focused her gaze on Isabella. "My new book has a character in it who's a psychiatrist. You'd make excellent research material."

"I'm honoured." Maddie could tell Isabella wasn't joking —and she completely understood. "Stop by any time."

"Should I make an appointment?" Nat sipped from her glass, but kept her eyes on Isabella.

"Depends." Isabella uncrossed her legs and bent over so her elbows rested on her knees, her face inches away from Nat's. "Does your soul need healing?"

Maybe Maddie had been too paranoid. Perhaps tonight wasn't about getting her and Alex better acquainted. Isabella seemed to have an agenda of her own.

"There's not enough money and time in the world to heal Orange's dysfunctional psyche. Her debut was based on a true story, you know," Alex said.

Maddie's awe spiked. Not just because of Alex's sharp tongue, but mostly because *My Family*, Nathalie's first novel that had won a slew of prizes when it was published seven years ago, was one of her favourite books.

"Alex is right." Nat kept her eyes glued to Isabella. "I may have some mommy issues." She slanted her upper body forward until her nose almost touched Isabella's. "Can you fix me, Doc?"

"I have time for an extra client tomorrow. Why don't you stop by around noon and find out?"

"I'm starting to feel like the third wheel." Alex turned to Maddie. "I hadn't seen this coming." She looked into her almost empty glass. "That must be some Scotch."

Maddie took that as her cue to pour them a refill. "I don't know about you, but this is the most fun I've had in ages." She looked Alex in the eyes. "Then again, my life has been lacking some excitement lately."

"Being a banker is not all it's cracked up to be?"

Maddie chuckled. "It's more my private life that's been a real mess."

"Same here." Before Alex looked away, Maddie could clearly spot the pain in her glance.

When Alex lifted her head back up, the sparkle in her eyes had returned. "Is Isabella even gay?" She whispered.

Maddie sighed. "It's complicated."

"It always is."

Concurring with a swift nod, Maddie leaned back and took a healthy gulp of champagne. Isabella and Nat continued their flirting match, but Maddie soon found herself losing interest—in favour of the pretty half-Chinese girl sitting next to her.

Alex and Maddie finished the bottle of Veuve Clicquot, while Nat opted for doubles every time Isabella topped up their glasses with more of her fine Scotch.

When Alex and Nat said their goodbyes an hour later, Maddie hugged Alex tighter than social elegance dictated and breathed in deeply to commit the fresh scent of her skin to memory.

"You may see me in one of your classes tomorrow," she whispered in Alex's ear before releasing her from her arms.

"If it keeps you out of the office." Something simmered in Alex's eyes when she said it. "I look forward to it."

ALEX

Alex woke up with a start and frantically searched for her alarm clock in the dark. Half a bottle of champagne and she wasn't herself in the morning. The red digits told her it was only five a.m. Plenty of time before her nine o'clock session. She turned on her belly and closed her eyes again. Ten seconds later she knew she wouldn't be able to fall asleep again, and if, by chance she did, she'd be too groggy to get up in time for work. She settled on her back and that's when she heard the noise.

Soft moans mingled with high-pitched giggles penetrated through the thin wall between her and Nat's room.

"For heaven's sake," she whispered in the darkness. "So bloody predictable."

It was hard to determine Isabella's exact age but Alex estimated it to be about twenty years above Nat's limit of interest. Despite flirting readily with the psychiatrist last night —as she did with everyone—Alex was certain it wasn't the regal penthouse inhabitant producing those yelps of pleasure in Nat's bed.

Spurred on by too much single malt, Nat had gone out after they arrived back at their flat, into the never-ending Hong Kong night. No doubt with the intention of bringing home one of many interchangeable Hello Kitty girls, and succeeding. The sounds on the other side of the wall were proof of that.

Alex sighed and shook her head. She actually hoped Nat would take Isabella up on her offer and book an appointment to discuss the state of her soul—and the bitterness in her heart driving her into the arms of these young, practically mute, but always admiring girls.

One day not long after she had moved in, Nat's helper had gotten some of Alex's laundry mixed up and she'd gone to look for her favourite white tank top in Nat's room. She hadn't snooped but she'd had to have been blind to not have noticed the big purple strap-on casually residing on Nat's pillow.

She'd laughed hard, picturing Nat wielding the enormous dildo in front of one of her tiny girls. Which is probably what she was doing now.

Alex shut her eyes and focused on the cries of ecstasy, more as an experiment, to see if they could excite her at all. She'd been starved of any kind of sexual affection long before her break-up with Rita, who'd obviously been getting it elsewhere.

The closest she came these days was with her vibrator. Short, almost mechanical orgasms, just to relieve the tension. The thought of it sparked something in her gut, a small desire for the tiny treat it represented. She might as well. It wasn't as if she'd still be able to sleep and moping around the flat while her roommate was getting off wasn't exactly an appealing prospect.

She reached for the bottom drawer of her night stand and dug the pastel pink toy out. It would only take a few minutes and the anticipation of the short but sweet relief made her a little giddy. While spreading her legs, she threw the sheets off, exposing her naked body to the conditioned air of her bedroom.

The advantage of using this particular aid was that it vibrated so vigorously it didn't require any mental stimulation. Otherwise, Alex's thoughts always, most inadvertently so, drifted to Rita. How Rita looked into her eyes as she parted her pussy lips with her fingers. Always, as if she owned her. That was Rita's thing in the bedroom—and Alex loved it.

Rita was the last person Alex wanted to think about. Rita and her power plays. Rita and her ability to always just hit the spot, whether spanking or fucking. When it came to Alex, Rita always knew what she was doing. Alex pushed any lingering thought of her ex as far back into her mind as possible. She'd shove her out if she could, but six years was a long time to forget about.

Instead, she cleared her head and let the mixture of giggles and groans coming from the other room wash over her. She brought the toy between her legs and just the soft buzzing of it was enough to make her clit throb. The plastic was cold against her pussy lips, which added to the sensation. She shut her eyes and concentrated on the vibrations pulsing through her clit and body. She knew that if she allowed her thoughts to wander, if she allowed herself to think of someone taking her—claiming her like Rita did—she'd come much harder. But that wasn't the point. This was her orgasm and Rita had nothing to do with it. If anything, this was the expulsion of Rita. The freeing of Alessandra Pozzato from her greedy shackles.

She wasn't far now. Alex felt some juice trickle out of her, down her buttocks. The vibrator was working its magic and her breathing intensified. Her pussy started clutching around nothing and, just before it happened, just before she came with a low whimper and a quick tremble, she imagined Maddie's face hovering above hers.

* * *

Alex ignored the twinge of disappointment sneaking through the back of her brain when Maddie didn't show up for her nine a.m. class. She wrestled her body through the different positions, making sure not to display any signs of fatigue to the group in front of her. One more session and she was done. She didn't teach on Sunday and Monday, but sometimes came in anyway to catch a colleague's class. A day without exercise was a day badly spent and it was important to experience a fitness class from the other side as well.

In between her two Saturday morning sessions, she flicked through a copy of Vogue—only purchased because of a spectacular cover shot of Charlize Theron's endless legs—at The Bean, keeping a watchful eye on the door. The way Maddie had hugged her goodbye last night didn't leave much room for misinterpretation. It was a lingering embrace expressing that first inkling of interest. If Maddie didn't show up for her next class, Alex would have to doubt her sincerity. After what Rita did to her, there weren't many qualities Alex valued more than sincerity.

While Alex stowed her belongings in her locker before her last session of the week, Maddie breezed into the dressing room—her presence sparking a prompt change in Alex, as if enough to squash her doubts. Without revealing she was there, Alex peeped at Maddie from around the corner as she changed into her workout clothes. She had good legs, long and toned, and—to Alex's experienced eye—revealing hours of personal training.

"Hey." Alex wasn't really the peeping type. "You made it."

Maddie pinned her eyes on Alex. The same burning glance Alex had seen in her fantasy that morning. "Of course."

MADDIE

After class, Maddie waited for Alex outside the studio. The mixture of yoga and tai chi had given her a peace of mind hard to come by of late. Alex stood surrounded by a group of enthusiastic local ladies ooh-ing and aah-ing at something she explained in Chinese. When Alex caught Maddie's glance through the glass door, she nodded and excused herself to her posse of admirers.

"That was truly wonderful." Without thinking, Maddie patted Alex's shoulder. "I haven't felt this relaxed in a long time."

"I aim to please." Alex shot her a wink. She really had to stop doing that. As innocent as the gesture was probably meant, it seemed to connect with some untouched spot in Maddie's soul. Oh, who was she kidding? She didn't use the word soul and the area she meant lay a tad further down south than where one would assume the soul to reside.

"I was wondering if you wanted to grab some lunch."

Alex raised her eye-brows. "Sure. How does organic pizza sound?"

"Cardboard-ish, but I'll give it a try."

"I hope you didn't just try to offend my taste in pizza. I am half-Italian, you know."

"I wouldn't dare." Maddie had guessed some Mediterranean blood flowed through Alex's veins.

"Good." They walked towards the changing room together. "Have you cleared this with your weekend boss?"

"I believe Isabella is keeping her lunch time schedule wide open for a certain unexpected client." Alex held the door for Maddie and shook her head.

"She shouldn't." They stopped at Maddie's locker. "When I left, Nat was still in bed with a massive hangover and a twenty-year-old girl."

"That must be quite the den of love on the forty-second floor." Maddie narrowed her eyes, ready to scan Alex's face for a reaction.

"Maybe on Nat's side of the hallway. Sometimes I think I'm only there to give the place a touch of wholesomeness." Alex sipped from her bottle of water and some drops ran down her chin. "What about the forty-third floor?"

Maddie looked around her. "Let's save that conversation for lunch."

"You'd better not leave me hanging." The drops of water trickled down Alex's neck, tracing a slow path to her collar bone. "I'm going to hit the steam cabin for five minutes. Care to join?"

Maddie had to swallow before she could answer. "Sure," she tried to say with as much nonchalance as she could muster.

They undressed and chastely wrapped towels around their bodies. Alex led the way to the steam cabin and Maddie simultaneously feared and hoped her new friend would keep the towel in its current position. Sitting down across from Maddie, Alex leaned her head against the wall and released the pressure of her hands from the towel. It split slightly, not wide enough to show anything, yet revealing enough to make Maddie gasp for air.

Alex's breasts and pubic area were covered, but Maddie's eyes had plenty to feast on. A hint of rock hard abdominal muscles for instance, and that strong shoulder line. Droplets of sweat streamed down Alex's pronounced biceps and, despite probably only sampling a fraction of what Nathalie Orange had, she had to agree with her. Alex must have the best body in Hong Kong.

Maddie's clit stood to attention and she had to close her eyes to calm her nerves. Not that it helped the tiniest bit. As soon as her eyelids fell shut, far more revealing images of Alex were projected on the back of them. Alex dropping the towel entirely. Alex beckoning her with just one glance. Maddie's lips on her collar bone, her tongue catching the descending drops of sweat. Her finger…

"Ready?" Alex towered over her. "I'm starving." Her towel clung to her body again.

Maddie quickly regained composure—or at least tried—and followed Alex to the shower area where she cooled herself off under cold water.

* * *

"How did you meet Nathalie?" All the way to the restaurant, squashed between the rush of tourists and shoppers crowding Central on a Saturday, Maddie had racked her brain for an innocent but interesting question to ask. This was the conversation starter she'd come up with.

"How do you think?" Alex crooked her lips into a lop-sided grin. "How does anyone on this island ever meet Nathalie?"

The question didn't appear to be so innocent after all. "I see." Maddie nodded. "She hit on you."

"She's gone for younger ever since." Alex took a bite of her pizza, unceremoniously squashing it between her fingers and discarding the provided cutlery. "And that was three years ago."

"Did you—" Maddie, who was never that much of a blusher, felt the heat rise to her cheeks. "—reciprocate?"

"The love between Nathalie and me has gone unconsummated so far." Maddie felt an irrational bout of jealousy stir inside of her at the casual mention of the word love. "I'm also very much a one-woman kind of girl and I was in a relationship when we met." Alex chuckled. "Nat and I would also make about the worst couple ever."

"I can kind of see why." Maddie tore her gaze away from Alex's tank top clad chest—did she ever wear anything else?—and focused on the food in front of her. Despite being used to more upscale eateries, she really enjoyed the pizza.

"So?" Alex slanted over the small table. They'd managed to score one in the corner of the roof terrace, away from the hum drum of the busy lunch service.

"So… what?"

"Earlier, you expertly derailed our conversation when it went into the direction of your bedroom." Alex put a good amount of emphasis on the *your* in that sentence.

"Mostly because there isn't that much to tell." Maddie felt her cheeks flush pink again. "I haven't had the best of luck with the ladies in Hong Kong." Her mind wandered to June, who was probably grocery shopping with Mark right now, or eating dim sum with her in-laws. "Made some wrong choices along the way." She couldn't help but notice a twinkle of amusement in Alex's eyes. "Suffice it to say the master bedroom in unit A on the forty-third floor has not seen a lot of action in the two years I've lived there."

"Maybe you prefer to play out games?" Alex wasn't letting up, and she clearly enjoyed this line of questioning. Maddie concluded it must be the Italian in her.

"If that's how you would categorise an illicit office romance, then yes. Out games are my forte." Maddie usually knew better than to spill her secrets to people she'd only just met. At least she thought she did.

"Really?" Alex's eyes grew wide. "I'm sorry, I didn't mean to pry." Judging by the flabbergasted look on her face, this was not the reply Alex had expected. Maddie could hardly blame her for that.

"And I didn't mean to shock you." Maddie sighed. "Anyway, it's over now. It had no future. She was never going to pick me."

ALEX

Disappointment rushed over Alex. Maddie was really starting

to grow on her, so much so that she was beginning to think she could overlook the fact she was a banker, but this, this was so much worse. She could never overlook cheating.

"She was with someone?" She leaned back in her chair, wanting to put physical distance between her and Maddie.

The thin lines bracketing Maddie's mouth deepened as she drew her lips into a pained pout. "Still is. Married to a man. A fight I can never win."

"How long did it go on for?" Alex might as well extract as much information as possible. She couldn't hide the disapproval on her face though. She never could.

"About six months, on and off. Look, we don't—"

"And she never told him?" The poor sod is just like me, she thought. Betrayed by banker bitches. Alex never used the b-word lightly, not even in her thoughts.

"You know what it's like for Chinese women. The pressure from the family is immense. I know you're out, but for most of them, it's just not an option."

"Oh, I know exactly what it's like. Just as I know exactly what it feels like to have someone you trust completely, someone you trust with your life, cheat on you."

Alex felt all the pent-up rage well up. Maybe Maddie didn't deserve an outburst like that, but, again, as far as she could tell, she was just like Rita. She appropriated things— people—that didn't belong to her. Alex could never see past that. She threw her napkin on the table and delved in her bag for some money.

"I'm sorry." She flung two hundred dollar bills on the table, which was surely too much but she didn't want to owe Maddie anything. "This was clearly a mistake."

She cast one more glance at Maddie's startled face and headed towards the stairs. She needed to be alone, away from someone like that. Tears stung her eyes as she exited the restaurant.

She'd allowed herself to entertain the notion of the two of them… the two of them what? As if she hadn't seen

Maddie gawk at her in the steam room. As if that hadn't been the reason Alex had invited her.

Instead of gliding up slowly on the escalator, Alex took the stairs to her building, eager to burn off her frustration. She hoped Nat's toy girl would have left. At least Nat was always honest about her intentions. She didn't pretend to be something she wasn't. She didn't make someone believe she loved them—for six full years—and then stab them in the heart.

As soon as Alex arrived home she sank down in the couch and cried. She cried for Rita. And for Maddie. For herself. She realised she was feeling mighty sorry for herself. But was honesty really so much to ask for?

"Hey," Nat came storming out of her office. "What happened?" She squatted next to Alex and placed her hands on Alex's trembling knees.

One look was enough to convey to Nat that she shouldn't ask too many questions. She'd know anyway. She made a living out of describing people's behaviour and she knew what people were like. If anyone, Nat would understand.

"They're all just a bunch of cold-hearted bitches. Cheating and betraying their way through life. It disgusts me, Nat. I can't help it, but I find it all so revolting."

Nat stood up and took a seat next to Alex. She put her arm around her shoulder and drew her towards her. "Come here." She patted Alex's hair. "I'm sorry for pushing you, Pizza. I know you better by now."

"It's hardly your fault," Alex sobbed. "I really liked her."

"Gosh, I would never have guessed." This was why Alex loved Nat so much. She was an expert at relieving tension with silly remarks. She was starting to feel a bit ridiculous, crying over a woman she barely knew. She'd spilled enough tears on Rita—she wasn't wasting any more on her.

"I can't believe I stormed out of there." Alex buried her face in her hands. "She must think I'm one of the crazy ones."

"Trust me. No one will ever accuse you of being crazy.

You are the most grounded, sane person I know. If only we all had a bit of Pozzato in us, the world would be better for it." Nat coaxed Alex's fingers away from her wet face. "Now, tell me what happened. I was just lacking some inspiration and there's nothing like a good dose of lesbian drama to get me going again."

Alex told Nat about the discovery of Maddie's flaws and her own—admittedly—somewhat disproportionate reaction to them. She collapsed back into the couch while uttering a big sigh.

"Wait here. Don't move." Nat walked to the liquor cabinet and poured a generous amount of Amaretto into a glass. She padded back and offered it to Alex. "Drink this."

Alex didn't protest. She brought the glass to her lips and let the sweet alcohol soothe her.

"I fully realise I often abuse it, but booze is not always bad for you." Nat plastered a crooked smirk on her face. "What do you say we get out of here for the rest of the weekend? I'll check with Henry if his place on Lantau is available. Just you and me, the beach, some books and some really bad movies."

"It's not because my taste in cinema is different from yours that it's necessarily bad." Alex threw a cushion in Nat's direction, intentionally only hitting the side of her arm.

"Let's agree to disagree on that one."

MADDIE

Maddie could hardly ignore June's existence. She was there, in the office, every day of every week, with her low-plunging necklines and well-shaped calves, and she looked good. She glowed. As if her body had suddenly decided to thrive after Maddie's last break-up with her three weeks ago.

For Maddie, on the other hand, those weeks had been the

loneliest in a long time. So lonely, in fact, she'd begun doing research on going back home. Back to Melbourne, where her sister lived with her two boys. Her parents. And Emma.

Maddie let the memory of Emma swamp her. Five years ago she'd been convinced of making the right choice: her career over love. Emma didn't want to relocate to Singapore with her. Fine. She'd go alone. Piece of cake. Yeah right.

Expat regret, Maddie called it, when she browsed the internet for job opportunities in Melbourne. For the first time ever, after a year in Singapore, two in Shanghai and two in Hong Kong, she realised she had sacrificed too much. It's not as if happiness was that easy to come by for anyone, and Maddie had made it especially hard on herself.

A great view over the harbour was not happiness. An after-hours fumble against her office door certainly wasn't happiness. Going home to an empty flat was most dreadful of all.

Perhaps it was Alex who'd made her face the truth about herself. Good-hearted, wholesome Alex who needed organic food and honesty. She'd felt it with Alex—that glimmer of instant attraction. That afterthought, after first meeting, that this could be more. That it had potential. And then it had just faded out before it even started.

A knock on the door yanked Maddie out of her pensive mood.

"Come." She straightened her posture.

June walked in and closed the door behind her. Maddie cast a quick glance at the wall clock. It was eight-thirty, well past regular office hours.

"Can I talk to you for a second?" June slanted her body against the door, like she'd done so many times before. What did she want? Was this the time for rekindling their affair? Maddie wasn't really in the mood for that.

"Sure." She gestured at a chair. "Please, have a seat."

June took a deep breath and strutted towards the desk. She sank down in one of the brown leather visitor chairs and crossed her legs.

"I thought you should hear it from me before word got out."

This peaked Maddie's interest. She leaned forward, planting her elbows on her desk.

June gazed at her hands in her lap. Why couldn't she look Maddie in the eye? She'd certainly never had a problem with that before.

"I'm listening." Maddie tried to keep her voice as soft as possible. "What is it, ba—" She corrected herself before she could fully say it.

"I'm pregnant."

Of all the things running through her brain, this was the last one Maddie had expected. She'd always, naively of course, assumed June and Mark didn't have a sexual relationship. That it was more a marriage of convenience. That June only fucked her. A life of misconceptions, Maddie thought, that's exactly what I'm living here.

"I suppose congratulations are in order." Maddie's voice broke a little. She couldn't help it. It wasn't so much that she'd lost June forever, she'd been half-way on the road to accepting that, it was more that she, at last, clearly saw all the mistakes she had made.

They spun in front of her eyes as if on display on a big wheel of fortune. Where would the wheel stop? At the bright pink 'left long-term girlfriend in Australia'? Or maybe at the scolding harsh yellow of 'only visited my nephews twice since they were born'? Or perhaps, more fitting for her current situation, at the devilish red of 'fucked straight married co-worker for six months, and not once in a good old bed'.

"I'm sorry I didn't tell you before. It was difficult for me." June sat there, an expression of defeat on her face—sad eyes, trembling bottom lip and, now that Maddie looked closer, a hint of black circles under her eyes.

Maddie could tell her domestic bliss might not be the thing June was searching for. That she wasn't heterosexual by a long shot. That the fact this kid was conceived while its mother was banging the boss were hard odds to start a life with, but it wasn't her battle to fight anymore. And she had plenty of her own.

"I understand. I wish you all the best." Gone was every trace of desire to slam June against the wall. To spread her legs and snake her fingers up along her thigh. This changed everything.

"I suppose there's not much more to say." June rose from her chair and Maddie could have sworn she saw a tear dangle from an eyelash. She started for the door, her head bent and a hand across her mouth.

"Hey. Wait." Maddie sprang up and raced around her desk. "Come here." She held out her arms for June, who turned around and greedily surrendered herself to them.

"You could leave him and we could raise the baby together," Maddie wanted to say, but it wasn't the right time for jokes like that, even though it might not have been that much of a joke. Instead, she patted June on the head while hugging her tightly.

"It'll be all right," Maddie whispered in her ex-lover's ear. "You're going to be a mother. How amazing is that?"

June lifted her head from Maddie's shoulder, her face blotched and her eyes puffy. "It's absolutely wonderful. But… this is the final curtain for us."

"I know, baby. I know." Maddie pulled June close again and embraced her for the last time.

ALEX

"I could do with a holiday." Alex stretched her arms over her head. The pain in her shoulder was still there. "My body is exhausted." Alex had been doubly busy, team-teaching classes with trainee instructors at a newly opened branch in Admiralty while learning choreographies of the latest releases herself.

"Stop doing everyone else's job." Nat slurped from her cappuccino. "And let them fill in for you for a change." Some froth clung to her nose. "You're too good for this world, Pizza. And definitely too good for this city."

"Could you tell that to my mother, please? Ever since Rita and I broke up, she thinks I'm doomed."

Nat shook her head. "For someone who puts so much stock in honesty, I find it extremely surprising you didn't tell her the truth about your lovely ex."

"She worshipped Rita. I couldn't do that to her."

"That's my point proven again." Nat slapped Alex playfully on the arm. "You're crazy. And your mom's old enough to handle the truth, no matter how vile."

Alex froze as she stared at the door. In walked Isabella with Maddie following in her tracks.

"It's just two ladies. Good-looking ladies at that. Hardly meriting that expression of utter shock on your face." Nat instantly waved them over.

"What are you doing?" Alex had time to flee. Maddie and Isabella were second in line to place their order. "I haven't seen her in weeks."

"Just because you had a little melt-down, doesn't mean you can't be friendly to your neighbour. Forget about that."

Nat was so easy about these things. Alex guessed that's what happened when you slept with another girl every week on an overcrowded island with too small a surface. She had no choice but to practice casualness. Alex wasn't really one for being casual though. And why would she be? She believed in taking things seriously.

The ladies approached their table and Nat was already pulling up extra chairs.

"What a sight for sore eyes on this dreary Saturday afternoon." She kissed them both on the cheek.

Alex exchanged a shy glance with Maddie. Ever since storming out of the pizza restaurant three weeks ago, she'd declined any offer of Nat to meet up with their neighbours. Apart from feeling mortified, she'd also doubted herself. She feared she couldn't trust herself around Maddie and the blue-grey stare of her eyes, which, most inappropriately, kept popping up in her fantasies.

"Hello stranger." Isabella addressed Alex. "Where the hell have you been? At a certain point, I believed you'd moved out of the building and quit your job."

"You know what The Ivy is like. You can go weeks without running into a familiar face." Alex had been lucky—if that was the right word—to not have bumped into Maddie for a few weeks, but she felt quite flustered to be in her company now.

Isabella nodded and took the chair next to Nat, leaving the one next to Alex free for Maddie.

"What about the gym?" Maddie turned to her, fixing those eyes on Alex. "That guy replacing you isn't half as fun to look at as you."

"I'll be back next week." The few of her regular classes Alex had taught, Maddie had not attended. "Still going strong then?"

"Can't you tell?" Maddie flexed her bicep. "I've even started doing weights."

Alex couldn't help but smile—and sneak a peek at Maddie's toned arm. "Impressive. Looks like you don't need me at all."

"Don't be fooled by these guns. I did some push-ups this morning and they're still pumped."

"That's even more impressive."

"Not half as much as what you've got going on." Alex remembered the five minutes they'd spent in the steam room a few weeks ago, and how she'd subtly flashed some abs at Maddie. She was also rather stunned to, off the bat, find herself in the middle of a flirty conversation with Maddie. As if her little scene had never happened. As if they'd sat opposite each other in that steam cabin only yesterday.

"I think I may owe you an apology." Alex leaned a little closer to Maddie. "For storming out so dramatically."

"You were upset. I get that." Maddie laid three fingers on Alex's arm. "You don't owe me anything." The smile she flashed Alex was glorious enough to make her forget about Rita altogether. It was about time for that anyway. A now-or-never feeling descended upon Alex. For some reason, this had turned into a significant moment. A sort of confirmation of that early attraction towards Maddie. The premonition that they could be more than friendly neighbours.

"Would you like…" Alex hesitated for a split second. The pain in her shoulder flared up, fatigue crushing both her body and her mind—and that guard she'd been keeping up for weeks. A layer of resistance peeled away, drifted off in her weariness. "…to have dinner some time?" Heat rose to Alex's cheeks. She hadn't asked anyone out on a date in years. And yes, this most certainly would be a date.

"I'd be absolutely delighted." A softness glowed in Maddie's eyes. "How about tonight?"

"Why the hell not?" The only plan Alex had for tonight was falling asleep in the couch around nine and dragging herself to bed at midnight—and possibly being woken in the middle of the night when Nat came home, alone or otherwise.

"I'll cook for you. I do the best spaghetti carbonara. Real Italian style." Maddie slapped herself on the forehead. "Oh shit. That usually works on women, but you're half-Italian so I may have to eat my words later."

"Don't worry. My mom did all the cooking in our house. I was raised on soup noodles instead of home-made pasta."

"Thank god for that."

"Well, I wouldn't say that. She's a terrible cook."

They burst out laughing.

"Hey, lovebirds," Nat chimed in. "Excuse me for interrupting your intimate moment." She winked at Alex, in plain view of Maddie's eye-line. "But I must take my leave. Life awaits."

Behind Nat, Alex saw Isabella shake her head. If she and Maddie experienced a lull in conversation tonight, they could always turn to the fruitful topic of Nathalie Orange—and how Isabella's interest was clearly growing beyond the professional.

MADDIE

Maddie filled her shopping basket with parmesan and pecorino to grate over the pasta. She was desperate to impress Alex, although she may have picked the wrong dish for that. Alex's question had surprised her, but she hadn't hesitated for a second. With June's recent news and her mind drifting off more and more to a departure from Hong Kong, a successful date was the only thing that could keep her from having to make a difficult decision.

She hurried to the cashier while keeping an eye on her watch. Cooking wouldn't take long, but making herself presentable would. She wanted to look her best tonight. Every inch the lady she, admittedly, really wasn't. If she were to stand a chance at all with Alex, she had to make up for her previous impromptu confession about June. Alex didn't strike her as the type to be fooled by some make-up and a fancy dress, but Maddie wanted to make the effort anyway. She wanted to impress, like earlier that afternoon when she'd flaunted her bicep. Maddie giggled at the memory. Who did that? Who boasted about a bulging muscle in front of the most well-toned fitness instructor ever?

Alex arrived at eight o'clock on the dot. Maddie hadn't expected anything else. She wore a white tank top—of course —and tight-fitting jeans. For the first time, Maddie saw her with her hair loose. It fell to her shoulders in dark wavy strands. Maddie could barely hide her excitement at what stood in front of her. Perhaps she had overdressed for the occasion though. Maybe this red number was a bit too statuesque for a relaxed home dinner. Still, she felt Alex's gaze glide appreciatively along the length of her body.

They kissed each other on the cheek a bit awkwardly before Maddie stepped aside and invited Alex to sit down.

"You're not working tomorrow, are you? With your changed schedule." She pointed at the bottle of Veuve Clicquot chilling in an ice bucket on the coffee table. "I have a nice Rioja to go with the pasta as well." There's nothing like making your intentions clear from the start.

"Heaven's no." Alex sat down with a sigh. "This new club opening has really done me in." Maddie saw her eyeing the bubbles with gusto. Maybe she needed something to take the edge off as well. "And taking my responsibility as a senior member of staff has led to a few senior moments, I'm afraid." Alex rubbed a hand over her neck and shoulder. "Perhaps for the first time in my life, I'm feeling my age."

Maddie unscrewed the cage of the bottle, but waited to pop the cork. "You speak as if you're over forty, while you don't look a day over twenty-five."

"Flattery will get you nowhere." Alex chuckled and held out the two glasses Maddie had prepared.

"Pity." She locked eyes with Alex as she poured the champagne and shot her a little smile.

They clinked rims and sipped eagerly.

* * *

After dinner—which Alex had praised as 'very authentic to the Chinese palate'—and half a bottle of red wine, they retreated back to the couch. Maddie couldn't remember the last time she'd sat in her living room with an attractive woman—and half-tipsy at that. She relaxed and heeled her shoes off.

"I'm really glad we did this."

"Me too." Alex had kicked her shoes off as well and slipped one foot under her knee. She sat with her body facing Maddie. "I figured I owed you another chance after going MIA on you." She rubbed her shoulder again.

"You've no idea how relieved I am you still want to hang

with the sordid likes of me." Maddie figured they'd consumed enough alcohol to allow some gentle teasing. "What's with your shoulder? You keep touching it."

"One too many push-ups, I presume. And it's a hard spot to reach to apply tiger balm. Nothing too serious though, just a body in dire need of some rest."

"Well, I simply can't stand for someone suffering in my home." She stood up. "Don't move." Maddie quickly darted off to the bathroom and unearthed a bottle of massage oil from the cabinet beneath the sink. She dusted it off before taking it into the living room. "You've come to the right place."

"If I remember correctly, I owe you a massage." Alex's eyes sparkled. Maddie was sure the wine was partly to blame, but she refused to believe that was all it was.

"As I said before, you don't owe me a thing." Maddie took position behind the couch. "Sit up straight, please."

Alex dropped her leg and leaned back.

"Where does it hurt?"

"Around here." Alex pointed at a spot above her right shoulder blade.

"At your service, madam." Maddie scanned Alex's tank top-clad back. "I wouldn't want to stain your clothes though. Would you mind if I pulled your top up?"

"Of course not." Alex beat her to it and in one swift movement her back was bare, apart from the straps supporting her bra. Maddie stood there swallowing the dryness out of her throat. A naked back usually didn't have this effect on her, but not all naked backs looked as perfectly sculpted as this one. She was almost afraid to touch it, scared she would ruin it somehow.

"Thanks." She reached out her hand until her fingertips touched Alex's shoulder, the electricity zapping through her flesh overwhelming her. "I'm going to lower these a bit." Slowly, she brushed the straps of Alex's bra down shoulders. "Just for better access." Maddie squirted some oil in her hand and heated it between her palms.

She took a deep but discreet breath, aware of the sudden throbbing between her legs, and got to work. Placing two lubricated hands on the soft skin of Alex's magnificent shoulders, she massaged gently but with focus. Not that she really knew what she was doing.

ALEX

Lust tumbled down Alex's belly. The pressure on her sore muscle was nice, but it wasn't what was causing her to gasp for air. She was glad she sat with her back to Maddie—the gentleness of her touch almost moving her to tears. She had drunk too much, had gone way over her quota, but that's what dates were for. And Alex really needed to let go a bit. She'd been too caught up in her own head of late, working crazy hours and pushing any thought of Maddie straight to the back of her mind. Until this afternoon.

"Does that feel all right?" Maddie's voice seemed to have dropped an octave.

Alex wanted to reply, but she was afraid her voice would come out as a yelp, or a whimper. It wasn't just that she hadn't been touched like this in months. It was also—mostly—that she could clearly feel, despite not being able to see her, Maddie's intent behind it. And her own desire was playing tricks on her as well.

"Like heaven." Alex tilted back into Maddie's hands, wanting to feel more of them on her body—not just her back. She closed her eyes and surrendered to Maddie's fingertips dancing over her skin. The hair on her arms rose as Maddie's thumbs pressed against a vertebrae. "I could get used to this," she hummed.

"I wouldn't mind if you did." Maddie's hands ventured upwards, over Alex's shoulders, her fingers stroking her collar bone. Instantly, Alex's nipples crinkled up. Maddie's fingers caressed her neck next, her nails trailing over her skin. This was no longer a massage. This was foreplay.

Maddie's fingers, red-nailed and long, travelled down, into the direction of Alex's bra cup. They trailed along the seam, teasing. As much as this excited Alex, and as much as she'd been willing to let go of restraints earlier, this was not something Alessandra Pozzato did on a first date. Ever.

"Stop," she whispered. Her voice a far cry from its usual mock-menacing tone—the one she used in class. She wrestled her hands free from her tank top and put them on Maddie's. "Too soon." Alex seemed incapable of forming sentences. "Sorry." Her tank top fell to the couch as Maddie's fingers halted their descent.

"I got a little carried away." Maddie retracted her hands and Alex suddenly felt very naked. She was scantily dressed. Her bra barely covering her nipples and her top a crumpled mess on the couch. She reached for it and clutched it to her chest, unable to pull it over her head. "I'm the one who's sorry." Alex heard Maddie swallow behind her.

"I should probably go." Alex said the words but didn't take any action towards making them happen.

"Stay a while." Maddie padded to the front of the couch and sat down on the coffee table. She looked gorgeous flustered, lust glinting in her eyes and the thinnest layer of sweat covering her brow. "It was just a massage, after all. Nothing actually happened."

Alex couldn't say no to that smile. Already she wondered what her reaction would be to Maddie's bedroom scowl. Instant surrender.

"You may want to put something on if you want it to stay that way." Maddie stood up and refilled their glasses and Alex took advantage of her looking away to slip her tank top over her shoulders.

"I need to take things slowly," Alex said in between drinking greedily from the wine. "I can't just dive into bed with you. That's not how I do things."

"I respect that." Maddie sat down next to her again, a little closer this time, their arms a whisper away from touching. "I hope you know I mean that sincerely."

Alex nodded. She took another gulp and braved Maddie's stare. "Have you always wanted to be a banker?" This was not what she wanted to say. She really wanted to ask Maddie if she could kiss her—as if the question needed asking. Instead, she'd opted for caution.

Maddie shot her the most disarming smile ever, a smile so generous and warm, Alex had to suppress the urge to snuggle up to her and luxuriate in an embrace of those luscious arms. "Of course not. Who does?" Maddie put her hands on Alex's knee, zapping sparks of electricity through the flesh beneath. "I wanted to be a vet, just like any other girl with lesbian tendencies in the Melbourne suburbs. When I was fourteen, I wanted to be a flying doctor for a while, but only because I had a crush on nurse Kate in the TV show."

Alex allowed herself a silly chuckle. "You must think I'm terribly uptight."

Maddie shook her head while digging her nails into Alex's jeans. "The only thing I think is that you've been hurt. Anyway, you must think I'm quite the floozy."

"Floozy?" Alex suppressed a fit of giggles. "Yeah, that about sums it up. A banker floozy with a seriously deranged moral compass."

"I'll take that as a compliment." Alex adored Maddie's self-deprecating sense of humour. "Now." Maddie leaned a little closer and put her wine glass on the table. "This floozy would really like to kiss those uptight lips of yours." Maddie took Alex's glass from her hand and put it away. "No tongue, I promise."

"That's about the most romantic proposal I've ever had."

"I thought so." Maddie slanted her head sideways as she inched closer. Alex smelled wine and that expensive banker perfume she remembered—often and usually when alone in bed—from the evening on Isabella's roof top. Maddie's lips tasted salty and promising. She brought her hand to Alex's neck and softly dug her fingertips into her muscles while parting her lips. Slowly, she trailed her tongue over Alex's lips. Alex immediately reciprocated by opening her mouth and allowing Maddie's tongue to slip in.

Alex's blood hammered in her veins as Maddie sank her teeth into her bottom lip before sucking it into her mouth. Alex grabbed Maddie's head and pulled her closer. She ran her fingers through Maddie's hair to keep them from exploring anywhere else—somewhere with a point of no return.

When Maddie eased her head back, a big smile etched around the corners of her mouth, Alex yanked it back towards her immediately. Maddie brought her lips close to Alex's ear.

"Don't you want me to stop?" She finished her question with a peck on Alex's ear lobe, soft, but enough to set Alex's flesh on fire again.

"God no," Alex moaned. Maddie's lips travelled along her neck, tracing a moist path of kisses on the way to her clavicle. "Kissing is perfectly acceptable on the first date."

MADDIE

"Are you seeing her tonight?" Isabella sipped from her protein smoothie while waiting for an answer. Maddie had barely touched hers, her stomach too fragile to take anything in. After Alex had left last night, after a few more rounds of extensive —but chaste—kissing, she hadn't slept a wink. Although exhausted, physically as well as emotionally, her mind had fallen prey to an onslaught of questions. What if Alex changed her mind again? What if she decided she didn't want to be with a banker after all? What if she wasn't ready? What if… she didn't feel the same way? Questions Maddie hadn't bothered with in years.

"No, she has a family dinner." Maddie looked at Isabella. She was so happy to have a psychiatrist as a friend, someone with a soothing, sane influence. Maddie desperately needed some grounding—and the yoga class they just took hadn't really helped. Possibly because it wasn't taught by Alex, although that would probably have made it worse. "And she's hardly the type to pop in after midnight for a quickie."

Maddie giggled at the memory of last night. They'd made out like teenagers in a dark corner at a dance party. Kissing like crazy, but hands always in check. It was the most spectacular night Maddie had had in five years. Because, unlike any other woman she'd slept with since moving abroad—since leaving Emma—Alex was worth waiting for.

"You look shattered but still, you're glowing." Isabella winked.

"How things can change in twenty-four hours." Maddie brought her hand to her chin and stroked it, still caught up in disbelief. "I was honestly thinking of leaving. What with June's big announcement and having to face my mistakes every day. I was so bloody unhappy and I didn't even realise." Maddie opened her hands. "And look at me now. Smitten like a fool."

"I sincerely hope it works out." Isabella slurped the last remnants of her smoothie through the straw.

"I know this will sound dramatic, maybe even a bit fatalistic. But I seriously believe my decision to ultimately stay or go will depend on Alex." Maddie sighed. "If this crashes and burns, I can't see how I can possibly stay."

"Don't get ahead of yourself. Just let things take their natural course." Isabella reached out her hand to pat Maddie's arm.

"I know. I sound like a sixteen-year-old. But I haven't felt like this in a very long time." Maddie's head felt as if it were about to implode. So much impulsive emotion thrashing through her body, she hardly recognised herself. This was not how bankers operated. They stayed cool and responsible under every circumstance. They had to.

"Really? You could have fooled me, Madison." Grinning, Isabella squeezed her arm. "What am I going to do with you for the rest of the day?"

"Well, we've had our exercise and this is Hong Kong. We're faced with the impossible dilemma of choosing between this city's two favourite pass times—shopping or drinking. What would the doctor advise?"

"I have a really nice bottle of Shiraz and a killer view. Let's go to my place."

Maddie shoved her untouched smoothie to the side and, together, they exited the gym.

* * *

At work the next day, everything seemed different. Gone was the sense of gloom that had been hanging in Maddie's office for too long. Impatiently, she waited until ten to text Alex. It was her day off and she wanted to invite her for lunch. Nerves eating at her stomach, she waited for the reply. It came almost instantly. *How about organic pizza?* Ludicrously hot, kind, principled and funny. This is meant to be, Maddie thought. If I don't get this woman I will move to the Australian wilderness and live like an old maid for the rest of my days.

They ended up in a small Vietnamese place around the corner from Maddie's office. As soon as they sat down opposite each other, Maddie couldn't stop grinning.

"How was your family dinner?" Maddie didn't really want to talk. She just wanted to stare at Alex's face for an hour, memorise the curve of her lips and get lost in the darkness of her eyes.

"You'd think growing up in a half-European family would make your parents less judgmental, but you would be hugely mistaken." Alex shot her a weary smile. "After having been a fitness instructor for more than ten years, my mother still thinks it's a big waste of time."

"How can she look at you and think that?" Maddie was glad the wine arrived. She needed something to calm her down. Her heart drummed in her chest.

"She doesn't look at me with the same eyes as you do." Alex's foot found Maddie's under the table. "Her intentions are more honourable."

"Would you care to explain what might not be honourable about this appreciative glance?" Maddie's exaggerated fluttering of eyelids and licking of lips made Alex grin.

"Not enough words in a dictionary for that." Alex had kicked off her flip-flop and ran a toe over Maddie's open-shoed foot. "Anyway, she'd rather have me wither away in some dull physics lab than do what I love. Same old song and dance." Alex was getting agitated and, to Maddie's dismay, had withdrawn her foot.

"Physics lab?" Maddie couldn't connect the dots. "It would be a crime against humanity to hide that shoulder line under a lab coat." Alex was wearing a white tank top again. She must have a few shelves reserved in her wardrobe for them, if not all. The memory of Alex lifting her tank top over her back the other night slammed into Maddie's mind again, resulting in a moist tingle between her legs.

"I have a Master's in Physics. An education my parents paid for, with the single hope of getting a great return on their investment."

Full of surprises, Maddie thought. So much to learn. "You're a brainiac, then. Not just a hot bod. Colour me impressed."

"For someone with such a high-up corporate job, you have surprisingly basic language skills." Alex bored her black eyes into Maddie's, which only intensified the sensation between Maddie's legs.

"I'll readily admit my brain function is a bit stumped at the moment. An event for which you are entirely responsible."

Alex's foot was back on Maddie's, her toe snaking up Maddie's calf. "Feeling frisky, Madison?" She bit her bottom lip after she asked the question, while keeping her gaze on Maddie.

"Does this count as our second date?" Maddie caught Alex's foot under the table and tickled its sole. "Because I sure hope you put out on the third."

ALEX

"You haven't fucked her yet?" Nat was sprawled out in the sofa, one leg dangling over the back rest, the other stretched out in front of her, a battered paperback resting in her lap. "What is wrong with you, Pizza?"

Alex knew this conversation was inevitable. Just as she knew Nat was joking. "Sod off, Orange. We're not all sluts like you." She sat down on the arm rest of the sofa, her bare feet planted on the bottom cushion. "What surprises me is that you haven't put the moves on the fair lady Isabella yet."

"Why on earth would I do that?" Nat pulled a grossed out face. "She's hardly my type."

"Oh, sure." Alex kicked Nat gently against the shin with the side of her foot. "And everything you say always corresponds exactly with how you feel."

"One shrink in the building is enough, thank you very much. If I need some analysing, I'll go two floors up." Nat bounced Alex's foot back.

"There's an idea." The arrival of a text message made Nat's phone buzz. She reached for it on the coffee table. Probably the arrangement of another meaningless date.

"Excuse me, but I don't seem to have planned time in my busy schedule for moralising." Nat glued her eyes to the screen of her phone, her face lighting up at what she saw. She looked up briefly. "Don't you have a date to get ready for? Armpits to shave?"

"I got them lasered." Alex kicked Nat in the shin again, a bit harder this time.

"Just get laid tonight, please. I'm tired of living with your dryness."

Nat was right. Alex did have a date to get ready for. The fourth date to be exact. If a quick drink—in a public place—after last night's body combat class counted as the third.

"Don't wait up tonight." She rose from the sofa and jumped off while winking at Nat.

Alex wouldn't call herself prudish, just careful. She wanted nothing more than to dive between the sheets with Maddie, but it was her nature to always think one step ahead. She probably got it from her ever-prudent mother, who did nothing without serious risk calculation first.

Alex was not a cheap thrill chaser like Nat. The only reason she went all the way with someone was because she had a serious interest in them. She didn't adhere to the let's-see-where-it-goes philosophy so many people in this town believed in. It was either the real deal, or it wasn't. Maddie could be the real deal.

Deciding to be adventurous, Alex opted for a navy tank top, an extra tight one. She wasn't fooling herself. Tonight would be the night. She'd been dreaming about it for weeks. Maddie's hands all over her, Maddie's fingers inside of her. If she had to be alone with Maddie one more time without touching every little bit of her, certain body parts might spontaneously self-combust. She was ready.

Half an hour later, she knocked on Maddie's door, a bottle of Perrier in each hand.

"Hey, neighbour." Maddie leaned against the door jamb and looked her over. "Need a cup of sugar?"

"If that's what you want to call it." She held up the two bottles. "I suggest we stay sober tonight."

Maddie pulled her in by her arms, shut the door and pressed her against it. "I suggest we skip the eating and drinking part altogether." They stood at the same height and Maddie pinned her banker stare on Alex.

"I usually wouldn't advise such madness, but I'll make an exception just this once." Alex still clutched the two bottles of sparkling water in her hands, preventing her from touching Maddie.

"I won't tell anyone." Maddie traced a finger along her jawline before letting it plunge down to her collar bone. "I'm going to kiss you now."

"Oh yeah?" Alex inhaled Maddie's scent.

Maddie inched closer until her lips almost touched Alex's. "Any objections?"

"Can you do it a little faster? Or are you feeling your age?"

"I'll make you pay for that remark one day." Maddie's fingers curled around Alex's neck.

"I look forward to it."

Maddie shot her a sly grin, one that promised certain things Alex would surely agree with. Then, at last, she planted her lips on Alex's mouth.

Alex still couldn't touch Maddie without dropping the glass bottles and she got the distinct impression Maddie got a kick out of being in control like that. Then again, Alex hadn't expected anything else. It was a huge part of her attraction to Maddie.

"Let me take these. At my age, you can't expect me to do all the work." Last night, at the bar, Maddie had revealed her age. Her ID card said she was forty, but she certainly looked much younger. They'd cracked jokes about it the rest of the evening.

Maddie liberated her from the bottles of Perrier and put them on the nearest surface she could find, a hallway cabinet.

"I've been here five minutes and we haven't made it further than the hall. How on earth will you ever get me into your bedroom at this pace?" Alex quipped.

"Like this." Maddie grabbed her by the hand and dragged her through the hallway, across the living room and into her bedroom. "Fast enough for you?"

"You must have been working out." Maddie pushed her against the door, against her bedroom door this time. Alex had to gasp for air for a split second. She was finally here.

"Correct. The instructor is so hot. I just can't stay away."

Maddie kissed her again and this time Alex didn't waste any time ruffling her fingers through Maddie's hair, along her neck, her sides.

"I want you so much," she whispered in Maddie's ear while she kissed her neck.

MADDIE

Maddie couldn't believe Alex would finally be hers. Her knees buckled at the magnitude of the thought. She'd known her for how long? A few weeks? Of which they didn't speak for three… and already it felt like so much longer. This was not just a dalliance against her office door. The woman gasping between her arms, responding to every little flick of her fingers, was available, gay and heartstoppingly beautiful.

The door. That was what was wrong with this picture. As if a door was to Maddie what a bed was to every other normal human being.

"I want you too," she hissed in Alex's ear and ushered her away from the door. This occasion, more than any other, deserved a bed.

Their arms tangling up, they stumbled further into the room. Maddie wanted to tear Alex's clothes off and bury her fingers inside of her, but at the same time she needed to savour this moment, draw it out so as to have more to hold on to later. They were making a memory for the ages, Maddie was certain of that.

Alex's fingers were in her hair, intertwining themselves with strands of blond locks. She exhaled soft moans driving Maddie to early ecstasy. Maddie deliberately tempered her movements, which had become too frantic too quickly. She broke from their lip lock and scanned Alex's face. All she saw was pure want, raw desire, her eyes darker than Maddie had ever seen them, blazing with need. Going slow would be a challenge.

Without taking her eyes off Alex's face, Maddie trailed her right hand along her neck, over her collar bone and in between her breasts. She'd only inadvertently touched them, but now, she'd do much more than touch. She let her hand glide all the way down Alex's top and slid a finger under. Rock hard abs responded to her touch. They both inhaled sharply, craving more oxygen to process this desire.

"Take it off." Alex's voice came out in stutters. Even saying only three words seemed too much. Maddie feared she'd lost the ability to speak altogether the moment she'd laid hands on Alex's belly.

Slowly, she eased Alex's tank top up, revealing her copper-skinned abdomen inch by inch. Maddie felt heat pool in her core. And she hadn't gotten to the best bit yet. Her hands arrived at Alex's bra, which, much to her surprise, was a sexy number in black lace—in all honesty, Maddie had expected a sports bra. Clearly, Alex had dressed for the occasion.

Alex lifted her arms and Maddie pulled the tank top over her head. Alex in a tank top had always been a glorious sight, but Alex in a black lace bra was a whole new story. Just like her eyes, the black of the fabric contrasted with the ochre colour of her skin. For once, Maddie was happy to admit she was suffering from a serious case of yellow fever.

Alex reached for Maddie. She didn't practice the same amount of patience and tugged feverishly at the buttons of her blouse. Maddie put her hands on Alex's to steady her grip. Together, they undid her blouse until it slid to the floor where it crumpled into a white silk puddle.

Maddie took the lead and edged another step closer to the bed. Alex followed swiftly and Maddie eased her down. She lowered herself onto the bed and slid next to Alex. Their bra-clad breasts touched as Maddie pressed her body against

Alex's and their lips found each other again.

Maddie fondled the cup of Alex's bra. It wasn't enough. She curled a finger underneath and found Alex's nipple. It stood tall and crunched upwards at her touch. She pulled down the cup, exposing Alex's nipple. Eager to taste the perky, dark bud, Maddie tore her mouth away from Alex's lips.

Alex groaned as Maddie's tongue made contact. A sound so guttural it connected with Maddie's pussy instantly, releasing a fresh wave of heat to rush through her. Maddie pushed herself up to free Alex's other nipple, baring it so she could taste it on her hungry lips.

"Jesus," Alex sighed, her fingers laced through Maddie's hair, her head thrown back into the pillows.

Maddie sucked and nibbled on Alex's nipples, and, before heading south, grazed them with her teeth, which coaxed an even louder moan from Alex's mouth.

Tracing a moist path with her lips to Alex's belly button, Maddie slipped her fingers under the waistband of Alex's jeans. Alex's body tensed at her touch there. She reacted by pushing her pelvis upwards.

Exercising a restraint she normally wouldn't bother with —when you're fucking someone in your office, speed is always of the essence—she only undid Alex's button and left the zipper nicely done up. It was enough to give her lips and tongue access to Alex's lower abdomen, that delicious part of her body gradually disappearing into her underwear.

"You're driving me insane." Alex shoved Maddie's head down, as if that would make her put her tongue where it mattered sooner. Instead, Maddie let a finger slip in between Alex's legs. Even through the thick fabric of her jeans, she could feel a warm glow. It was practically a crime against humanity to not set her free from these trousers.

"I've only just started." Maddie sat up and locked eyes with Alex. She brought her hands behind her back and unclasped her bra. She waited a few seconds before lowering it off her body, three seconds in which she drove Alex a little bit crazier. She lay there panting, her lips parted and her eyes glinting with hunger, incapacitated. Quickly, Maddie removed her own pants, leaving her underwear, before going to work on Alex.

As slow as she could muster, Maddie unzipped Alex's jeans. Gradually pushing them over her hipbones and revealing Alex's toned legs. Alex's underwear matched the black lace of her already discarded bra, reaffirming to Maddie she had come here for one thing only.

ALEX

Sweat prickled Alex's overheated skin and her clit was about to burst out of her undies. Maddie crouched half-naked in front of her, her breasts creamy-white and delicious, her panties looking about ready to be ripped off. For someone with such stamina, someone trained to perspire for hours, Alex had been reduced to a paralysed bundle of desire quite quickly—and efficiently. Alex liked a woman who knew what she was doing. A woman who teased her and took control in the bedroom. She suspected a high level of sexual compatibility between Maddie and her. Those bossy banker types were always the same, which is why Alex found them so hard to resist.

Alex's breath quickened—nearly stopped in her throat— as Maddie trailed her fingers along the seam of her panties. Juices gathered where Maddie's hands stalled, circling above the fabric. These panties would be ruined, but Alex couldn't care less. She'd only bought them for tonight. She was more the comfortable boy shorts type, anyway.

Maddie's finger slipped under now, just one, exploring the wetness pooling between her legs. Alex dug her nails into the mattress, fearing she may not be able to stand this tension any longer. She was sure one expertly placed flick would be all it took. She was also sure Maddie would postpone that as long as possible.

At last, Maddie tugged at the waistband of her panties. Alex pushed her bottom up to give Maddie better access—anything to speed up this sensually torturous process. And there she lay, all naked and on display for this woman who'd gotten her into this blissful state. Panting. Ready. Limp and damp.

Alex hoped Maddie would remove her own underwear as well. She didn't have it in her to reach over and take them off. Gravity seemed to work against her. And lust. She was floored by lust. Floored by the desire to have Maddie inside of her. Not long now. That recurring dream was about to come true.

Maddie didn't slip out of her undies, instead she poured her body over Alex's useless limbs. Their nipples met and fire soared through Alex's flesh. Maddie's knee rested inches from her throbbing clit.

They lost themselves in a passionate kiss, tongues probing and exploring, skating over lips. Maddie's knee was on her now, pushing into her and Alex couldn't help but rub herself against it. Sparks rushed up her spine as she felt her dampness spread on Maddie's skin.

Maddie shifted her body weight to one side, resting on her left elbow, and releasing the pressure her knee was applying. Her mouth was drawn into a confident smirk—one that said, *I'll fuck you now.*

With her gaze firmly pinned on Alex, Maddie brought two fingers two Alex's mouth. Instinctively, Alex parted her lips and let them slip in. She licked Maddie's fingers while drowning in the light grey of her eyes, more juices leaking from her aching pussy as a result. As far as foreplay went, she was done.

As soon as Maddie retracted her fingers, Alex swallowed and said, "Fuck me now. Please." Her eyes pleading, her body trembling.

Maddie responded by narrowing her eyes and broadening the smirk on her face. She traced her wet fingers over Alex's nipple on their way down, slip-sliding them over her belly.

Alex spread her legs wider in anticipation. With the back of her hand, Maddie stroked her pubes and dipped lower, not really touching her nether lips yet, just brushing them. Alex's body reacted nonetheless, her muscles flexing and her breath hitching in her throat.

Maddie's eyes were still pinned on her, reading her, scanning her face. Alex had trouble keeping her eyes open—lust tugging her eyelids shut—but she kept her gaze on Maddie, not wanting to miss any emotion displayed on her face.

Then, there it was. A finger gliding along her lips, sailing through her wetness. Tentative at first, as if wanting to acquaint itself, but then, suddenly, it was inside. Alex gripped the sheets between her fingers and buried her toes in the mattress. It was just one finger, but it was almost too much.

"Oh," she moaned, and in between the fluttering of her lashes, she witnessed how Maddie's smirk shifted from confident to sentimental, from wide to narrow. Maddie added another finger and started moving inside of her, fucking her. Stars started exploding on the back of Alex's half-closed eyelids. She wouldn't last long. She already felt it build in her belly. That fire. The big swell of a wave. Tingling through her, sparking colours in front of her eyes.

Maddie owned her in that moment, she had her. Alex didn't give herself that easily, but she had done it now. Beyond the point of no return.

"You're so gorgeous." Maddie's voice was close when she said it. Her lips grazing Alex's ear. "I'm going to fuck you all night long."

Alex could only whimper, and tremble at Maddie's fingertips. And surrender. And agree. The fire intensified, picking up speed as it spread through her muscles. Alex pushed her groin into Maddie's fingers, wanting more—all—of her.

Maddie's face wasn't close to hers anymore when Alex

opened her eyes next. It hovered over her hand, the one she was using to fuck Alex. Maddie's tongue brushed her clit, the roaring centre of the fire swirling over her body, back and forth. She flicked once, and the wave started crashing into Alex. Seizing her. Dipping her under. Another flick and the wave took her. Everything collapsed in her brain and in her belly and in her cunt. One more flick and Alex was done. Spent. The stars falling from the black sky on her eyelids. The walls of her pussy contracting around Maddie's fingers, as if wanting to keep them there forever. The tingles in her belly erupting into a symphony of fireworks.

"Oh god," Alex screamed. "Oh my g—" The words froze in her throat as another wave rose and engulfed her. Maddie kept fucking her, spreading her fingers inside of her, wanting to claim the last bit of her. This one was different, calmer and easier to enjoy. Not that avalanche of emotion and cramped muscles crushing her like before. Alex rode it out, on Maddie's able fingers, until she collapsed on the bed, her body spent and her mind empty.

MADDIE

Maddie let Alex pull her close, let her nuzzle her neck and bury her nose in her tousled hair. Alex's biceps twitched their way through aftershock as they locked around Maddie's neck.

After a few seconds of hard hugging, the kind expressing much more than words, Maddie freed herself from Alex's strong arms. She needed to see her face, scan her eyes for signs of satisfaction. Maddie wasn't expecting tears.

"Are you all right?" With her thumb, she brushed away a teardrop lingering on Alex's majestic cheekbone.

"Perfectly." Alex shot her a joyous smile. "This is why I don't do one-night-stands. Too embarrassing."

"And here I was thinking it was your virtuous nature."

Maddie leaned down and pecked Alex on the nose. "Your secret's safe with me."

"Come here." Alex drew her in for a deep kiss, her tongue probing more aggressively this time, as if liberated from first-time inhibitions. She bent her leg and pushed her knee against Maddie's groin. The instant Maddie's clit—still chastely covered by dampening panties—connected she was reminded of the pent-up tension strumming in her veins.

Maddie tried to steady her breath while Alex pushed herself up and toppled Maddie off of her.

"I'm starving." She looked down at Maddie, her defined shoulders glistening with tiny drops of sweat. "Someone made me miss dinner." Her eyes sparkled with mischief.

"The all-night buffet has been declared open."

"At last." Alex leaned in for one more kiss, before moving her lips down. First stop, Maddie's breasts. Her nipples pierced the air. Alex kissed them gently, licking them to peaks, twirling her tongue around them before sucking them into her mouth one after the other.

Maddie couldn't keep her eyes off Alex's shoulders. The way the muscles underneath Alex's smooth skin responded so elegantly sent shiver after shiver of red hot desire through her blood. She wasn't so hypocritical to claim a good body didn't matter—because it did—but Maddie had never had the likes of Alex in her bed. Luckily, she was too far gone, too wrapped up in pleasure to feel self-conscious about her own lack of muscle definition in certain places.

Her gaze alternating between the sight of Alex's lips around her nipples and her out-of-this-world shoulder line, Maddie felt her juices drench the fabric of her panties. And as much as she loved the attention Alex gave to her breasts, she couldn't wait for that mouth to travel down.

Alex looked her straight in the eyes as she locked a nipple between her teeth and gently pulled it upwards. An action of which Maddie felt the consequences shudder throughout her entire body. Alex smiled, tiny laughter lines—almost invisible

—creasing around her black eyes. "At last, dinner time," she said, while licking her lips. Maddie's clit thumped with anticipation.

Trailing a moist path with her lips down Maddie's belly, which she—admittedly—pulled in a little, Alex made her way down to where the feast was being offered. Alex traced her tongue along the edge of Maddie's undies, then kissed her way, on top of the fabric, to just above Maddie's clit, before finally ridding Maddie of her soaked underwear with a few quick tugs.

Maddie's pussy pulsed violently with want, her lips swollen and wet. Just the thought of having Alex look down on her cunt, glistening with lust, made her shudder all over.

Alex took her time, kissing Maddie's inner thighs first—as a starter, no doubt. Excruciatingly slowly, she inched closer to Maddie's lips. The first lick barely grazed her flesh, but, nevertheless, thundered all the way to her core. The second one went a little deeper, probing between her lips and veering off just before reaching Maddie's clit.

At last, Alex zoned in on her clit, starting with a tentative peck, a soft lick, and another one, before she sucked Maddie's clit into her mouth. Maddie was so on edge, so ready to explode, she nearly came there and then. As if Alex sensed it, she withdrew and refocused on her pussy lips. She pushed her tongue inside, deeper than Maddie could have imagined, withdrew, and licked her up and down, only casually skidding over her clit.

Maddie's heart banged furiously beneath her chest. She pushed herself onto Alex's mouth, wanting to feel as much of it as possible on her wanting cunt. Alex sucked her pussy lips into her mouth, one after the other and then, oh bliss, both of them together.

"Aah," Maddie murmured, converting the wimpy yelp building inside of her into something more suitable and mature. This seemed to spur Alex on, as she traced her tongue back to Maddie's clit. If Alex didn't hold back now, this would be it. Maddie's first climax delivered by Alessandra Pozzato. Her new lover. Potential girlfriend. Her reason to stay.

Alex flicked her tongue over Maddie's clit from left to right, so quickly, so deftly. Maddie extended her arms and buried one hand in Alex's hair while placing the other on the shoulder nearest to her. She needed to feel those muscles flex for her. Alex sucked Maddie's clit back into her mouth and left it there to play with, let her tongue dance over it.

A storm raged inside Maddie's bones, a hot wind beating against her flesh. She squeezed Alex shoulder, hard, her nails digging into her skin as the storm breezed over her, only to return with more force, as Alex exposed her clit to the air again and licked her into complete oblivion.

Maddie came with Alex's face pressed into her, her nails no doubt leaving their mark on her shoulder. Good, she thought. She's mine now. That's my territory marked.

Pushing Alex gently away from her too sensitive clit, Maddie couldn't suppress a grin. When meeting someone you really connected with, there was always a chance the love-making would lack. That the chemistry would not translate into the bedroom. Not in this case. She wanted to purr with delight. Not just because she'd just had a massive orgasm, but because of the new beginning it represented. And because, for once, she didn't have to smooth the wrinkles out of her skirt and go back to work.

ALEX

Alex woke with a start. A loud buzz broke the silence in the room. Pale sunlight slanted under the blinds. An arm was slung over her middle.

"Morning," Maddie whispered from behind her, her lips on Alex's shoulder blade. "I'll take care of that." Alex heard a slap and the beeping stopped. She turned on her other side and faced Maddie.

"I'm a fitness professional who's trained to work all the muscles in the human body, but I think last night may have activated a few underused ones."

They'd barely gotten any sleep, going for round after round of discovering each other's body as the hours ticked away. Alex searched for the alarm clock on Maddie's side of the bed. Six-thirty. She heaved a sigh of relief as she didn't have a class until lunch.

"Are you saying you're unfit to work?" Maddie's smile was a glorious sight to behold in the early light of dawn. She even looked good waking up. Alex suspected the fucked-all-night-glow might have something to do with that as well.

"At this moment? Yes. But I can sleep for at least four more hours. You?"

"God, you're mean before your morning coffee." Maddie snuggled up a little closer. Alex wrapped her arms around her and kissed her on the head.

"I'll make it up to you tonight." Alex felt Maddie's lips curl into a smile against her chest.

"How about right now?" Maddie looked up and found her eyes.

"Won't you get fired if you're as much as ten minutes late?"

"I'm pretty high up." Maddie's lips already hummed across Alex's chest. "And anyway, I think I should call in sick."

Alex grinned. "What terrible affliction might you be suffering from?"

"Let's see." Maddie sighed. "Definitely inexplicable heart palpitations. And worst of all, a terminally wet pussy."

Alex succumbed to a fit of giggles. "That does sound bad. Do you need me to examine you?"

Maddie nodded. "I don't think you have much choice." Maddie shuffled her body upwards until she was at eye-height with Alex. "But all jokes aside, last night was spectacular."

"I have a strong tendency to agree."

"Is there anything I can do to sway that tendency into a definite agreement?" Maddie's teeth grazed the flesh above Alex's nipple while her hand darted off between her legs.

"One is free to try." Alex grabbed Maddie's head and pulled it towards her face. She slipped her tongue into Maddie's mouth, as Maddie slid a finger into Alex's pussy. Just like that. Without warning. Alex gasped, breaking their kiss.

"Is this working in my favour?" Maddie pinned her eyes on Alex.

"Fuck yeah." Alex, past the shock of Maddie's sudden, but not unwelcome intrusion, found the damp heat between Maddie's thighs. Maddie didn't need any coaxing to spread them. She felt silky and wet, ready to be fucked. Again.

Alex inserted a finger into Maddie's pussy and they found a matching rhythm. Alex went in as Maddie slicked out, over and over again, all the while staring into each other's eyes. Maddie's long fingers burrowed deep, demanding more pleasure from Alex—and she thought she'd given up everything she had last night, screaming into darkness.

Alex knew then that she'd made the right decision. It wasn't serious yet, but it had the right hint of earnestness. She saw it in Maddie's eyes as she thundered towards orgasm. This was no ordinary fuck.

"Oh, baby," Maddie whispered and Alex felt the walls of her pussy clench around her fingers. *Baby.* It was enough to send her over the edge. Alex responded to Maddie's orgasm by coming herself, hard and fast, on Maddie's fingers.

* * *

After a shower and leaving a note to Maddie's helper that, whatever she did that day, it had to include changing the sheets, they had an early brunch in The Bean. Maddie had effectively called her assistant and told her she was not well.

"That fake sick note will not do for my class tonight. I hope you realise that." Alex slurped from her mochaccino, which seemed to taste better today, just like the bite of egg sandwich she'd just had. "You can't be complacent at your age."

"I realise we're both raging lesbians, but we've only just had our first night of pleasure. We can't be inseparable just yet."

Alex leaned over the table, chuckling. "Just don't expect me to give you any leeway because you're fucking me."

A smile tugged at the corners of Maddie's mouth. "Good god, that language of yours. I may need to speak with your mother."

Alex realised she might never win any future arguments with Maddie. She looked her over and acquiesced with open palms, exhausted from not enough sleep and the prospect of teaching three strenuous classes later.

"And I may need a full body massage tonight."

Maddie reached for her hand and grabbed it, rubbing her thumb across Alex's knuckles. The gesture ignited a shiver to dance up Alex's spine.

"I don't want to influence you with my appalling behaviour, but is there any way you can take tomorrow off work? And if it can bribe you in any way, yes I will bring you breakfast in bed."

"I do have about a dozen favours I can call in." Alex squeezed Maddie's hand. "The real question is whether you'll let me enjoy my well-deserved rest."

Maddie brought Alex's hand to her lips and kissed her knuckles. "What a silly question. Of course not."

MADDIE

"I was seriously contemplating leaving before you came along." Maddie and Alex sat opposite each other in Maddie's sofa, their bare legs stretched out in front of them, touching. Maddie had needed two glasses of wine before she could say it, but she thought it significant enough to make the effort—

and to get tipsy for.

They'd spent the day in bed, luxuriating in the unquenchable thirst of early passion. It was Saturday and Alex had called in her favours at work, resulting in hours of uninterrupted pleasure. They'd barely spoken, only tearing their lips away from each other to attend to acute hunger or engage in silly banter. Alex was good at banter. Alex was good at many things involving her lips and tongue.

"You either love or hate this town, I guess. But it's different for me because I was born here."

"I was really starting to hate it. And all the mistakes I've made in it." Maddie buried her eyes in her glass, not usually this shy.

"I think it's important to get out at regular intervals. Breathe in some fresh air on a beach. Get away from the crowds." Alex pursed her lips together before she continued. "So, I'm your reason to stay?"

"I…" Maddie hesitated, wondering if she was saying too much too soon. "This is the first time since moving here that I…" What was she trying to say, anyway? "You know… met someone like you."

"Someone who knows how to dramatically storm out of a restaurant, you mean? And is not afraid to judge people by their profession?" Alex contracted her impressive thigh muscles and shuffled closer.

"We can't all be perfect." It was so easy to deflect things with a silly quip. Maddie corrected herself. She had some more things to say. Before sliding towards Alex, she put her glass on the coffee table. They weaved their legs over each other and Maddie wrapped her arms around Alex's half-naked neck— tank top, no bra. "I've done some things in my life you may not agree with. Treated lovers badly. Abandoned someone in Melbourne I really cared for. But, as I've grown older, I've become much more serious about love and relationships and I started to realise this city isn't made for it."

Alex snaked her hands up Maddie's back, squeezing

gently. "No one I know is a saint. Nor am I. I believe in certain things, but I've learnt that the best things in life tend to happen when you step away from your most rigid principles. When you let go a little." Alex drew Maddie closer, until her lips grazed her ear. "I count what is happening between us among those things."

"I guess I'll stay for a while then." Maddie found Alex's earlobe and gently sank her teeth into the soft flesh.

"That'd be nice." Alex ran her tongue over Maddie's neck. "Nat and I are very happy with our upstairs neighbour."

"If you play your cards right, you're looking at spending a considerable amount of time on the floor above you." Maddie's fingers kneaded Alex's shoulders. She couldn't get enough of her shoulders.

"Do you propose I sleep my way to the top?" The back of Alex's fingers skated along the side of Maddie's breasts.

"Heaven's no. I'm not the kind to ever suggest such a thing." She noticed a scratch under the strap of Alex's tank top, no doubt left by her nails. She traced a finger over it. "But if you must… please stick to this floor."

"I think Isabella might have other interests than me."

"Excellent observation skills." Maddie felt her nipples go hard as Alex's hands hovered in their vicinity. "Something's definitely going on with her. Something Orange-related."

"Maybe we can help." Alex dropped her hands down and slipped them under Maddie's t-shirt.

"I thought Nat would never go for someone like Isabella." Maddie slipped the strap of Alex's tank top off her shoulders and dug her fingers into her muscles there.

"Nat is aimlessly fucking her life away. She's not really interested in any of these girls she brings home. She got hurt badly a couple of years ago." Alex's hands arrived at Maddie's breasts, causing her to take a sharp breath of air. "I think Isabella might be just what Nathalie Orange needs. But she'll need a lot of discreet cajoling to ever come to that conclusion on her own."

"We have time." Maddie gasped as Alex's hands cupped her breasts and her palms rolled over her nipples. "We're not going anywhere."

"You seem to be more of a fan of coming, anyway." Alex dark eyes were on her as she moved her fingers over Maddie's nipples.

"That was a really lousy joke." Maddie tugged at Alex's tank top and started to pull it over her head. "One deserving of proper punishment."

Alex sat in front of her, bare-chested, dark-skinned nipples pointing straight ahead. "What did you have in mind?"

Maddie had to swallow before she could speak again. "For starters, you can't put that top back on until I say so."

"That's not punishment, that's taking advantage." Alex tweaked her nipple roughly. Maddie caught the yelp in her throat before it escaped. She yanked Alex's hands from under her t-shirt and held them together by the wrist.

"Don't you speculate about my definition of punishment." Alex's glance shifted from surprised to excited in a split second. Maddie pulled her arms above her head and pressed down until Alex lay on her back. "You'll find out soon enough."

Maddie rose to her knees and straddled Alex. She knew that look in someone's eyes. That look of total capitulation. She pinned Alex's arms above her head before she leaned down and planted the softest of kisses on her lover's lips. Alex didn't resist.

ALEX

"Oh my god. Who are you and what have you done to my flatmate?" As expected, Nat was being all dramatic about it. Alex had barely set foot in the flat since her date with Maddie last Thursday. It was late Sunday afternoon, dusk already settling into darkness outside. "Is that you, Alessandra?" Nat squinted into Alex's direction. "Oh, and if you're going straight back up, tell your girlfriend the ceilings in this building are ridiculously thin for the exorbitant amount of rent we pay."

"Imagine the things she must have heard coming from your room for the past two years then." Alex took the chair opposite Nat's computer.

"Ouch. It fights back." Nat leaned back in her chair, the illuminated screen of her laptop lighting up her face. "You are positively glowing, Pizza. Hallelujah." She pumped her fists into the air, punching nothing.

"What are you doing tonight?" Alex cut straight to the chase.

"Being a literary genius, as I do every Sunday night. Why does the seriously over-fucked lady want to know?"

Alex rolled her eyes at Nat. Maybe this plan she and Maddie had hatched was the worst one in the history of set-ups. It definitely looked like it from the outside. Come to think of it, from the inside as well.

"Maddie is inviting you and Isabella to dinner. And I'll be there as well, of course." Alex tried to keep her voice casual. She was bad at this sort of thing. Something always gave her away. An unfamiliar inflection in her voice. Or that twitch in her lip.

"You've barely been shagging a few days and are already playing house. How revoltingly lesbian and domesticated." Nat slapped down the lid of her computer. The room now solely lit by a small reading lamp on the floor—not its correct place, but Alex had long given up on adhering to the right spot of things in the flat. "Good for you. But I'm sorry, I can't make it tonight. It's a little too short notice."

Nothing was ever too short notice for Nat—especially if it involved a girl in her early twenties and the prospect of sex. "Oh really? What pressing matter is keeping you from a home-cooked meal with friends?"

"Work. I can see the end looming. Just a few more hours

and my first draft is done."

"Fair enough, but you've got to eat, right?"

"Not today." Alex noticed how Nat deflated, her voice almost breaking. "I'll have a liquid dinner tonight." Just like that, Nat went from mouthy brat to broken girl. She drummed her fingers on the table, as if mustering up the courage to say something but not quite getting there. "I'm very happy for you. I honestly am. But I don't have it in me to look young love in the face tonight." Alex noticed how Nat swallowed hard before continuing, how she hesitated to say the next words. "Today's the day, you know. My drunkest day of the year."

That's when Alex remembered. Nat had the morbid habit of commemorating the day Claire had dumped her three years ago. Claire, the woman Nat had left Brooklyn and moved to Hong Kong for. She got up and walked around the table, sitting down in the chair next to Nat.

"I say this with the biggest amount of love in my heart." She took Nat's hand in hers. "But isn't it time you broke that habit?"

Nat brought both their hands to her face. "Good grief, Pizza. You could have washed. You reek of sex."

"Don't do what you always do, Orange."

"Don't try to fix me." Alex hadn't counted on this display of grief. It made her all the more determined to hook Nat up with Isabella, if only for a talk.

"I'm just trying to help you." She gave Nat's hand one final squeeze before releasing it. "Just like you would do for me."

"One drink and the shrink'd better bring some of that Cadenhead."

"You got it." Alex risked a wink. Nat responded with the beginning of a sly smile, the cocky one all the girls fell for.

"And none of that lovey-dovey stuff, okay? Be kind to single lesbians."

"Cross my heart." Alex got up. "Come on. Stand up."

"What for?" Nat pinched her eyebrows together. Alex pulled her up by her arms.

"Because I want to hug the silliness out of you." She slung her arms around Nat's firm frame and held her tight. Nat fell into the embrace with a desperation Alex hadn't expected.

* * *

Two hours later, all four of them sat around Maddie's round dining table. She'd prepared roasted chicken thighs, grilled asparagus and baked potatoes and Alex was quite impressed with her cooking skills. Isabella had brought a few bottles of Bardolino. Nat had purchased a bottle of the strong stuff herself. Her blue eyes were already a bit glazed over, but Alex knew she was better trained than that. She could drink a bottle and still be standing.

Maddie's hand rested on Alex's thigh while Isabella poured the wine. Her best friend, a little broken but not unfixable, sat across from her. Not bad for a fitness instructor who, a few weeks ago, was still nursing a badly broken heart. Moving into The Ivy, one of the poshest high rises in Hong Kong, had been one of the best decisions she'd ever made.

UNDISCLOSED DESIRES

ISABELLA

"Claire was a proud serial monogamist."

Isabella had found Nat waiting for her, sunk to the floor, an almost empty bottle of Scotch in hand, in front of her door after she returned from Maddie's apartment. She now sat across from Isabella, her back slouched against the sofa cushions, her speech slurred and her eyes droopy. All it did was make her even more attractive, in that lost child bohemian kind of way Isabella found so hard to resist. She believed in causes and rescuing people from themselves. She was convinced Nat needed her. Even at well past midnight on a Sunday evening.

"Just like every other fool who came before me, I thought I could change her." Nat eyed the glass of water on the coffee table, but didn't reach for it. As if she had a point to prove. She shook her head. "Obviously, I couldn't."

Isabella had done her research months ago, after first recognising Nat in the elevator. It was all over the internet. How Nathalie Orange had left her native Brooklyn for Hong Kong to be with Claire. How she'd fallen for the neon-lit city and the peace she found in its crowded, anonymous streets. How the warm winters agreed with her night time wanderlust.

"She said she believed in relationships, just not forever." Nat's chuckle hesitated between pained and disdainful. "At least she was always honest. As if she warned me beforehand that, surely, at one point she'd lose interest." She pushed some hair away from her forehead. "It didn't hurt any less when she finally did."

Isabella had to lean forward the catch the next words tumbling from Nat's lips.

"Only more." She sagged down a little lower, the muscles of her back giving way to the alcohol, slackening her posture. "She just left. Dumped me and went back to New York within a month. Moving on as if I'd never even existed. That's when I decided…" Nat's blue eyes glistened, a sudden tear moistening them. "That no one would ever do something like that to me again." She didn't bother brushing away the teardrop rolling down her cheekbone. "And guess what? They haven't." She balled her fists in mock victory.

Isabella ignored her shrink instincts. This wasn't a therapy session after all, more like a drunk friend letting it all out on her couch—no doubt because she was, in fact, a psychiatrist by profession—but professional rules didn't apply. She got up and sat down next to Nat, offering her the glass of water.

"Drink this."

Nat held up her hands. "I'd prefer something with a bit more colour and bite." She fixed her eyes on the liquor cabinet flanking the opposite wall.

"Do you have any idea how the Chinese treat alcohol poisoning?"

"Do you?" Despite the mistiness of her gaze, Nat was quick to respond.

"Not really, but I'm fairly certain it involves a concoction including donkey testicles."

"You're the doctor." Nat grinned, a boyish, brazen smirk taking over her face. "I suppose I have to take your word for it."

"At last, she accepts my authority." Isabella held out the glass of water again. "Drink."

Nat sipped carefully at first, then knocked it all back in greedy gulps. Licking the last drops from her lips, she stared into Isabella's eyes. "Can I have some more?"

Those eyes, Isabella thought as she refilled the glass from a bottle of Evian. Who can ever refuse them anything? The clearest of blue, like the Hong Kong sky after a cleansing tropical storm, hiding oceans of pain and lifetimes of running away.

After downing another glass of water, Nat repositioned. She slung one leg over the other and folded her fingers behind her head, as if settling in for a long night of deep conversation.

"What's your story, Doc? Why are you single?"

Isabella wasn't used to being on the receiving end of a probing question. This one was easy though, and she had a well-prepared answer. "I was married for fifteen years. I felt like a change." It was the truth.

Nat smiled and sucked her bottom lip into her mouth briefly while fixing her gaze on Isabella. "Fair enough, but you know, everyone needs a little tenderness now and then."

"Is that what you call it? Tenderness?" Isabella wondered what was tender about bringing home a new girl every Saturday night.

"I have a lot of respect for my elders. I refrain from using crass language in front of them."

"At least it excludes me from your advances. Being old and such." It stung more than Isabella had expected.

"A dog like me?" Nat spread her elbows wide, pushing her chest forward. "No one's safe as far as I'm concerned."

"I'll remember to double lock my door at night." Isabella reluctantly peeled her eyes away from the cleavage peeking through the V of Nat's t-shirt. "Now, can I give you some friendly advice?"

"I thought you'd never ask, Doc." Nat let her hands fall into her lap, fatigue suddenly conquering her face—that and the amount of Scotch she'd ingested.

"For the next two weeks, don't give in to your baser instincts. Don't pursue *tenderness* as if there's no tomorrow.

Focus on something else. For instance, why after three years, you still feel the need to get shit-faced in remembrance of Claire leaving you."

"I get shit-faced on a much more regular—"

"I don't need arguments," Isabella cut her off. "I only need a yes or a no."

"Fine. No sweat." Nat uncrossed her legs and rested her elbows on them, her breath so close Isabella heard it sing in her ears. "But quid pro quo, Doc. It's the least you can do."

"What do you have in mind?" Intrigued, Isabella leaned in a little closer.

"You let me set you up with a friend of mine."

A small pang of disappointment flared in Isabella's stomach. "Deal," she said anyway.

NAT

Nat wasn't completely oblivious to Isabella's interest in her. She noticed it in the twitch of her muscles as she restrained herself from putting a hand on Nat's thigh. In the widening of her pupils when Nat shed that tear earlier. In the way her features deflated when Nat suggested she'd set her up with a friend. For a shrink, Isabella had a really bad poker face.

"Sophie's a class act, I'm sure you'll like her." All this banter of other women—and the sudden promise of abstinence—had gotten Nat's mind off Claire. She had to give Isabella that. Truth be told, her yearly pilgrimage into complete drunkenness because of Claire was bordering on ridiculous, but one day a year of self-pity wasn't too bad. Nat cursed herself because she was the last person to believe her own lies. "When are you free?"

"I'll let you know." Isabella massaged her temples. "What will you do with all this time freeing up in your schedule?"

"What I always do when I have some time on my hands."

Nat straightened her back, getting ready to leave. "Dream of a better future."

"I'd love to know what that entails." Isabella's eyes flashed with intensity again, one last sparkle before the day ended.

"Let's save that for the next session, Doc." Nat winked at Isabella and stood up. "I'll let myself out."

Later, alone in bed—and in the flat, as Alex spent most nights at Maddie's—Nat wondered if this was what an existential crisis felt like. Or if it was all still down to Claire. Claire, the one woman she couldn't have, who, out of the blue had turned up on her doorstep and told Nat she'd broken up with Amy and that she was available now. Claire Foster and Amy Perez, banker and literary agent, New York's ultra-power lesbian couple, at least throughout 2005 and a good chunk of 2006. You couldn't find a woman more loyal than Claire, until she was done with you. Then you might as well not have existed anymore.

Nat had managed to keep hold of her for three years. "Longer than anyone else that came before you," Claire used to tease, in better days, before her heart programmed to serially kill relationships prevailed again.

It has been three years since those three years, was the last thought drifting through Nat's mind before she dozed off. Maybe it was time to get her act together.

* * *

The next day, while crafting an elaborate email to Sophie in which she raved about Isabella—an easier task than expected —Alex stormed in.

"You're up early. Date with the muse?" She joked. She had that satiated look about her only young lovers display during the first months of courtship.

"You know me too well, Pizza." Nat flipped the lid of her laptop down. "Actually, I'm working on a master plan plotting the happiness of one Miss Isabella Douglas."

"Really?" Alex settled on a chair opposite from Nat. "Are

you making arrangements to offer yourself to her on a silver platter?"

"Nice try." Nat pouted her lips. "But we both know I'm in no state to fit into anyone's plans during their pursuit of happiness."

"You'd be surprised." Nat noticed scratches—old and fresh ones—on Alex's shoulder. "And don't sell yourself short like that."

"I'm arranging a blind date with her and Sophie from my book club."

Alex raised her eyebrows and wolf-whistled. "You're setting yourself up with some stiff competition there. Sophie's gorgeous."

"That's the whole point. And let's leave me out of the equation, please. I know you and Maddie are desperate to go on double dates with us once the novelty of your affair wears off, but it's never going to happen. I like her, just not in that way."

"Whatever you say, Orange. But remember, I know you too well." Alex shoved her chair back and rose. "Want to grab some lunch?"

"Not today. I'll be living a more indoor lifestyle for the next two weeks." Nat opened the lid of her laptop again, the email to Sophie brightly flickering on the screen.

"What the hell is going on here?" Alex planted both her hands on the wooden table top. "What have I missed?" She fixed her eyes on Nat.

"I made a deal with Isabella last night." Nat hesitated a split second too long and Alex jumped in.

"Last night? When? I thought you went out?"

"I ended up having a late night conversation with Isabella and we agreed that I could organise a date with Sophie if I refrained from picking up girls for two weeks."

Alex sank back down into her chair. "This is a historic moment, Orange." Alex reached across the table and grabbed Nat's arms. "It took her one conversation to get you to do what I've been trying to accomplish for months."

"Apparently you don't seem to have the same powers of persuasion." Nat shook Alex's hands off her. "And don't go making more out of it than it is. I'd like to keep Isabella as a friend."

Alex held her hands up in defence. "You have my word, roomie, I swear. If Isabella's friendship has this effect on you, who am I to question something so powerful?" Alex's eyes glowed, maybe with hope or compassion, but most probably satisfaction.

"If you will excuse me, Pizza. I have a blind date to arrange."

ISABELLA

When it came to picking other people's dates, Nat had impeccable taste. The woman sitting across from Isabella at Le Petit Duc, another brand new French restaurant catering to the ever-growing French population of Hong Kong, was a real stunner. Milk chocolate skin stretching tautly around almond-shaped eyes. An Irish accent to die for, curls for days and not half bad at conversation either.

"This city is not exactly littered with eligible bachelorettes of our persuasion," Sophie said, before taking another sip of the Bordeaux Isabella had chosen.

"About that." Isabella cleared her throat before continuing. "I don't know what Nat has told you about me but I may not be the full-time lesbian you take me for."

Sophie smoothed the napkin in her lap before speaking. "She told me you were enough of one to risk going on a blind date." She flashed Isabella a small smile. "And that's a quote."

A loud laugh escaped Isabella. She wasn't in the habit of discussing her sexuality at length—like all the youngsters did these days. "All my significant relationships have been with men. I was married to one for fifteen years. But I've had my fair share of…" Isabella racked her brain for the least offensive words.

"Experiments?" Sophie asked, a sudden tightness around her mouth.

"Same-sex affairs involving enough feelings to merit the label relationship."

"But not enough to be significant?" Sophie reached for the bottle, refilling her empty glass.

For all her degrees and years of studying human interaction, Isabella always had trouble explaining, which was why she usually chose not to—and shied away from blind dates.

"My ex-husband and I had an open relationship the last five years of our marriage." Isabella tried hard to not sound like a professor explaining a math problem. "During that time I started a relationship with a woman that lasted almost three years, but my marriage always came first. After my divorce I made the conscious choice to stay single for a while."

"Jesus Christ." Sophie snorted. "And I thought lesbians were champions at complicating things."

"It's not complicated anymore. I'm single, available, and into women." Despite that last statement, Isabella was well aware she was sabotaging the date. She hadn't set out to do so, not really, but most sane women looking for a relationship—thus going on blind dates—would not go for someone with her complex past.

"Just not significantly," Sophie shot back. "I'm sorry." She regrouped, taking a sip of water. "I don't mean to be rude. I'm old and wise enough to know love is more fluid than girl meets girl."

"It's my fault entirely." Isabella leaned over the table. "I shouldn't have mentioned my messy marriage before the main course."

A waiter approached with two plates. Duck breast salad for Sophie and bouillabaisse for Isabella. They halted conversation until he left.

"Let's chalk it up to blind date nerves," Sophie whispered. "And please excuse me for my über-lesbian reaction."

"Shall we start afresh over our mains?" Isabella extended her hand. "Hi, I'm Isabella and I'm your complicated date for tonight."

Sophie chuckled and shook her hand. "Sophie, your judgemental dinner companion."

"Glad we got off on the right foot."

"Better than any date I've been on this past year." Sophie speared a piece of duck on her fork. "Let's see." She found Isabella's eyes. "There was a completely self-obsessed French woman who could not stop talking about herself and all her wonderful accomplishments. A very cute Chinese woman with whom I got totally lost in translation. And a Canadian who was really only after a job at my firm, including a work visa." Sophie nibbled her duck like someone brought up with a lot of emphasis on table manners.

Isabella giggled, amused by Sophie's candour. Maybe Nat had found her a good match. And perhaps she owed it to herself to give Sophie a fair chance, seeing as Nat clearly had no interest in her. "Can I ask you something personal?"

"That's what I'm here for, right?" Sophie shot her a smile bordering on flirtatious. Isabella responded by chewing her bottom lip.

"Have you and Nat ever, you know…" Isabella's pulse picked up speed as she waited for the reply, as if this was the million dollar question and everything depended on its answer.

"God no, you know what she's like." Sophie rolled her eyes. "She'd flirt with your grandmother for hours, but would end up taking your impressionable teenage niece home."

"How long have you known her?" Isabella realised Sophie could be a valuable source of information.

"About four years. She joined our book club after we invited her to read for us. A year before it all went south with Claire." Sophie put down her cutlery and continued in a conspiring manner. "Dreadful that was. Nearly destroyed her. She didn't show up for months. Until one day she re-appeared with a twenty-year-old English Lit student on her arm. The ladies were not impressed, but they let it go because she's Nathalie Orange." Sophie sought Isabella's glance. "Have you?"

"Have I what?" Isabella's brain was too busy processing all the data on Nat to follow Sophie's train of thought.

"You know, you and Nat? Two single women living in the same building." Sophie scrunched her eyebrows together twice in quick succession.

Heat flared on Isabella's cheeks. Just the assumption was enough to awaken long-sleeping butterflies in her stomach. "No, no," she stuttered, a mere shadow of the confident psychiatrist she believed to be. "Of course not."

"I see." Sophie nodded, her lips bunched in a knowing pout. "I do like you, Isabella, but it seems to me that you have some issues to work out."

Isabella wondered what the right thing to do was. What would she, as an objective sounding board, advise someone else to do next? Full disclosure, of course, but it was much harder to practice than to preach.

"Look, it's—" She started.

"Complicated?" The smile on Sophie's face was much friendlier than Isabella had expected. "You don't have to explain. Just tell me this… if you have a thing for Nat, what are you doing here?"

"We're going to need another bottle of wine." Isabella raised her hand and called for the waiter.

NAT

Nat punched the air with more vigour than usual.

"Final round, team," Alex shouted from the front. "Time

to empty that tank."

Nat balled her fists tighter and slammed them into nothing. She focused on Maddie and Isabella's rhythmically bouncing shoulders in front of her. They boxed against their invisible enemy in perfect sync, as if they had practiced it beforehand.

"Well done, guys." Alex slapped her hands together. "Give yourself a well-deserved round of applause." A smile graced her flatmate's lips, the same smile Nat had been forced to watch for days. Not that she wasn't happy for Alex, but after years of self-chosen singlehood and loose midnight encounters, their flat seemed to burst with early romance hormones. It was her flat—and Alex was hardly ever there—but somehow Nat felt as if she belonged there less now that a different vibe had taken over.

They gathered outside the studio, the four of them, a tangled-up blend of neighbours, friends and lovers. A few months ago they'd barely nodded in recognition and now Alex was sleeping with Maddie and Isabella knew more about Nat than she felt comfortable with.

"A decaf at The Bean before bed?" Maddie asked.

New friends, new habits. On any other Wednesday Nat would have either holed up in her office with a bottle of Scotch or ventured out into the night in search of distraction. Now she spent her evenings in brightly lit coffee shops in the company of self-assured lesbians with well-rounded personalities. "Sure, I have a certain esteemed psychiatrist to grill on a blind date, anyway."

"There's really not that much to say." Isabella's head was flushed red, sweat dripping from every pore. For a woman her age, she had spectacular arms. "I possibly made a new friend and that's it."

"Come on. How can you look at Sophie and not want to ravage her? She's by far the hottest Hong Kong has to offer in the more mature lesbian department" They made their way to the changing rooms. "And anyway, that's not what I heard."

All three of them turned to Nat with an inquisitive look on their face. Isabella was the only one who spoke.

"Oh really? Do share your information." She brushed a drop of sweat from her forehead, hiding her eyes behind the towel.

"Sophie said that, provided some kinks got worked out, there could be something." Nat yanked Isabella's towel from her hands. "I presume the kinks are most persistent on your end?"

"I have absolutely no idea what you're talking about."

Scottish skin is so revealing, Nat thought. She didn't say it out loud so as not to embarrass Isabella, whose neck and ears had turned a deep shade of crimson, while the blush of their workout should have receded by then.

"Whether you're expecting it or not, you should prepare for a second date invitation. Apparently you made quite the impression on Sophie. Of course, she's a sucker for lesbian drama. She can't help herself."

Nat wisely left out what else Sophie had told her. That is was clear Isabella had the hots for her. That throughout the date she had displayed a subtle but stubborn interest in details about Nat's life, quizzing Sophie on her friend's most obvious psychological shortcomings. "Nevertheless," Sophie had said to Nat, "she needs as much rescuing from herself as she believes that you do from yourself. I think I'm the right woman at the right time."

To have it spelled out like that by Sophie had confused Nat. She knew Isabella was interested in her, but she'd thought it to be more in a professional way—the save the poor-little-rich-girl routine.

"Thanks for the heads-up," Isabella mumbled and clumsily headed for her locker. She was so damn cute when she lost composure.

Still, despite the banter between them, and the deeper connection established the previous Sunday night, Nat couldn't picture them together at all. Isabella was almost fifteen years older than her. She'd been married to a man for a decade and a half and had no proven track record of successful lesbian relationships. They were from a different generation—and world—altogether. Isabella probably didn't know what dubstep was. She'd probably never set foot in Volt or Fortune or Munchies, Nat's favourite hang-outs.

Later, in The Bean, Isabella was uncharacteristically quiet, like a child caught stealing cookies, not exactly a gloomy silence, more a guilty one.

"Why don't you join our book club?" Nat focused her attention on Isabella. Maddie and Alex were wrapped up in their own little loved-up world. "That way you can get to know her better, but from a distance. With less pressure."

"Which book are you reading? *Fifty Shades of Grey*?" Isabella immediately went on the defence. "I have more classic taste in literature."

"You'll fit in perfectly then." Nat ruffled through her bag and dug up a battered copy of Camus's *The Stranger*. "I've read it a dozen times, so you can have this one if you want. The next meeting is on Tuesday, if you're a fast reader."

Despite having her own copy at home, Isabella accepted the book and thumbed through it. "It's one of my favourites." Her eyes glistened with recognition, like they do when people find unexpected common ground.

"It's a deal then?" Nat glanced at Isabella, unable to predict her reply.

"Can we talk in private for a minute?" She held the book close to her chest before rising out of her chair. "My place in half an hour?"

ISABELLA

Innocent flirting was no problem for Isabella, nor was the odd innuendo now and again, but the instant deeper feelings became involved, she got serious. Which is why she paced the length of her flat, nervously waiting for Nat, racking her brain for a good way to say what she had to say.

A few minutes later Nat rang her bell. Isabella opened the door and Nat stood there, leaning against the door frame, a grin on her face, looking ten years younger than her age.

"I hope this is not a booty call because my doctor prescribed abstinence." She fiddled with one of the two small silver crucifixes dangling from her neck, glowering at Isabella from under long dark lashes, head tilted sideways.

If charming cockiness were a person, I'd be looking at them right now, Isabella thought. "Come in."

Isabella had prepared two glasses and started pouring from a bottle of Cadenhead.

"Not for me. I'm cleansing my liver as well as my…" Nat paused for effect. "You know what."

In response, Isabella poured herself a double. She headed to the sofa and gestured for Nat to follow. She cleared her throat before speaking.

"I'm not going to date your friend. And I'd appreciate it if you didn't pressure me about it." Isabella buried her eyes in the golden liquid of her glass. "Don't get me wrong, she was perfectly lovely but Sophie is not what I'm looking for. In fact, I'm not looking at all."

When Isabella dared to look up, Nat leaned back in the couch, her lips drawn into a smirk, her arms spread wide on the backrest. Was everything really a joke to her?

"Give it to me straight, Doc. Quid pro quo, remember?"

Isabella had guessed Nat wouldn't let her off the hook so easily. "I kept my end of the bargain. I met up with Sophie. It didn't work out."

Nat sighed and shook her head. "If that's your definition of giving it to me straight, I do wonder about the mental health of your clients."

Refusing to take that kind of bait, Isabella let the insult wash over her. "Are you really going to make me say it?" She locked eyes with Nat briefly before downing a good gulp of Scotch.

"Say what, Doc? Why am I here?" Nat played the innocent. She probably knew what was going on inside Isabella's head better than Isabella did herself.

"I'm sorry. I shouldn't have asked you here. It was a mistake." Isabella became acutely aware of the fact that she had allowed emotion to cloud her judgement. She wasn't going to succumb to confessing a foolish crush on Nathalie Orange. She hardly knew the person sitting across from her. Nat might as well be a client. She might as well mean nothing to her. This entire situation was ludicrous to say the least. Isabella was no match for a skinny-jeaned hipster with wax in her hair.

"Suit yourself." Nat hoisted herself out of the couch and sauntered over to Isabella, where she crouched in front of her. "Hope to see you at book club, if not before, neighbour."

Isabella's eyes followed Nat, and the ridiculous swagger of her walk, as she exited the apartment, the door crashing behind her with a loud bang.

* * *

"Look who just returned from the planet of love." Isabella kissed Maddie hello and threw in a quick hug, eager to absorb some of the good vibrations radiating from her body. "What does it feel like to sleep with the hottest trainer in town?"

"Incredibly inadequate at times, I must confess." Maddie chuckled. "But overall, it has nothing but perks."

"I'd ask for details, but I'm not sure I can handle them in my current condition."

A waiter appeared and took their drinks order, a bottle of Sauvignon Blanc and two glasses of water. This was lunch, after all. Isabella had two clients this afternoon and Maddie must have a few millions to make.

"I'm the one who needs details. What's going on with you? I get myself a girlfriend and you go off the rails?" Maddie pinned her blue-grey eyes on Isabella, calming her. Why couldn't Nat's eyes have the same effect? Why did the mere presence of them have to set her flesh on fire? Surely, that wasn't normal behaviour for a woman of her age—and wisdom.

"I honestly think I'm losing my mind." Isabella held her head between spread-out fingertips. "It started as an almost purely professional interest and in a matter of weeks it has turned into this massive…" She pointed her palms upwards in despair. "Infatuation." She slapped her hands down on the soft table cloth. "I find it hard to even be in the same room with her these days. I lose my nerve. I'm not myself. I go on disastrous blind dates with gorgeous women. It's madness." Isabella giggled nervously. "Look at me. I'm a wreck."

The waiter arrived with the wine and filled their glasses. Isabella didn't wait for him to turn his back before taking a greedy gulp. "I've even started mimicking her drinking habits."

"You enjoyed a stiff drink long before Nathalie Orange entered the scene." Maddie shot her a knowing smile.

"I managed it fine until last Sunday, when she turned up on my doorstep out of the blue. Before, she was merely an attractive woman with a huge guard up. Someone unattainable. Someone to dream of when your attention was loose and floundering. A flirt with no consequences. But I saw the real Nat that night, for the briefest of moments she opened up to me, and all I've wanted to do since then is hold her in my arms and kiss it better. And I'm a psychiatrist for heaven's sake."

"Don't be so hard on yourself. Alex and I invited you both to dinner that night for a reason. Sparks have been flying since you met. You'd have to be blind not to see that." Maddie leaned over the table and grabbed Isabella's arm. "But she's a difficult one. According to Alex, complicated doesn't even begin to describe it. And it doesn't help that she's stubborn as a mule. Alex's words."

"I think you're wrong. We do have a connection, but it's not the same for her as it is for me. And we're polar opposites." Just talking about it was a huge weight off Isabella's shoulders.

"You couldn't be more different, that's true, but Alex is convinced Nat feels something for you. She may never admit to it. She may prefer a faceless shag every other day over owning up to her emotions, but we both agree there's something there."

"Then what is she doing setting me up with her friend? Insisting on me getting to know her better?"

"Beats me. You're the shrink." They both burst out in giggles. The waiter interrupted to take their food order and they both ordered the set lunch.

Isabella was none the wiser after lunch than before, but at least she'd gotten it off her chest. A powerful remedy to all sorts of mental aches, she knew from experience.

NAT

"Pizza, come here." Nat felt strangely satisfied to be able to call her flatmate's name and actually have her show up. She'd caught herself doing it before, to no avail, because Alex was chained to their upstairs neighbour's bed, confined to spend most of her free time one floor above.

"What?" Alex had a towel wrapped around her body and big drops of water rained from her hair.

"I've found a TV show we can both enjoy." Nat pointed the remote control to the screen. "It's enough of a bubblegum soap to get you hooked and it's layered enough to keep me entertained." Nat pressed the play button. "And check this." She kept her eyes glued to the screen. "Isn't that the most adorable little lesbian you've ever seen? If this was reality TV, I'd move to Chicago in a heartbeat."

Alex rolled her eyes. "What is it?"

"It's called *Underemployed* and it's light and smart at the same time." Nat pinned a hopeful gaze on Alex. "And the cute Asian lesbian character is a writer. Can you believe it?"

"Couldn't this unveiling of your TV crush have waited until after I'd finished my bath?" Alex leaned down on the armrest of the sofa, uncharacteristically not caring about the amount of water she was shedding on the rug. "And how much longer will this dry spell go on for? I'm getting worried about you."

"I'm just refocusing my energy. This TV show is what it has landed on." Nat shifted her body to better face Alex. "And look how the tables have turned. Not long ago we were talking about your dry spell, Pizza. Which, if I may remind you, lasted much longer than the six days I've had."

"Maybe Isabella had something else in mind than substituting real life Asian lesbian tweens with fictional ones." Alex's towel started to split, revealing sensational obliques.

"We both know what Isabella really wants." Nat arched her eyebrows. "And you'd better take care of that towel because I'm feeling dangerously frisky."

"Tough luck, Orange." Alex held the ends of the towel open a bit more. "This body is spoken for."

"Bankers get everything good in this town." Nat winked at Alex. "Hot date tonight?"

"Yes, with you, that couch, and this new TV show. Maddie has a work thing."

"You've no idea how honoured I am." Beneath the banter, Nat was truly grateful. She hadn't allowed herself to even feel the smallest pang of loneliness. It wasn't the intimacy she missed, or the girls. It was more the simple act of being with someone, of being distracted. With Alex spending more time out of their flat than inside of it, and her own new lifestyle choice, Nat had to face a degree of being alone she'd always carefully managed to avoid.

"Let me put some clothes on." Alex beamed her a warm smile. "Before your frustrated hands ravage me."

Frustration was the last thing Nat felt. It was more a blend of small bouts of jealousy for the early romance bliss Alex found herself in and the dawning realisation that she'd gotten a lot of things very wrong. That, since Claire left, she'd been coasting through life, getting by, instead of really living it.

"Will you have coffee with Sophie and me tomorrow afternoon?" Nat asked Alex when she returned to the living room, sporting the inevitable black sweat pants and white tank top. "I need a second opinion on this whole setting her up with Isabella business. I need to know if I'm doing the right thing."

"That should be interesting." Alex settled in the sofa next to her, their shoulders touching the way they'd grown accustomed to. "Now hit me with some brainless entertainment."

* * *

It wasn't often that Nat witnessed Alex openly ogle someone, but she was doing just that. Sophie's striking appearance had that effect on people, even on someone as in control as Alex.

"I've called her, but she doesn't pick up. Doesn't get back to me either. It's pretty clear to me." Sophie stirred sweetener into her coffee, the movement of her arm making her curls dance on her shoulders. "It's simply not meant to be."

"Not so fast." Nat felt responsible, and she wasn't very good at failing. "That's not what you said last time we spoke."

"That was before I called her five times. We all have our ego to take into consideration when it comes to matters like this." Sophie buried her eyes in her coffee cup, avoiding Nat's glare.

"I know, but meanwhile, there's been a breakthrough." Nat noticed how Alex raised her eyebrows. Otherwise, she was a respectfully quiet audience. "This mild crush she may have on me. It's never going to go anywhere."

"Oh, and I get promoted to sloppy seconds. Whoopee." Sophie pursed her lips into a pout and shook her head.

"I know you like her, Sophie. Give her another chance."

"If she wants another chance, she'd better give me one first. The ball's in her court." Sophie shifted her gaze to Alex. "What do you think?"

Alex cleared her throat. "I think you're all grown-ups who indulge too much in teenage-like hormonal behaviour."

Sophie burst out laughing. Nat was less amused.

"I promise she'll call you before the end of the weekend."

"And who are you to make that kind of promise?" Sophie refocused her attention on Nat. "Stop trying. It's no big deal. She didn't lie to me, didn't behave dishonestly. And I didn't get my feelings hurt. It was one blind date, not the end of the world."

"But it does sting a little, doesn't it?" Nat kept on trying. "I'll make it right."

ISABELLA

Isabella was more than surprised when the call came. She'd skipped body combat class on Friday to avoid Nat, but had, much against her own advice, started reading *The Stranger* again —not because she wanted to join the book club, but because the book belonged to Nat.

"I have in my possession," Nat had said over the phone, her voice brimming with *the Nat swag* as Isabella had coined it, "Blu-ray discs of *Casablanca* and *North by Northwest*. A bottle of your favourite Bordeaux and an array of French cheeses I can never eat on my own. Care to join me on an indoor evening of decadence?"

The mixed messages swirled in Isabella's brain. Was it a date? An apology? And if so, for what? Or was Nat lonely and needing to talk?

"How can I possibly say no to that?" It had been raining all morning and Isabella had planned a cosy night in, safely shielded from the elements. Why not spend it in charming company? All she had to do was take the elevator two floors down. And it would give her a chance to see Nat's flat.

* * *

"I see you're taking your vow of abstinence seriously." Isabella presented Nat with another bottle of Bordeaux.

"At least one of us has to honour our arrangement. Otherwise, it would just cease to exist."

"Mm." Isabella ignored Nat's comment. If she didn't, she would be in for a long night of torment. "Nice place."

Nat had obviously had work done on the place. Flats in The Ivy didn't come equipped with wall-length book cases and white-washed floorboards. Drawn to the colourful spines of Nat's book collection, Isabella inched closer and let a finger glide over them.

"At least you have good taste in literature." Did she really say that out loud?

"Taste is so subjective." Nat came to stand next to her, eyeing Kafka and Bukowski paperbacks together with Isabella. "Take the lovely Sophie for example. Ninety percent of this city's lesbian population would jump at the chance of a date with her, but what does Isabella Douglas do?" Nat turned to her, her blue eyes already piercing through Isabella's resolve. "She doesn't return her calls."

At least the mystery of the impromptu invitation had been solved. This was about Sophie.

"That's not very polite, is it? Or is that how they do things in Scotland?" Nat continued, her gaze scanning Isabella's face for signs of weakness—at least, that's how it felt.

"I was still considering it." It wasn't a complete lie. Sophie had been pleasant enough company and she had called Isabella five times. No matter what Maddie claimed to know about Nat, she would never fall into Isabella's arms without a long, drawn-out fight. And even if she did, then what? Isabella didn't feel like becoming another of Nathalie Orange's one-night-stands. She needed a distraction and, as far as distractions went, Sophie fit the bill more than perfectly.

"How about a renegotiation of our deal?" Isabella asked.

Nat stared at a shelf completely dedicated to hardcovers of Elizabeth George's Thomas Linley mysteries. "Don't you think *With No One As Witness* is one of the best crime novels ever written?"

"I wholeheartedly agree." Isabella had trouble ignoring the image of her and Nat's bare feet propped up on an ottoman on a Sunday afternoon. The beginning of a typhoon raging outside while they were both immersed in a book, sharing a bottle of wine between them. Out of nowhere, it had popped into her head. As if Nat were the type to engage in some gentle afternoon reading. She seemed more like someone who nursed a vile weekend hangover with another round of Scotch. Possibly something stronger. "How about I commit to at least two more dates with Sophie. I'll call her tomorrow. And you add another week to your new way of life."

"Well-played, Doc." Nat gave her a half-smile. "It's a deal. Now, can I interest you in some light snacks and beverages?"

Halfway through the first movie—*North by Northwest*—Nat fell asleep. First her eyelids shut, then her lips opened slightly, letting out gentle puffs of air with every breath, followed by her body sagging deeper into the cushions—and closer to Isabella. As her breathing got heavier, her bare arm slumped closer toward Isabella's shoulder.

Oblivious to the suspense on the screen, Isabella waited patiently until that final breath, the one that would catapult Nathalie Orange, if not into, at least against her arms. She fixed her eyes on Nat's heaving shape and waited, immobile and with a mounting tension in her muscles.

"Oh damn." Nat smacked her lips together and hoisted herself up. She'd been so close, perhaps only five breaths away from touching. "I dozed off for a minute."

"That was a nice snoring symphony you performed there," Isabella joked while her blood hammered in her veins. "Do you want me to rewind?"

"Not necessary. I've seen this movie about twenty times.

I can tell you exactly what's going to happen in the next scene."

"So can I, as a matter of fact." Isabella chuckled.

"But it's perfect for a gloomy Saturday night cheese-and-wine fest." Nat straightened her posture, widening the distance between Isabella and her.

"Why gloomy?" Isabella could never keep herself from asking such questions.

Nat shrugged. "I've had a lot of time to think lately. Maybe too much. No booze, except for the occasional glass of wine." She reached out her hand to grab her drink. "No girls. An absent flat mate. A finished first draft. It hasn't exactly been fun and games on the forty-second floor of late."

"It surprises me you would include a finished first draft in that list. Isn't that a good thing?" Isabella spun herself towards Nat to better pick up on her body language.

"I love writing the first draft. Pounding out the words as if there's no tomorrow, as if no one will ever read them. The first draft is the fun bit. It's all bloody hard work from there. And endless as well."

"It also sounds like a cause for celebration, though. Have you celebrated at all?"

"I haven't been in the most celebratory of moods lately, Doc. Seem to have lost my mojo. Don't really know what's going on."

Isabella witnessed Nat deflating in front of her, just like a week ago when she'd found her perched on her doorstep. As a matter of self-protection, she decided to retreat into professional mode. No almost touching of arms this time around and no succumbing to the vulnerability of Nathalie Orange. Isabella was smart enough to know that this was the Nat she had fallen for. This bruised but proud person trying to find her way, not the loud-mouthing philanderer with alcohol on her breath.

"It may take a little while before you feel better, but, trust me, it will get better." Isabella eyed her glass of wine but thought it wiser to not drink anymore. "You're on the right track. Changing your behaviour. Confronting yourself. You're doing important work."

"If I understand you right, it needs to get worse before it gets better though?" The blue in Nat's glance had shed some of its sparkle.

"Not necessarily. Try to focus on positive things. Events you look forward to. People whose company you enjoy." Isabella returned Nat's broken stare with a confident smile. She realised Nat had a long way to go, and her journey was more important than any hormones waging war in her own menopausal blood.

NAT

Nat woke up in the sofa at three in the morning with a blanket thrown over her body. The cheese had been transported back to the fridge. The wine bottle had a metal cork popped in its neck and the glasses and crockery awaited a wash-up in the sink. Good thing last night wasn't a date because she prided herself on never falling asleep on a date—except when they involved sleep-overs of course, but even then she always waited until the other party nodded off first.

She dragged herself to bed and, before settling her head onto the pillow, pointed her ears towards the ceiling to check if the upstairs neighbours were getting any sleep at all. Except for the never-ending rush of cars outside, everything was silent.

Before allowing herself to drift off again, she remembered the talk she'd had with Isabella. It was so easy to confide in her. It must be her shrink vibe, as if she could see right through Nat and all her antics. As if, with her only, there was no need for pretending.

When she woke up again five hours later, hangover-free

and with a surprising spring in her step, she threw the windows open and inhaled the damp air. Hong Kong always felt reborn after a good rainstorm. And it didn't get glacially cold in November.

After a shower, Nat grabbed her laptop and made her way to The Bean for some Sunday morning surfing and, who knew, maybe some revising of her work in progress, tentatively titled *In My Name*.

Cindy, the barista, who reminded Nat of the lesbian writer in *Underemployed* with her big nerdy glasses and shy smile, couldn't believe it when Nat showed up before ten a.m. on a Sunday morning.

"Morning, Nathalie," she cooed, batting her dark lashes twice. "Double espresso?"

Nat nodded. A week ago she wouldn't have hesitated. She would have inquired about the end of Cindy's shift. She would have waited or come back when she was done working and taken her to Fortune for a drink, then back to the flat for some Sunday afternoon fondling. How easy it would be to while away another day like that. Nat had no trouble imagining exactly how good it would feel.

"Thanks, Cindy." She planted an elbow on the counter and slanted her body sideways, looking up at Cindy with wide eyes. "Morning shift?"

"It's not so bad on a Sunday." The noise of the coffee machine temporarily halted their conversation. "You're up early." Cindy deposited a steaming green mug of coffee in front of Nat. The vapours rose up around Cindy's angelic face, framing it as if in a feverish erotic dream.

"I knew I had to be here on time if I wanted to catch you." Nat accompanied her statement with a broad smile.

Cindy reciprocated with a timid one.

"Can I buy you a…" Nat's next move was interrupted by the cheery door jingle announcing the arrival of another customer. Cindy's attention immediately shifted. She pushed her glasses high up her nose and painted a friendly smile on her face. Nat shot her a quick wink and left some money on the counter before turning to find a seat.

"Hey, Orange, ignoring's not going to work." Alex's bossy fitness instructor voice cut through the coffee house's snug Sunday morning atmosphere.

"Well, well. Look who managed to drag herself out of bed and was let out of the flat on her own on a weekend day. Shocking."

Alex ignored Nat's remark and kissed her on the cheek. "What happened to you?"

"Why don't you get yourself a coffee and I'll tell you all about it." Nat gestured at Cindy, whose grin had gone back to displaying small signs of being smitten. Or at least interested enough.

"Where's your woman?" Nat asked as soon as Alex sat down.

"Getting Isabella out of bed so she can join my special Sunday afternoon body combat class. I'm filling in for Jason. Want to come out and play?"

Nat peered at Cindy behind the counter. It was either body combat or break the deal with Isabella. If she lingered in The Bean on her own, she knew how it would end—the same way it always did.

"What time?"

"I wouldn't want to keep you from more important tasks, of course." Alex shot her a knowing smirk. "Two o'clock."

Nat cast one more longing glance at Cindy, who was occupied serving another customer. "Sure, I'll be there."

"How's your you-know-what going?" Alex leaned in closer. "And the grand Isabella-Sophie set-up scheme?"

"You're usually not one to gossip, Pizza. What's gotten into you?"

"I'd tell you in great detail, but I'm pretty sure you don't want to know."

"Don't be so certain. At least I'd get to live vicariously through you." Nat sighed. "Damn, that's sad."

"What?" Alex beamed a glorious smile brimming with sexual satisfaction. "Because for once I'm getting more than you?"

Nat bowed her head. "You said it, not me."

"Maddie is just…" Alex leaned back in her chair, bliss written all over her face. "So amazing. She instinctively knows what I want. I don't have to tell her. Don't even have to hint at it."

"I see, your affair has graduated to spanking already. I'm so happy for you, Pizza."

A flush crept along Alex's cheeks. "So, tell me about you." She changed the subject.

"Well, it looks like you arrived in the nick of time. I was about to fall off the wagon." From the corner of her eye, Nat caught Cindy ogling her.

"I thought as much." Alex emptied her mochaccino. "Come on, I'm taking you to brunch. You'll need the energy if you want to survive my class this afternoon."

Nat grabbed her laptop bag and notebook and made for the door with Alex, turning around once more to shoot Cindy an apologetic look.

ISABELLA

If Isabella had known Nat would be in body combat class, she probably wouldn't have invited Sophie. Then again, it was an excellent way to prove to Nat she was sticking to her end of the new deal. In Isabella's mind, having Sophie join Alex's body combat class counted as one of the two dates she had committed to. It was an inconspicuous way of spending time together. She'd attend the book club meeting next, and, depending on any sparks arising, that'd be that—and she'd have been true to her word.

Seeing them side by side, Nat with her scrawny hair and

boyish looks and Sophie with her skin the colour of caramel and her wavy dark hair was, in terms of assessing compatibility, quite the eye-opener.

"Dreaming of a threesome?" Maddie whispered in her ear during a short break between tracks.

It hadn't crossed her mind but now that Maddie had planted the seed, Isabella had trouble keeping up with the complicated hook-jab-cross combo Alex demonstrated in the front. The mere thought of it was enough to soak Isabella's skin in another layer of sweat. After class, she had trouble forming coherent sentences. Luckily, she could blame it on the strenuous workout.

"If there's no one else in there, the steam cabin should have enough room for the five of us," Alex said.

"We all know Alex loves the steam cabin. It's her favourite means of seduction," Maddie teased. "Are you sure you want three other women in there, babe?"

"It's good for you after a workout." Alex hooked her arm into Maddie's. "And don't you dare question my motives. Or my authority."

Isabella's skin already felt so flustered, she wasn't sure she could face even a minute in the sweaty cabin, certainly not if she was sitting in between Nat and Sophie. She followed along anyway. Before they walked in, steam greeting them, Maddie shot her a wink, her lips curled into a wicked grin.

Isabella chose the corner seat, next to Maddie and Alex and across from Sophie and Nat. Maybe suffer was a big word for it, but lately, she had found herself surprised more than once by a sudden flare of lust. In the five years after her marriage she'd been single, but not always celibate, although her last night of passion had occurred more than a year ago. Pre-menopausal or not, Isabella discovered her juices were still flowing. Especially in that steam cabin.

Alex and Maddie had let their heads fall back, their pinkies touching on a spread out towel on the bench. Sophie and Nat sat grinning opposite her, Nat's paler skin contrasting deliciously with Sophie's exotic complexion. To sit between them now, Isabella thought, would be the hottest sandwich ever. Hottest sandwich? She must have picked that up from Nat at some point because Isabella Douglas did not use expressions like that.

Was this her moment of choice? The goods on display at their finest, skin glistening with sweat, a good deal of naked body parts on offer. They were both equally striking, each in their own way. Nat in an unassuming but über-confident manner, eyes bright blue and up for anything. Sophie with her luscious mane of hair and white-teethed smile, dimples in her chin and her relaxed, everything-will-be-all-right demeanour.

Isabella understood this wasn't about looks. At her age, rapidly approaching fifty, compatibility was of much greater importance. In that respect, Sophie passed the test with flying colours. Nat not so much.

"Shall we go to Pierre's later and have ourselves a well-earned piece of triple chocolate cake?" Nat asked.

"Yes please," Maddie groaned, her eyes still closed.

"You ladies go ahead. I'd like to take Isabella somewhere special," Sophie said, fixing her glance on Isabella, who had almost forgotten this was a date. "Maybe we can meet for drinks later tonight."

"Oooh, have I heard of this special place before?" Nat cooed.

"Nope," Sophie rotated her body to face Nat. "For serious dates only." She turned back to Isabella and gave her a warm smile.

Something took flight in Isabella's stomach, maybe butterflies, but probably just nerves. Apart from that blind date, which had turned into more of a reluctant confession of her crush on Nat, she hadn't really been on one in years. She took a deep breath and returned the smile.

"I need to get out of here before I melt." She stood up and headed for the door. When she walked past Sophie, Sophie stood up and put her hand on the small of Isabella's back.

* * *

"Where are we going?" They waited for a cab at the bottom of the escalator on Hollywood Road.

"Somewhere nice and relaxing, I promise." Sophie hailed a cab and ushered Isabella in. "It's not far, but you'll think you're in another city."

The cab headed east. Isabella had to admit she never ventured much further than Sheung Wan to the west and Wan Chai to the east anymore. It was her habitat of comfort, her stomping ground. Everything she needed was within walking distance. She did go on hikes on the south of the island, and spent a few afternoons on the beach every summer. She occasionally took a boat out to another, less crowded island now and again, to enjoy the seafood and the calmer surroundings.

After fifteen years you stop exploring. Once it felt as if it had become her town, the urge to wander and discover had dissipated. She knew all she needed to know about Hong Kong.

The cab curved along the expressway flanking Causeway Bay, probably the most crowded shopping area in the world, and took a right.

"I'm intrigued." Isabella looked out of the window on Sophie's side and noticed the self-satisfied smirk on her face.

"It's a well-kept secret. Although I suspect not for much longer. More and more expats are discovering the place."

"The curse of every nice spot in this city." Isabella lay a hand on her chest. "I plead guilty as charged."

The taxi pulled up on a wide street with cars parked on either side.

"Welcome to Tai Hang," Sophie said. "I'm looking to buy here and am desperate for a second opinion."

NAT

"What's with the frown, Hemingway?" Nat was about to take the first bite out of her chocolate bomb—a small, perfectly shaped dome of nothing but dark chocolate. Alex interrupted her most pleasurable moment of the day.

"It's my dessert biting face."

"Allow me to disagree." Alex sipped her coffee. If anyone worked her body hard enough to deserve a luscious piece of pastry on a Sunday afternoon, it was Alex, but she was more the abstaining type. Her restraint drove Nat crazy sometimes. "I think it resembles more of a jealous scowl."

"You reap what you sow," Maddie cut in. "If you hadn't insisted on Isabella going out with Sophie again, you wouldn't be sitting here feeling sorry for yourself."

Nat tuned out Alex and Maddie's voices. She should have stayed in The Bean this morning and waited for Cindy. The day had begun so full of promise. Bright blue skies after two days of rain. A clear head. Good intentions. An innocent flirt. She bit into the dome, too big a bite for a posh establishment like Pierre's, and didn't wipe the chocolate from her lips. As far as acts of rebellion went, it was the only one she could resort to at the moment.

She could be in bed with Cindy. Or revising her novel. Or just cruising through the city on this lovely sunny day. Instead, she was watching the worst pair of matchmakers on the planet lick crème patissière from each other's fingers.

Nat swallowed and fixed her eyes on both of them. "Here's the deal, lovebirds. Whatever strange kick you think you might get out of Isabella and me getting together, the time has come to forget about it. It's not going to happen. We're friends. She and Sophie are a good fit. It's how I want it. Deal with it."

"So defensive." Alex half-smiled. "Who are you trying to convince, Orange?"

"Leave her be, babe. Let things play out naturally." Maddie winked at Nat and jabbed Alex softly in the bicep.

"It's all right, honey." Alex didn't let up. "She can take it."

"Please buy your self-righteous girlfriend a strawberry tartlet so she'll shut up for five minutes."

Maddie touched the fingers of her right hand to the palm of her left in a ninety degree angle. "Time out, you two." She turned to Alex. "Babe, give her a break." She pinned her glance on Nat. "And you, everyone's entitled to a bout of grumpiness from time to time, no matter the reason. Ignore Alex. Oh, and…" She leaned a little closer. "Maybe you should consider a shag."

"You know I mean no harm." Alex joined the huddle and put a hand on Nat's arm.

"I know, Pizza. I love you too." Nat finished her dessert and said her goodbyes. When her poker face failed, she knew it was time for solitude.

On her way up the escalator, she passed The Bean and looked inside. Cindy's shift had ended long ago.

Alex had read her like an open book. At first Nat had tricked herself into believing it was the-third-wheel blues. Alex and Maddie being so ridiculously happy in front of her and Isabella going off with Sophie to that *special place*. All four of them building something meaningful. Nat had a phone bursting with numbers to call, but none of the women those numbers belonged to would ever mean anything to her.

She was jealous.

When she arrived home she poured the remainder of the wine Isabella had brought the previous night in a glass and settled in the couch with another copy of *The Stranger*. She guessed Isabella would join the book club now. Another twosome to see flourish in close proximity.

Fuck this, she thought once she'd drained the wine in a few greedy gulps. She tossed the book aside and glared out of the window, into the million lights of the Hong Kong evening. She straightened her t-shirt in the reflection, shot herself a wink and was out of the door in a matter of seconds.

When she arrived at Volt, a primarily gay hang-out of which the lesbian clientele had increased substantially once Nat had started frequenting the place, it was packed with goodies.

"Scotch on the rocks?" Freddy, the bartender, asked.

"No need for ice today." Nat leaned on the bar with one arm and scanned the small venue. It had its very own lesbian corner now. A slew of tables pressed together tightly where gay boys feared to tread. The little waves of recognition started quickly. Tiny-fingered hands greeting her. These girls weren't so much literary groupies. It was more a fame kind of thing. Chinese girls seemed to love famous people more than anyone else in the world. Nat had taken great advantage of that fact and she was about to resort to it again.

Nat slammed the Scotch back in one long gulp. It burned her throat a little but only a fraction of how it set her insides on fire the first time she had tried it, with Claire back in New York.

One of the girls felt bold and walked over to her. Nat recognised her face but couldn't immediately place it. She gestured at Freddie for a refill. Was that Cindy approaching her, sans glasses? This day could be saved after all.

"Hey." Cindy waved nervously, the beginning of a smile conquering her lips, waiting for Nat to instigate further conversation.

"I hardly recognised you out of your uniform and without those glasses." Her hair was down, reaching her neck, and her tiny body was squeezed into a tight black dress. "You look very glamourous." Nat shot her *The Smile*. God, this was almost too easy.

"I heard you come here often." Cindy's voice sounded pitchier than at The Bean, more girlie and frivolous.

"I do." Always the same conversations, and never about anything interesting, like a Hitchcock film or a Vonnegut book. "Can I get you a drink?"

"I'll have what you're having." Cindy eyed Nat's Scotch

with a hint of fear in her glance.

Nat raised her eyebrows. "Are you sure? This is pretty heavy stuff."

"Yes." Cindy's voice trembled. She probably didn't even drink alcohol.

"How about we both have a glass of wine?"

"Sure." Cindy nodded, her hair bobbing up and down.

Nat placed the order and returned her attention to the girl. That's what she was, a girl. Hardly a woman. Probably wore a Hello Kitty backpack to work. "What have you been up to today?"

As she asked the question, Nat realised she had absolutely no interest in the answer. She used to enjoy this endless small talk. This nothingness. All these conversations going in the same direction—her bed. What would Sophie and Isabella be talking about? Knowing Sophie, she wouldn't wait too long to make a move. Had they kissed yet?

"I went to Times Square mall with my friends. Just hanging out after work." Cindy's eyes started sparkling. "We saw a picture of you in the bookshop. I told my friends I knew you."

Nat shot her a weary grin. "That's nice." She handed Cindy her glass of wine and they clinked rims.

ISABELLA

"I've been here before, but back then it was mainly auto repair shops. Taxis parked all over the place, waiting for an oil change." Isabella sat across from Sophie on a sidewalk terrace, sipping an oversized cappuccino. Cosy outdoor space like this was rare in this city. "The neighbourhood has a very un-Hong Kong vibe to it. It almost feels like escaping. I love it."

"Did you like the flat?" Sophie's eyes glinted with the hope of newness and positive change.

"Definitely."

"Would you come visit me here?" Sophie glued a wide smile on her face.

"Without question." Isabella shot Sophie a seductive grin back. She was happy to be out of her every day environment, away from the crowds and the noise. Her muscles relaxed and her mood improved by the minute. "I should speak to Graham about this neighbourhood. In a few years it'll be crawling with expats and prices will skyrocket. He invests a lot in property."

"That's your ex-husband, right?" Sophie's eyes narrowed.

"The one and only." Isabella briefly looked away to check out a cute corgi padding by. "We split on good terms."

Sophie nodded pensively and hesitated. "I was surprised you called me this morning."

"I can imagine." Isabella pulled her lips into an apologetic pout. "Sorry for stalling."

"I suppose our friend Nathalie had something to do with that?"

"With stalling or calling?" Isabella gave in to the urgent need to inspect her hands.

"Both." A sharp edge manifested itself in Sophie's voice.

"Full disclosure time." Isabella prided herself on being able to look Sophie in the eyes now that it mattered. "I don't believe in starting something based on assumptions and half-truths."

Sophie didn't blink. She sat there awaiting the verdict, legs crossed and lips tight.

"I do feel something for Nat, but I'm a grown woman and I can deal with it. Especially because I fully realise Nathalie Orange would be about the worst choice of partner for me. She's going through certain issues she has to deal with on her own and at her own pace. I'll be there for her, as a friend." Isabella slanted her upper body over the table and let her hands rest inches away from Sophie's. "And I'd be a total nutcase to not be grateful for what I have sitting right in front of me."

Sophie sipped from her coffee before responding. "I appreciate your candour." She withdrew her hands and put them in her lap. "And I like you enough to see where this might go, but I refuse to be messed with." She drew a breath. "Despite knowing full well how you feel about Nat, this is not exactly what I was hoping to hear."

Isabella grabbed onto the spoon Sophie had discarded on the table, just to hold on to something. "I totally understand. Which is why I'm asking for a fresh start. You wouldn't be here if you didn't think it possible."

"True." The stiffness seemed to recede out of Sophie's muscles. "It's not every day one meets an attractive, intelligent woman like yourself on this island, even if she has taken temporary leave of her senses." A small smile tugged at the edge of her mouth. "Are you up for a little hike?" Sophie cast a glance under the table and checked out Isabella's shoes.

"I guess." Isabella pinched her eyebrows together. "You're full of surprises today."

"Oh yeah." Sophie stood up. "Come on."

She guided them out of the cluster of low-rises, all the streets lined with terraces and tiny restaurants. They crossed the main road and zigzagged through a couple of narrow alleyways until they arrived at the foot of a mountain.

"There's a small path over there." Sophie pointed to an unlit, impossibly steep gravel trail meandering uphill.

"Really?" Despite the cooler evening air, Isabella already had to wipe her brow. "Are you related to Indiana Jones by any chance?"

"The reward is worth it, trust me." Sophie grabbed Isabella by the hand and pulled her forward.

Isabella puffed her way up the path, grateful for the hours she put in at the gym but feeling her age nonetheless. She focused on Sophie's slender calves, the muscles underneath her skin flexing and relaxing with every step she took. They were all alone—no one would come here after dark. The city glow was growing ever more distant.

"This is it." Sophie spun around, her smile baring a sliver of white teeth. "Turn around."

Despite having one of the most spectacular views of the island at home, Isabella was floored by what lay beneath. It was the contrast of total darkness surrounding her and the scattered light pattern in the distance that did it. Sophie breathed heavily into her neck, her body heat radiating onto Isabella's back.

"Was I right or was I right?" Sophie's hand landed on Isabella's shoulders, soft and a little bit damp.

"Not bad." Isabella downplayed it because she knew it didn't matter what she said anymore. The next thing she knew Sophie's lips grazed the skin of her neck. Isabella had a lot of pent-up lust to deal with and Sophie's touch throbbed throughout her body.

"This way," Sophie whispered in her ear and coaxed her toward a tree just off the path.

Isabella stood with her back against the tree. Twinkling lights below and an unfamiliar silence around her. Sophie's eyes glinted in the dark, her body more contour than shape.

The kiss didn't come as a surprise, but it zapped through Isabella's bones like an electric shock—current after current making her head spin. It had been a while since she was last kissed.

Sophie's fingers found her cheekbones, tracing them while she caught her breath. "This is how I like to spend my Sundays." She leaned in for another kiss, another round of reducing Isabella's synapses to breaking fuses.

"I can see why," Isabella said, in between biting Sophie's lips and, slowly, finding her breasts with her hands.

"Do you need to process before this goes any further?" Sophie's lips were at Isabella's ear. She could feel them stretch into a smile.

"Heavens no." It was more a sigh than a reply.

"Good." Sophie clearly took this as the go sign. "Because we don't have all night." She slipped her hands under Isabella's top and caressed her nipples over the fabric of her bra.

All Isabella heard was the sound of her own breath deepening as her excitement grew. The rustling of clothes in the dark. The smacking sound of their lips as they connected over and over again.

She produced a bit of a yelp when Sophie squeezed her nipple, and responded by hiking up Sophie's skirt and slipping a finger under the waistband of her panties. To feel someone's skin react under her fingers again, to hear someone breathe sighs of pure excitement in her ear. The walk up the hill had been enough foreplay. Isabella let her finger dip down and was astounded by Sophie's wetness.

"You really do like me," she hissed.

Sophie's sole reply was a low grunt as Isabella pushed a finger inside.

Isabella retracted briefly to let Sophie gather her composure—and hoist up her skirt.

Nat. Blind dates. Unusual deals. Quid pro quo. It all didn't matter in that moment, the moment in which she knew she couldn't go on unless someone fucked her there and then.

Sophie brushed against her clit and Isabella's knees buckled. Isabella slipped two fingers inside Sophie and found a rhythm, her back grating against the tree as she moved up and down.

She stopped for a moment to let her fingers skate over Sophie's clit.

"Just fuck me," Sophie moaned.

Isabella obliged and plunged back in, feeling the rim of Sophie's pussy contract around her fingers every time she pushed up.

Sophie let her finger dance over Isabella's engorged clit, manipulating it with agile tenderness. This wasn't about a long drawn-out and gentle first time. This was about releasing tension—and creating an unforgettable memory. If it was the beginning of love, they'd have a long way to go from that hill in the dark, but it felt as if the entire city was bursting out of

Isabella's heart. It lay below her, bustling and glittering, as she thundered towards orgasm.

The walls of Sophie's pussy started clenching around her fingers as her moans grew hoarser. The guttural sounds uttered inches away from her ear didn't miss their effect on Isabella.

"Oh fuck," she exclaimed, just before a fire shot up from her toes and reached her core, like a rocket being launched through her body.

"God," Sophie murmured and collapsed onto Isabella.

They stood gasping against the tree for a bit, their clothes rumpled and their legs shaking.

"Better than any bed, don't you think?" Sophie planted a moist kiss on her lips.

Isabella could only agree.

NAT

Nat zipped up the escalator, Cindy's nervous giggles at the same time stirring anticipation in her blood and launching an assault on her nerves. What had Isabella said? *Don't you want something better for yourself than an endless slew of girls you deliberately choose because they won't mean anything to you? And what about the girls? Don't they deserve someone who can at least pretend to care for them for longer than a night? It's a lose-lose situation. No one gains anything in the long run.*

As the evening had progressed, flashes of Isabella's advice had materialised in Nat's brain in between shots of Scotch—Cindy had wisely opted for another glass of wine. Then there was the memory of Isabella running her long fingers over the paperbacks on her book shelf. She'd done it reverently, with passion in her eyes. The look on her face betraying the desire to pull one out and settle in the sofa for the night.

The more her brain had suffered from Isabella-related images, the more Nat had put the moves on Cindy. She was cute as a button with her pouty lips, round cheeks and eyes as dark as the night—they all had eyes like that, no matter how glittery their jewellery and make-up.

She tested some first lines for a short story titled *The Darkness of the Hello Kitty Girls*. She could picture Cindy on the cover. Eyes blazing and mouth giggling. *As if the bubblegum factor of their cheery-pink exterior is all a means to hide the blackness of their stare.* Nat had soon aborted the little writing session in her head. If Isabella was fucking Sophie tonight, she'd be taking Cindy home. And even if Sophie and Isabella were all chaste about it and decided that the first date after a blind date should be platonic, then at least Nat would have one up on Isabella.

She could easily imagine how Isabella would look at her if she were to confess to having thoughts—or was it more like a strategy?—like this. Ever-accepting eyes peering over dark-rimmed glasses—the ones she put on for watching TV—her face drawn into a serious expression but the sparkle in her glance revealing her true feelings.

They were almost at the top of the escalator, at the street of The Ivy, when Nat realised what the real question was. Why had she insisted on setting them up? Why had it been so important? Deep down, it started dawning, but she'd need a few more processing sessions with Isabella before she could actually admit it.

Cindy grabbed her hand as they turned the corner, her tiny clammy fingers probing their way between Nat's.

"Are you sure?" Nat faced her one last time. Not that she questioned Cindy's eagerness, more her own.

Cindy's only response was a squeeze in Nat's hand accompanied by an unexpected confident smirk. And people claim these girls are interchangeable, Nat scoffed inwardly—mostly for the benefit of her own self-esteem.

Spencer, the doorman, held the glass doors wide open for them, his face as professionally blank as ever. Nat always shot him a wink.

"Sorry, Miss Nathalie," Vivian at reception said. "Only one elevator available right now. The other one under maintenance."

"Sure." Nat nodded at Vivian. "No worries."

Upon reaching the elevator bank Nat stopped dead in her tracks when she noticed the two women with their backs to her, their clothes wrinkled and their arms hooked into one another. Her heart thrashed in her throat. Losing face was never easy, but confined to the secluded space of an elevator it would sting at least twice as hard. Nat dropped Cindy's hand and cleared her throat. Isabella and Sophie spun around as if they were in a ballet performance together.

"Successful date, I presume?" Nat needed to get the first word in. Perhaps it could give her the upper hand as well.

"Looks like we're not the only ones." Confusion and disappointment battled for the upper hand in Isabella's expression.

A high-pitched bell announced the arrival of the lift. They all stepped aside to make room for the exiting passengers, then shuffled in. Isabella stood with Sophie on one side, Nat with Cindy on the other, as if divided by a secret line of decency. People with strong morals who kept their end of the deal on one side, the more loosely-principled ones on the other.

Nat tried to hold her head up high, but she was crumbling inside. Not only was Isabella the last person she wanted to run into while bringing Cindy home, but the sight of her with Sophie, so at ease together and strangely satisfied —like couples on a sexy Sunday—caused her stomach to knot. Sophie's eyes sparkled and hinted that she wasn't merely being taken to the penthouse for a pousse-café.

Mistakes And How To Make Them, Nat thought. Another good book title, maybe for my memoir some day.

"I've persuaded Isabella to join our book club," Sophie said, trying to break the suffocating silence in the cabin. "Even though I'm not sure she'll have time to finish the book before then."

If she had talked like that about any other woman, Nat would have given her a pat on the back, but this was about Isabella and all Nat wanted was to slap her friend in the face—the friend she'd deliberately set Isabella up with.

"Great." Nat seemed to have lost the power of speech as well as the ability to look anyone in the eye. Thank goodness the elevator was speedy and about to deliver her and Cindy to the forty-second floor.

"See you then," Nat mumbled and dragged Cindy out of there as soon as the doors opened.

Once safely inside her flat she went straight for the liquor cabinet and poured herself and Cindy a large Scotch—neat.

ISABELLA

"Here's a drink." Isabella planted a glass of Bordeaux between Sophie's fingers. "Make yourself comfortable, please." She brought her hand to her chest. "Give me five minutes. I'll be right back."

"You're going to see Nat?" Sophie's face tensed.

"Something's wrong. She wouldn't so flagrantly piss over our arrangement if there weren't. I just want to assess the damage." Isabella placed her hands on Sophie's shoulders. "As a friend." She tried to put as much sincerity into her smile as possible. "I swear."

"No need to swear." Sophie spun on her heels. "Hurry back." Sophie positioned herself in front of the full-length windows overlooking the city and didn't say another word.

Isabella hurried out of the flat and didn't wait for the elevator. She'd never before taken the stairs and her heels echoed in the concrete stair well. Two floors lower she emerged and rang Nat's bell.

"Not a good time to forget your keys, Pizza." Isabella heard from the other end of the door as she waited for Nat to open. When she did, Isabella noticed how Nat's fingers loosened around her glass of Scotch and she regained composure just before dropping it.

"Oh. Looking for a foursome?"

"No, are you?" Isabella dragged Nat out of the flat by her arm. "Come outside for a minute."

Nat made light work of the remainder of liquid in her glass. By the mistiness of her gaze, Isabella could tell it wasn't her first drink of the night.

"What are you doing?" Isabella tried to keep the disappointment out of her voice, for her own sake as much as for Nat's.

"Exactly what it looks like, Sherlock." Nat shrugged. "I guess our deal is off. You can send Sophie home if you want. No need to consummate the date."

"Why are you doing this?" Isabella leaned against the marble wall. The Ivy wasn't built for drunken arguments outside its many front doors. This was a place of discreet class. People kept to themselves and didn't raise their voices once they left the privacy of their flat. This conversation was pointless. Nat was tipsy and looking for a fight. If Isabella had more than a few minutes she might be able to get through to her, but Sophie was waiting upstairs. Sophie, who had already given her the benefit of the doubt once today when it came to Nat.

"Go back to your date, Doc." Nat made for the door. "Give me a shout if you need any sex toys." Nat had locked herself out and had to knock on the door until Cindy— Isabella recognised her from The Bean—opened it, a startled look etched across her face.

"Suit yourself." Isabella watched as Nat slipped inside, one arm already draped around Cindy's shoulder. Jealousy, frustration and disappointment fought for the upper hand in her mind. She shook her head and climbed the stairs to the penthouse where Sophie waited.

"And?" Sophie's features had softened. She walked toward Isabella as she entered the flat, handing her a glass of wine.

Isabella shook her head and accepted the drink. "In the end, it's her choice."

"Maybe she needs something else than abstinence." Sophie coaxed Isabella to the sofa. "Maybe it's our turn to set *her* up."

The thought terrified Isabella. "Do you have someone in mind?"

"I'll have to think about it. She's not an easy one to match."

"Judging from what she told me about Claire, it'll have to be someone who's willing to play hard to get. Too eager won't do it for Nat." Isabella sank down in the couch. "It's a near impossible task."

"Whatever it is, it's not a task for us to worry about on a Sunday evening." Sophie inched closer. "I think it's time I found out what it's like to kiss you indoors."

Isabella smiled, hoping it would relax her, but her muscles tensed under her skin when Sophie touched her. Her head filled with images of Nat and Cindy—all of them indecent and painful.

Sophie kissed her and it didn't change a thing. Their lips touched and their tongues swirled around one another and Isabella only had one person on her mind. It wasn't the one whose tongue darted in and out of her mouth.

Sophie wasn't the kind of woman you pushed away twice. It was already quite the surprise she was sitting here now, her hands snaking toward Isabella's breasts. She started pushing Isabella down, covering her with her body.

Isabella didn't feel the same exhilaration rushing through her flesh as earlier on the mountain. Her mind didn't shut off, allowing her body to enjoy Sophie's caresses. All she saw was the sadness in Nat's eyes, the desperation of her drooped shoulders, the pleading of her glance.

She knew what she had to do.

"I'm sorry." Isabella pushed herself up on her elbows, breaking Sophie's lip-lock.

"What?" Sophie's eyes glistened through narrowed eyelids, desire clinging to her voice.

Isabella thrust herself up some more, forcing Sophie off her completely. "I thought I was being honest with you."

Sophie's mouth fell open, her eyes still confused.

"But I failed to be honest with myself." Isabella placed a hand on Sophie's forearm. "I'm sorry, but I can't do this."

"What the—" The mist in Sophie's head seemed to clear. Her eyes darkened and she shook herself free from Isabella's gentle hold. "This is about Nat, isn't it?"

"Yes." Isabella nodded. "I'm afraid it is."

"I'm beginning to think you two deserve each other." Sophie straightened her skirt. Her voice was calm, but her eyes were shooting daggers at Isabella.

"She…" Isabella knew full well how stupid it sounded. "She needs me."

"Sure." Sophie looked around for her bag. "But don't pretend you don't want to fuck her as well." She found it on the floor next to the sofa. "Good luck with that." Once she reached the door she turned around one more time. "Don't call me again."

Years of training and experience in all kinds of matters of the heart and mind and Isabella had ignored her own the most. She was crazy about Nathalie Orange and it was about time she did something about it.

NAT

Isabella's little visit had been the nail in the coffin of Nat's already dwindling desire for Cindy. She'd excused herself and hid in the bathroom, head spinning and heart hurting, but she couldn't stay there much longer without crossing even more boundaries of decency. She checked herself in the mirror before heading back into the living room. This morning she'd looked so healthy and energetic. That seemed like weeks ago. She took a deep breath and faced Cindy.

"I'm so sorry." She crouched next to her. "I'm not feeling very well." She rubbed her tummy for effect. She could hardly tell Cindy the truth and expect her to understand. Nat barely got it herself.

"Oh." Cindy drew her mouth into an O, making her look even more perplexed. "What can I do?"

"Nothing." Here comes the blow, Nat thought, and she truly felt sorry for the girl. "I think I just need to rest a bit, sleep it off." Or maybe she'd just saved her. "I'm sure I'll feel better in the morning."

"I can get you some medicine."

Cindy was way too sweet for this situation, her kindness stirring endless guilt in Nat.

"No, that's fine." Nat squeezed Cindy's thigh. "I'm sorry for dragging you all the way up here."

"It's okay. I just want you to feel better."

"I will. I just…" Nat stretched herself upward. Why did she do this to herself? This is why Isabella had insisted on her abandoning her antics of picking up and swiftly abandoning girls. To shield her from even more emptiness.

"I'll go now." Cindy rose from the sofa. "Please rest."

"I will." Nat accompanied her to the door. "See you at The Bean this week."

"Yeah." All hope had left Cindy's eyes. She might be young but she wasn't stupid.

Nat let the door fall shut behind her and leaned against it, banging her head into the wood a few times. Cindy was gone, but Isabella was still sharing her bed with Sophie two floors above. If only Alex were here. They'd watch a stupid movie together, shoulder to shoulder, and Nat would give her hell about it. Alex, who had only moved in two months ago and who Nat missed as if she'd lived in the flat for two years before she started seeing Maddie.

Nat knew Alex's absence wasn't the real issue.

This would make an excellent black comedy, Nat thought as she wandered to the liquor cabinet. She poured herself another drink, but only sniffed it. It didn't taste as good as before.

A soft knock on the door startled her. She checked the wall clock. It was almost eleven. Either Cindy had forgotten something or Alex had had her first row with Maddie. She secretly hoped for the latter, then immediately felt guilty for doing so.

For the second time that day, Isabella appeared in her doorframe. A crushing weight seemed to lift from Nat's shoulders at the sight of her.

"You have to stop showing up like this, Doc." Nat couldn't suppress a wide beaming smile. "You may put thoughts in my head."

"And what if I do?" Isabella fiddled with her fingers and a blush crept up her cheeks. "I don't mean to intrude on you and Cindy, but—"

"Cindy left."

"Oh." Isabella pinched her eyebrows together. "So did Sophie."

"Did she get sick of you running down to scold me?" Nat opened the door wide to invite Isabella in.

"Something like that." Isabella entered and eyed the open bottle of Scotch. Nat took the hint and poured her a glass. They both settled in the sofa. "What a day."

Nat found Isabella's eyes. "Crazy." Her throat seemed to constrict around the word. She took a quick sip to hide her nerves. "I shouldn't have pushed you into Sophie's arms. It was a mistake."

"Why was it a mistake?" Isabella didn't take her eyes off Nat when she drank.

"I think you know why."

Isabella shook her head. "Too much has been left unsaid between us. We need to change that."

"It's not that I disagree, but the written word is more my field of expertise." Nat's heart jumped in her chest.

"I noticed." A small smile played around Isabella's lips. "But it's as much my fault as any. I just… thought I didn't stand a chance." Isabella's voice trembled. "Which is a pretty lame excuse, I know."

"Is that really your definition of clearing the air?" It was Nat's turn to smile now. "I believe I asked you once before, after which you took the cowardly way out and completely shut down." Nat inched closer until their hands almost touched. "Here's your second chance to give it to me straight, Doc."

Isabella adjusted her posture and swallowed before speaking. "I believe I may be falling for your charms."

Butterflies rose in Nat's stomach. She set her glass aside. "I'm fairly certain the feeling is entirely mutual."

They both giggled like Hello Kitty girls.

"Are you going to kiss me or what?" Isabella got rid of her glass as well.

"Patience, Doc. You've waited this long." If Nat inched any closer she'd be on top of Isabella—which wouldn't be a bad place to be.

"True and I've run out of patience." Isabella put one hand on Nat's neck and drew her near. She brushed her lips against Nat's lightly then retracted. "Before this goes any further." She gave Nat a crooked smile. "You're not the first woman I've kissed today, but the only one I've wanted to kiss for weeks."

Then, at last, she surrendered. Their lips met and, instead of the usual frenzy taking over, that unstoppable drive to almost literally take the other, to pin them down and drive out her demons, Nat let herself drift off into the soft caresses of Isabella's lips. She let them carry her to a place of gentle bliss she hadn't visited in years.

ISABELLA

Isabella was struck by the difference in emotions coursing through her when Nat kissed her. Earlier that day, when Sophie had pushed her against the tree, it had been exciting but more because of the circumstances than because of the woman. Now, it felt like a life-changing event.

Nat broke free from their embrace and hoisted herself out of the sofa. She extended her hand and Isabella eagerly accepted it. They rushed to Nat's bedroom at the end of the hallway.

"Did you do it?" Nat asked as she dragged her onto the bed. It was unmade, a pile of books on either side.

"Do what?" Isabella's brain had stopped performing anything but basic functions.

"You and Sophie. Did you hook up?"

Isabella scanned Nat's eyes for signs of jealousy. All she saw was an amused smile and big blue eyes glinting with desire. "Yes."

Nat stretched her grin a little further. "And now you're about to jump into bed with me. How promiscuous for a woman your age."

Isabella ran her fingers down Nat's neck. "Oh yeah, I sure am the promiscuous one here."

Nat pushed herself up and toppled Isabella off her. "My days of promiscuity might be over, but I am still a top." She slid her body over Isabella's, her knee hitching up her skirt.

Isabella noticed Nat casting her glance to the side of the bed. She followed Nat's line of vision and her eyes met with a sizeable purple strap-on. She wanted Nat, but not like this. Not as if she was just one of her girls.

"Why don't we go to my place?"

Nat stared down at her. She drew her lips into a pout before speaking. "I don't suppose you want me to take that thing?" She nodded at the toy. She was more than smart enough to get it.

* * *

"I think it's only fair I shower first before inviting you into my boudoir." Isabella needed to wash the day—and Sophie—off her.

"I hope that's an invitation." Nat responded by pulling her t-shirt over her head.

A tingle crept up Isabella's spine. "I can hardly leave you alone with my Scotch collection." Nat stood in front of her, with only a bra covering her breasts and her hands on her hips. Isabella reached for her, hooked three fingers in the waistband of her jeans and pulled her close. She dragged her nails over Nat's naked skin while finding her lips. If they didn't make it to the shower soon she'd be a lost cause. "Come on."

They left a trail of discarded clothes on their way to the bathroom. Isabella hesitated to take her underwear off. Gym sessions and subsequent locker room encounters aside, she hadn't taken it all off for someone in a long time.

Lust brimmed in Nat's eyes as she took the final step towards Isabella. She curled a hand around Isabella's neck and drew her in for another kiss, while her other hand crept up her back and, with one quick snap of the fingers, undid her bra. Years of practice, Isabella guessed, but abandoned the thought as soon as the back of Nat's hand flitted along the side of her left breast.

Isabella stepped out of her panties and opened the glass door of the walk-in shower. She turned the tab to steamy hot, eager for some clouds of fog to rise between them now that the differences between a late forty-year-old and an early thirty-year-old body became clear.

The skin that stretched tautly over Nat's abs glistened as the first drops of water rained down on her and Isabella had to question her motives again. Was this more than a subconscious desire to flirt with youth now she was approaching fifty? Nat didn't give her time to process. She pressed her against the tiled shower wall, taking control, no doubt because that's what she always did. Isabella would let her for now, but she had other plans for later.

"I believe someone needs a thorough scrub." Nat's words were hot in her ear, her fingers gripping her waist. She reached for the soap while pushing her pelvis into Isabella's, the crash of skin on skin swirling through Isabella's bones the way steam was slowly swirling toward the ceiling—moist and lingering.

While rubbing the soap to white foam between her hands, Nat pinned her eyes on Isabella, her crooked grin baring more teeth than usual. Her dark hair clung to her forehead in short wet strands, drops of water streaming down her face. A sight so sexy Isabella was glad she had the support of the wall against her back.

Nat brought her hands to Isabella's shoulders and started applying the bubbly soap in downward circles. Isabella's skin turned to gooseflesh under Nat's prolonged caresses. Her nipples puckered up as Nat's hands zoned in. The circles reached her breasts and Isabella became acutely aware of not just the wetness surrounding her, but, even more so, the juices drizzling from between her legs.

When Nat's fingers encircled her nipples, both of them at the same time being stroked to rock hard peaks, a deep throaty moan escaped her. Nat's breath came quicker as well, short puffs of air floating between them. Their lips, slippery and wet, found each other again and just as Nat bit down on Isabella's bottom lip she pinched both her nipples between soapy fingers.

"Mmm," Isabella groaned and spread her legs. Whatever this was—inevitable signs of a midlife crisis, a creative way of helping a friend or the beginning of something beautiful— Isabella was ready for Nat's fingers inside her.

Nat transported the foam to Isabella's abdomen, drawing more circles there, before letting her hands dip down slightly

—but nowhere near low enough.

"Turn around," she hissed into Isabella's ear. "It's so easy to neglect the back when you're in the shower."

Despite an overwhelming desire to grab Nat's hand and guide it to where she wanted it—inside—Isabella did as she was told. The touch of the tiles on her nipples stiffened them even more, or maybe it was the way Nat scratched her nails along her spine.

"More soap." Nat squirted more liquid into her hands and Isabella shut her eyes and surrendered to Nat's will. Her hand's floated like feathers over Isabella's back, slithering the soap over her skin in long, fluid motions. The first contact with her behind made Isabella's pussy throb so violently, so desperately, it made her knees buckle.

Isabella hadn't allowed herself this kind of desire for years, this kind of all-engulfing, all-encompassing lust that soared through her flesh and crushed her sanity.

Nat's hands kneaded her butt cheeks in ever-expanding circles. Soon her fingers dived between her legs, always halting just before touching too much. Wetness oozed out of Isabella. She pressed her entire torso against the wall for support, leaving her butt to stick out.

Nat moved the action of her hands to Isabella's inner thighs, stroking them again and again with the fingers of one hand while the other rested on Isabella's left cheek, nails digging deep, her thumb pointing to Isabella's moistening pussy.

Then, at last, Nat's fingers inched closer.

"Aah," Isabella cried out, just because of the long-awaited connection of fingers on lips. They tickled the length of her pussy.

"I think your back is clean now." Nat hunched over her and slid the tip of her finger inside briefly. "Turn around."

Isabella stood panting against the wall. She took a deep breath before spinning her body around to face Nat. The look in Nat's eyes had shifted from lustful to determined. This is what she does, Isabella concluded. This is her comfort zone. She had every intention of crashing through the walls around it later, but first, her own pleasure needed tending to.

Nat kissed her full on the mouth with soaking wet lips. Their bodies slicked against each other, lubricated by soap and water. Isabella spread her legs wide. Nat started circling again, around Isabella's clit this time. It swelled and pulsed and Isabella dug her hands into Nat's hair, threading a few strands around her fingers, and held on for dear life.

A fire started in her belly as Nat entered. Isabella had no idea how many fingers Nat was pushing inside of her. She was only aware of the pleasure sparking through her flesh and the way the fingers drew groan after groan from her throat.

Something came alive inside of Isabella, exactly in the spot where Nat kept touching her. It tingled its way through her blood, up her spine, all across the planes of her skin. As if Nat's fingers knocked on a long closed door, awakening a slumbering joy inside of her.

Then she knew it had nothing to do with her age or her will to free Nat from that crushing weight on her shoulders. This was emotion connecting with physicality, feelings colliding with hot, sweaty flesh. This was why this time, as opposed to this afternoon with Sophie, the stars came crashing down more with each of Nat's thrusts.

Nat flicked the thumb of her other hand over Isabella's clit while she kept digging her fingers inside. Isabella grabbed Nat's head with two hands and held it in position in front of her face, panting and moaning. She wanted to see Nat's eyes when it happened, needed to be as close to her as possible.

The expression on Nat's face was deadly serious—as if this was a matter of life and death for her. Water spilled down from above, raining on their skin, intensifying everything. Nat quickened the pace of both her thumb on Isabella's clit and her fingers inside of her. She bored her blue eyes, lashes dripping, into Isabella's.

Isabella dragged her thumb over Nat's lips, hard, before

allowing herself to tip over the edge. It spread from her cunt to her fingertips and toes in jerky waves, slapping her senseless in the process. It beat through her blood to the rhythm of Nat's fingers, insistent and confident. Warmth gathered in her belly and exploded before collapsing all over her.

To come on Nat's fingers was not just physical pleasure, it really was the beginning of so much more. She didn't need to be a psychiatrist to figure that one out.

NAT

Nat slowly slid her fingers out as Isabella peered at her through half-lidded eyes. Her long brown hair clung to her forehead and her lipstick had come off, but she'd never looked more beautiful. Nat searched her brain for something meaningful to say—something to mark the moment with—but her mind seemed to have turned into a blank space. Instead, she smiled sheepishly, an almost shy grin making its way across her face, and was floored by the intensity in Isabella's gaze. Her brown eyes shone with tenderness as she stood gasping for air against the tiled shower wall.

"What a waste of water," Isabella muttered. "I was already soaking wet."

Nat's grin transformed into a loud giggle and she flung herself at Isabella, covering her naked, dripping limbs with her body.

Isabella reached for the tab and turned off the water. The sudden silence, deafening and a bit too confrontational for Nat's taste, shocked her into recognising the significance of the moment. Nat had delivered countless climaxes after Claire had left, with her fingers, or her strap-on—and most likely also with whatever importance her bed partners attached to her name—but never with this kind of affection. Not after Claire.

Her first instinct was to towel off and bolt out of there,

but she stayed. Her instincts had betrayed her too much of late, like when she'd been convinced she had to set Isabella up with Sophie. And again, when after their first blind date Isabella had been reluctant to see Sophie again. Nat realised she'd conveniently mistaken fear for instinct. In front of her, joy painted across her face, promise dancing in her eyes, stood the woman who'd made her see.

"Your turn." Isabella freed herself from Nat's hug and opened the shower door. She held out a towel for Nat as she waited for her to follow. Mischief burned in her glance, her usual reserve replaced by something Nat couldn't put her finger on.

Isabella rubbed Nat dry, avoiding her breasts and behind —as if they hadn't just done what they'd just did. This was still their first time after all. Nat returned the favour and soaked up the water dripping from Isabella's hair with a soft white towel.

Their eyes met and a bubble of tenderness seemed to explode in Nat's belly. To think that, if they hadn't run into each other in the lobby with their respective mismatched dates, Nat could be lying in bed with Cindy right now, eyes wide open while she waited for the girl to fall asleep, the usual mixture of instant remorse and addictive satisfaction clouding her brain. Instead, here she stood, eye to eye with Isabella, the one woman who'd had the courage to call her out on her destructive behaviour. Nat suddenly felt quite vulnerable.

"Come on." Isabella grabbed her hand and led her into the bedroom. Like in the living room, two walls consisted solely of floor-length windows, revealing a sprawling view over the city.

"How much do you charge per hour?" Nat had found her voice again. "This place must have cost a fortune." With a towel wrapped around her she looked down on the glowing lights beneath them.

"A parting gift from my ex-husband." Isabella approached her from behind and put her hands on Nat's neck. "He's a generous man." She rubbed her thumbs into Nat's muscles—the ones that were always tense from hours of hunching over her laptop in a bad position. Her body reacted instantly, her clit and nipples reaching skyward.

Nat let the towel slip off her and spun around. Isabella hadn't bothered to cover her body and tiny droplets of water glittered on her skin in the dim glow of a floor lamp.

"I take it my boudoir has left you suitably impressed." Isabella's voice was a mere whisper. "Judging by how swiftly you just disrobed."

"It's more the owner." Nat brushed a lingering drop off of Isabella's cheek bone. "And perhaps her shower habits." Nat planted the softest of kisses on Isabella's nose before letting her lips travel to her open mouth.

Isabella started walking backwards to the bed, dragging Nat with her and, soon, on top of her. They shuffled upwards until completely supported by the mattress. Their breasts touched, then their nipples, and Nat felt a hot glow spread through her. Isabella's red-painted fingernails stood in stark contrast to her alabaster skin. Nat wished she could read her mind. She wanted to know if Isabella had dreamt of this moment, at night, when she lay alone in bed, but she was rendered mute once more. If only she knew, Nat thought, what power she holds over me.

And then, without seeing it coming, Nat was on her back. Isabella had flipped her over and stared down into her eyes, her lips drawn into a sly smirk.

"I let you have your way with me in the shower." Wet strands of Isabella's hair fell to Nat's breasts. "Quid pro quo time, once again."

Nat responded by pulling Isabella close and sucking her bottom lip into her mouth. In bed, she usually wasn't the one lying on her back, but with Isabella everything was different.

Isabella dug her knee between Nat's legs and the contact made her breath hitch in her throat. She'd happily take whatever Isabella had to offer.

Isabella pushed herself up, releasing the pressure from

her knee, and smiled down at Nat. She bent her elbows and lowered herself until her nipples grazed Nat's skin. Slowly, she traced a path across Nat's belly, the hard buds leaving gooseflesh in their wake. And up she came again, brushing her nipples against Nat's before manoeuvring upwards and skating one along Nat's lips and offering it to her eager mouth. Nat sucked it in and let her tongue dance over it while her hands buried themselves into Isabella's moist hair.

Isabella pulled her nipple out of Nat's mouth and replaced it with the other one as her knee found its way to Nat's pussy again. Nat let one hand slide down and cupped Isabella's breast, kneading it softly before pinching her nipple between two fingers. She couldn't wait to see her face surrender to joy again, to feel her body tremble on her fingers and her knees go weak with delight.

Pulling free from Nat's mouth and hand, Isabella let her breasts travel down again, halting at Nat's nipples and meandering across her abdomen. She bent down a little lower and guided one nipple along the length of Nat's pussy. The sensation was enough for Nat's lips to pucker up and release more moist heat.

The first connection of her clit with Isabella's nipple made all the muscles in her body contract wildly. Nat looked down and saw how Isabella curled her fingers around her breast to target the contact of her rock hard nipple more precisely. She deemed herself the centre of the the most erotic dream of her life.

Isabella's nipple picked up moisture between Nat's pussy lips—another heavenly sensation—and made its way back to Nat's clit, circling it relentlessly.

"Jesus." Nat heard herself cry out.

Isabella looked up, her breast still caught in her hand, her tongue licking her lips. She shifted her weight forward until their mouths met. Nat's pussy tingled and got wetter by the second. Isabella broke the lip-lock and scanned Nat's face, her full lips curling up at the sides. She removed herself from the embrace and flung her body sideways, her head dipping below the edge of the bed. Nat heard rummaging sounds. Within a few seconds, Isabella was back, cradling something in her hand that made Nat's mouth water and her clit pulse with anticipation.

"I thought you'd never ask." Nat reached for the dildo and harness, but Isabella pulled it away while shaking her head.

"I'll be doing the honours tonight."

Nat arched her eyebrows, but soon recovered from the surprise. In light of the day's events, it made sense, despite the fact that, since Claire, Nat was always—always—the one to strap it on.

Isabella had turned the tables on her during their unexpected conversations and now she was about to do it again.

"As long as you're okay with that." Isabella's voice was soft, but her tone insistent. Nat wouldn't dream of saying no. She knew she needed to do it. The time had come to completely surrender to someone once again, no matter the consequences.

"Even in the bedroom you're a shrink. Don't you ever relax?" Nat shot Isabella a wide grin. She was giddy with excitement and a new sense of freedom, as if the mere thought of letting Isabella fuck her was an act of liberation from the demons that had long haunted her.

"How easily youngsters forget." She shook her head and a few drops of water crashed down onto Nat's chest. "Remember the shower?" Isabella proceeded to lick the drops of Nat's chest, her tongue swirling close to Nat's nipples but not touching them.

"I'll be curious to see your strapping-on speed," Nat whispered in her ear. "I can do it in less than five seconds."

"Why don't you give me hand then, Miss Expert."

Nat noticed a slight crack in Isabella's confidence. She curled her fingers around her neck and pulled her close. "Anything for you, Doc."

Nat helped Isabella secure the greenish-blue dildo in the harness and pull the straps tight around her thighs. The sight of her neighbour sitting naked in front of her with a sizeable sex toy strapped to her pelvis, made her giggle and shudder with delight at the same time.

Isabella lay down next to her, the silicone poking against Nat's thigh. She let her fingers roam across the skin of Nat's breasts and belly, lazily making her way down. Light as a feather, she grazed the tip of her finger over Nat's pussy lips, which pulsed with anticipation. Where her nipple had drawn circles earlier—a memory etched in Nat's memory for life—she now traced her finger around Nat's clit.

Pushing herself up for better access, the dildo resting half in between Nat's legs and half on her upper thigh, Isabella positioned herself so the fingers of her right hand could wander freely while her face hovered close to Nat's. Nat's flesh burned with excitement, her pussy leaking juices onto the sheets.

When Isabella inserted the first finger, she licked Nat's earlobe at the same time and Nat shivered underneath her. Nat searched for Isabella's eyes and found them just as she let a second finger enter, gradually preparing her pussy for what was to come.

Nat wanted to say to Isabella how beautiful she was, and how necessary in her life, but her mind blanked once again and she was reduced to just feeling now, to surrendering to ripple after ripple of glorious sensation washing over her.

"You're so wet," Isabella whispered, her brown eyes locked on Nat's as she slicked her fingers back and forth.

Nat's breathing picked up, transforming into clipped moans. With every stroke a wave of pleasure crashed over her, and then subsided to allow her to catch her breath. Isabella expertly avoided her clit, instead focusing her attention on twisting her fingers inside of Nat—three now. Almost ready.

They didn't kiss, just gazed into each other's eyes. Isabella's face changed with every thrust, her lips narrowing and her cheeks flushing. Nat's fingers ran across Isabella's spine, dug into the muscles of her back and curled themselves into her hair. She bucked up her pelvis quicker and quicker, eager to take more of Isabella's fingers in.

Isabella nodded at her briefly, blinking, and Nat nodded back. She was ready.

Isabella sat up and quickly unearthed a small bottle of lube from the night stand drawer. She squirted some in her hands and rubbed it over the dildo until it glistened. Nat spread her legs wide, her mouth going dry and her heart thumping in her chest.

Isabella took position and shot Nat a smile, her eyes twinkling and lips so deliciously curved. She guided the head of the toy in between Nat's lips and moved it along the length of her pussy, skimming Nat's clit every time it went up. Slowly, she coaxed it in. Nat's pussy stretched wide—wider than she could remember—and filled up with warm silicone.

Isabella leaned over until her face was inches away from Nat's before she started thrusting her hips back and forth. Nat could feel how Isabella's breath quickened as it blew across her cheeks. She dug her nails into Isabella's buttocks and pushed her pelvis upward to meet her strokes. She hadn't surrendered like that in years.

Isabella's hair fell to one side of her head as she tilted it to kiss Nat's temple, her cheekbone, her mouth. "Never…" She groaned into Nat's ear. "In my wildest dreams."

The filling sensation spread from Nat's pussy to her belly and limbs. Heat pooled in her cunt as Isabella upped the speed of her thrusts, the pressure of her knees into the mattress making the bed shake.

Nat drew Isabella in for a kiss, her tongue frantically darting in and out of her mouth. She pulled Isabella's hair and scratched her shoulders and lost herself a bit more with every stroke inside of her. Heat pulsed through her body, hot wave after hot wave, and peaked when Isabella drilled her eyes into hers.

"Touch your clit," Isabella said.

The sound of her voice briefly brought Nat back to earth, before spiralling back into that parallel orbit where she was only body, only pleasure, only at Isabella's mercy as she fucked her senseless. Nat lowered her hand and gently strummed her clit with one finger, the back of her hand grazing Isabella's lower belly. One flick was enough to take her to that higher level, to that point of no return where only extreme joy lives. The dildo seemed to take over her entire body. She felt its movements in her toes and in her fingers and in every cell of her body.

"Oooh," Nat moaned as Isabella slammed into her and she surrendered to the lights from outside moving in and crashing down, to the dizziness in her head and a delicious, long-awaited harmony. The walls of her pussy contracted around the toy as she wrapped her arms around Isabella's neck. Isabella's grunts blended with her own, creating their own sexy, raunchy symphony.

"Oh yes," were Nat's final words before she crashed into the mattress one last time, her body tingling and her voice breaking.

ISABELLA

"Next time, I'm on top." Nat had barely come to her senses, Isabella could tell by the glassiness of her eyes and the twitching of her muscles, when she said it. After quickly removing the strap-on, Isabella curled her body over Nat while a deep satisfaction blossomed inside of her.

"What do you mean, next time?" Isabella pecked Nat's forehead. "I believed you to be the fuck-and-run type."

"I haven't fucked you yet." Nat kissed Isabella's chin. "And anyway, I thought you were a lady."

"I'm fairly certain you felt every inch of the lady I am."

Their eyes met and they burst out laughing.

"What a difference a day makes." Nat's voice seemed to have deepened somewhat.

"Poor Sophie. We couldn't have used her in a worse way." Isabella scrambled with the sheets, eager to get under as the air around them chilled. She settled her head in the crook of Nat's shoulder.

"I'll talk to her. It's my fault," Nat said.

They fell silent for a while. A crushing fatigue weighed on Isabella's bones. Her eyes started fluttering shut.

"Alex is going to have a field day with this." Nat didn't appear sleepy yet. "She's going to think she and Maddie arranged this in some way." She nuzzled her nose into Isabella's hair. "While it's clear you had the hots for me from the very beginning."

"Mmm." Isabella didn't have the strength left to quibble over details—not that there was a lot to argue about. She drifted off, her head gloriously empty and Nat's arms around her.

* * *

Isabella woke up with the sheets thrown off her, her legs spread wide and Nat in between them. At first she thought she was stuck in the kind of dream you never want to wake up from, but she extended her arm and Nat's hair bopping gently up and down was real and so was the pressure she applied to Isabella's clit with her tongue.

When she dug her fingertips into Nat's shoulder muscles, Nat looked up and grinned, her lips glistening with Isabella's juices.

"This is your wake-up call, Madam." She winked and a slew of butterflies fluttered in Isabella's stomach. "Orange Enterprises at your service. Please relax and enjoy." Nat's head ducked between her legs again and Isabella had no trouble doing what was asked of her.

Nat's tongue whispered along her lips with light, deft strokes. She'd barely been awake a few minutes, but already wetness trickled down Isabella's thighs. It might as well have been a dream.

Images from last night flashed through her mind and blended with her current arousal. Nat's tongue flicked over Isabella's clit, back and forth, while Isabella remembered the look on her face when she made it clear she'd be wielding the toy. No doubt Nat would get her back for that soon enough.

The tip of Nat's tongue circled the entrance of her pussy. Nat really seemed to have a thing for circles. When she pushed it inside, Isabella didn't bother to suppress the yelp escaping from her throat.

If only all alarm clocks operated like this.

Nat traced her tongue upwards again, gliding stoutly through Isabella's folds. Isabella wouldn't survive another round of clit stimulation. The fire inside her was building already, igniting from deep within her belly and starting to spread through her bones.

While zoning in on Isabella's clit with her tongue, lapping endless circles around it, Nat slid a fingertip along Isabella's lips. Ever so lightly, she trailed it along Isabella's entrance, as if preparing her for something bigger, but for Isabella it was more than enough to tip her over the edge. She dug her heels into the mattress and looped her finger around Nat's short strands of hair.

"Oh god," she moaned, pushing herself into Nat's mouth. Her muscles started to tremble, quick convulsions announcing climax. Nat's tongue danced over her clit, while her fingertip lingered at the rim of her pussy. The fire raged with full force, flaring up before the final explosion.

"Aah," Isabella groaned, reaching the pinnacle of pleasure and just then Nat pushed a finger deep inside of her. It startled and amazed her and catapulted her straight into another round of flames erupting in her belly, shooting straight to her limbs. Her pussy clenched around Nat's finger and her clit throbbed against her tongue.

With a sigh Isabella collapsed into the mattress as her

muscles relaxed. Nat gently slid out her finger and wiped her mouth with the back of her hand as she shuffled upward.

"Breakfast of champions." Nat shot her a broad smile and Isabella failed to hold back a tear. One drop tumbled out of the corner of her eye before she could blink it away.

Nat kissed her on the mouth, her lips still wet with juices. Isabella had trouble finding her voice. She replied by slipping her tongue deep into Nat's wet hot mouth.

* * *

"I suppose The Bean for brunch is out of the question." They stood in the kitchen, both drinking greedily from bottles of Evian after a quick shower. "What did you tell that girl, anyway?"

Nat's hair pointed in all directions and the t-shirt Isabella had lent her strained around her chest. She looked the very picture of delicious.

"That I wasn't feeling well, which wasn't far from the truth." The fly of her jeans was open and she wasn't wearing anything underneath. "I'll sort it out."

"Busy Monday for you, it would appear." Isabella didn't want to let her leave. Nat looked even better dishevelled, as if born for the post-fuck look. "A lot of bridges to reconstruct."

Nat merely nodded. "What do you have in your fridge?"

"See for yourself." Isabella pulled the door open for Nat. "But I have a client in exactly one hour."

"Not to worry, scrambled eggs *à l'Orange* coming up in five minutes." Nat licked her lips. "You go and put yourself together."

"I may need more than five minutes to make myself look presentable after last night."

"Then I suggest you clear your schedule tomorrow because tonight I'm on top." Nat's face peeked from next to the fridge's door, a gentleness glinting in her eyes that contradicted the implied dominance of her words.

"We'll see about that." Isabella laughed and turned on her heels.

NAT

When Nat opened the door to her flat, Alex sat cross-legged in the sofa staring at her phone. She barely looked up when Nat walked in.

"What's the matter, Pizza? Did Maddie just text you a picture of her privates?"

Alex shot her a confused look. "Where have you been?"

"One floor higher than you. And yes, your wettest dream has come true."

"What?" Was that a tear glistening in the corner of Alex's eye? She couldn't be *that* happy for Nat. "I thought Isabella left with Sophie yesterday afternoon."

"Long story." Nat perched on the arm rest next to Alex. "All in due time." She nodded at Alex's phone. "What's going on?"

"Nothing." Alex sighed. "Rita just sent me a long e-mail apologising for all the things she did wrong. Look." Alex held out her phone. "It has bullet points and everything."

Nat took the phone and skimmed over the e-mail. "She wants to meet?"

Alex nodded. "She claims she needs my forgiveness to move on."

"What are you going to do?"

"I don't know." Alex shrugged. "What do you think I should do?"

"Ask the expert, always a good plan." Nat winked, anxious to transform the scowl on Alex's face into a smile. "Whatever you do, don't give her the satisfaction of replying straight away. She tore you to pieces. I'm not sure she deserves your forgiveness. If you've forgiven her at all."

Alex shook her head. "I have been in a more forgiving mood lately." She tossed the phone on the coffee table. "But no, no matter how she puts it now, and no matter our history, what she did is inexcusable."

"But of course you can't ignore an e-mail from a woman you shared six happy years with. I get it." Nat knew how Alex's brain—and heart—operated.

Alex looked up at Nat, her lips trembling with hesitation. "What would you do if…" She fidgeted with her fingers. "If Claire, out of the blue, asked to meet after pointing out all the mistakes she made with astounding clarity?"

Nat blew some air through her nose. "I'd tell her to fuck right off." This was most probably a lie. "But hey, that's me. You're nothing like me."

"Whatever I do, I should tell Maddie."

"You should do whatever you think is best for you, Pizza." Nat slipped off the armrest and crouched in front of Alex. "Don't meet Rita because she wants to. Only agree to seeing her if you think it can help you."

Nat remembered the sad bundle of flesh and bones passing for Alex she'd taken in after Rita's affair with her Mandarin teacher had come to light. "You don't owe her anything." Alex squeezed her hand, her fingers trembling in Nat's palm. "And of course it didn't work out with the teacher. Of course, she regrets hurting you. What a fucking cliché." Nat searched for Alex's eyes. "You've got a good thing going with Maddie. You've moved on. Don't let Rita ruin that."

"I won't. I need some closure too, I guess."

"You don't have to decide right now. Think about it."

Alex pinned her eyes on Nat, looking her square in the face for longer than a second for the first time since Nat had walked in. "You wouldn't really say that to Claire though, would you?"

"It doesn't matter what I would do. Your situation is different, anyway."

"Did you and Isabella really hook up?" A glimmer of excitement sparked in Alex's eyes.

"Yes, we did." Nat couldn't suppress a huge smile from

bursting out all over her face. "And it was so bloody amazing we may very well do it again tonight."

"She gets two nights in a row with the elusive Nathalie Orange? Has she hypnotised you or something?"

"She's a psychiatrist, Pizza. Not a charlatan." Nat stood up and fell into the sofa next to Alex. "Come here." She threw her arms around Alex and hugged her. "I'm thinking this could really be something."

"I knew it. I didn't really dare believe in it, but I noticed it the first time we all got together on her roof terrace." Alex freed herself from the hug. "Nathalie Orange has feelings after all." Alex elbowed Nat in the bicep. "I'd never thought you'd go for someone older than the company I'm keeping these days."

"Age is just a number, Pizza."

They both exploded into a fit of giggles.

"This building surely has been good to us."

Nat narrowed her eyes and lifted a cautionary finger. "Don't let Rita come between you and Maddie."

"I won't. Speaking of which." Alex snagged her phone of the coffee table. "I have to call her at once and tell her about this miracle."

"Oh damn," Nat sighed. "It's going to be like this for a long time, isn't it? Lame jokes and a lot of I-told-you-so's."

"Oh yeah." Alex dialled and stood up. "Have you heard the news, babe?" Alex said into the receiver. They'd be all right. As for herself, she couldn't wait until Isabella's last client left and they could, at last, fairly settle their fight for top.

NO ORDINARY LOVE

ALEX

Alex lay with her hands cuffed to the railing of Maddie's bed. The cuffs were lined with fur, but still cut into Alex's flesh every time she moved.

She had scratches on her back, her buttocks, and a whole maze of them healing on her shoulders. Maddie always had that little extra to give when it came to Alex's shoulders. Her nails dug a little deeper and her moans grew higher whenever Alex flexed her shoulder muscles.

Her shoulders, no matter how strong, were quite useless now though. So were her legs, tied around the ankle to the foot end of the bed with two of Maddie's Hermès scarves.

Alex was totally at Maddie's mercy and she wouldn't want it any other way.

Maddie's gaze hovering over her naked, helpless flesh was enough to cause a wild throbbing in Alex's clit. But Maddie wasn't just using her eyes. She'd unearthed a short leather whip from the box under the bed where she kept all her valuables— as she called them—and traced it along Alex's abs. Alex's abs could take a lot of things, gentle teasing with what looked like a riding crop was not one of them. She squirmed under the touch of the leather and the more she squirmed the more Maddie loved it.

As usual, Maddie had undressed Alex with no intention of shedding her own clothes. She still wore her work outfit, a grey Ralph Lauren pencil skirt topped with a black pin-striped blouse that looked a little too tight for comfort at the office. Maddie's blond hair was tied together at the back of her head and, no doubt for effect, she hadn't taken off her dark-rimmed reading glasses. It was working.

The room was silent except for the soft swish of the whip as it glided along Alex's flesh and the ragged sound of Alex's breath, which escaped her at quickening intervals.

Maddie kneeled between Alex's legs, her face sporting that wicked smirk she only ever displayed in the bedroom. They'd only been dating a few weeks but Alex always knew the score when she spotted the bedroom smirk.

It was hard to notice the emotion in Maddie's eyes while they were protected by glasses, but Alex could see plenty of passion displayed in the way Maddie's mouth twitched upwards as she dragged the tip of the whip over Alex's breasts. Maddie's nipples had grown so stiff they pointed through the fabric of her bra and blouse.

For the first time that night Maddie cracked the whip, right next to Alex's left nipple. Alex let out a tiny gasp, loud enough to encourage Maddie to repeat the action, but controlled enough to not let her experience too much satisfaction. From the outside Maddie may have appeared completely in charge, but they both understood this game was a two-way street.

Maddie treated Alex's right breast to the same sensation, but added more power to her action. She trailed the whip between Alex's breasts, down to her belly and over her belly button to her upper thighs. A few quick snaps on each thigh, on that delicate spot just below her entrance, and Alex was lost.

A rapid succession of whip lashes on her nipples and outer thighs reduced Alex to a puddle of desire at Maddie's mercy. Then Maddie positioned the whip between her legs again. She traced it through the moistness gathering there, slowly but with such menace it made Alex shiver in her skin.

Maddie flicked the whip twice right on Alex's clit. Alex arched her back and the cuffs bit into the tender flesh of her wrists. The whip circled her pussy before coming down hard on her blood-shot lips. Wetness trickled between Alex's legs and suddenly the whip was gone.

Maddie removed her glasses, slowly unbuttoned her blouse, slid out of her skirt and sat in front of Alex clad only in a black lace bra and matching panties. Unlike Alex, Maddie always dressed to impress.

Her light blue eyes peered into Alex's. She didn't move a muscle for several seconds, just staring at Alex, her unflinching glare setting Alex's skin on fire.

Maddie had said it out loud enough for Alex to guess what she was thinking—that her body was a work of art. That marble statues should be carved to its likeness. That it should never be allowed to be covered by more than a tank top and boy shorts, and only if strictly necessary.

She had that ravaging expression on her face, her lips pursed together in a tight line and her eyes scanning prey.

Alex lay there panting, immobile and impatiently waiting for what was to come. She fiercely hoped Maddie would undo her bra and reveal her creamy white breasts and tiny nipples. They stood high, the pink buds of her nipples always pointing upwards, and Alex couldn't wait for one of them to coast along her lips.

Her prayers were answered as Maddie brought her hands behind her back to unclasp her bra. Alex inhaled sharply, her entire body pulsing with want. Foreplay between them wasn't always so unconventional, but either way, she was ready for the more advanced action to begin.

Maddie's breasts tumbled out of her bra. She slipped it off her shoulders and threw it behind her onto the floor. Maddie's gestures always had a flare for the dramatic, while it was Alex who was supposed to have fiery Mediterranean blood running through her veins.

Alex checked, if by any chance, the cuffs holding her

wrists in place hadn't come loose so she could cup Maddie's divine breasts—they fit so snugly in her hands. She wanted to roll Maddie's nipples between her fingers and pinch hard. Maddie could take as good as she could give. The cuffs held and Alex could tell her struggle with them—and the consequent flexing of her bicep—excited Maddie. She was fast to discard her underwear and position herself on all fours, hovering over Alex, her breasts inching close to Alex's wanting mouth.

Maddie traced her lips over Alex's collarbone, not quite kissing and not quite touching, blowing air on her skin until all the hairs on it reached skyward.

Her lips trailed down, only briefly stopping at Alex's nipples to lick them into even stiffer buttons. She blew air on Alex's inner thighs and pussy lips—hot moist air driving Alex crazy.

The only body part, apart from her head, that Alex could manoeuvre was her pelvis and she thrust it in the direction of Maddie's teasing mouth.

While digging her fingers into Alex's abs, Maddie flicked her tongue where the whip had done the same earlier. Short, quick snaps of her tongue skated across Alex's lips and Alex eased into it, relaxing, knowing it was only a matter of minutes now.

When Maddie's tongue found Alex's clit and circled it, she buried her nails in the muscles of Alex's belly, causing Alex to expel a loud moan. It wasn't the first time Maddie did it, but the effect it had on Alex still surprised her. Desire mingling with pain. Pleasure blending with lust. Alex was no stranger to it all—Rita had made sure of that—but a new lover always brings new tricks to the table, and Maddie certainly knew what she was doing.

Maddie sucked Alex's clit into her mouth and let her tongue dance over it. Exquisite sensations slammed into Alex, starting at her core and spreading through her well-kept muscles at lightning speed. Maddie kept working on the sensitive bud between Alex's legs, letting her tongue alternate between circling Alex's clit and lapping at her lips.

Shackled and bound, the sensation hit Alex twice as hard and when Maddie traced one hand from Alex's abs to between her legs and pushed the tip of her finger in, Alex couldn't stifle a scream.

Just like that, Maddie was inside of her while licking her, and the trembling started. For all the control Alex issued over her muscles in her daily life, they were useless when it came to this. Shaking and contracting of their own volition, leaving Alex spent in a matter of seconds.

Maddie added another finger and upped the pace of her tongue. Alex held on to the railing of the bed and shoved her heels into the mattress as the climax engulfed her. She felt the walls of her pussy clench around Maddie's fingers, again and again, as she rode out her orgasm and Maddie's tongue bestowed a few more strokes on her clit.

After slowly pulling her fingers out, and wiping Alex's juices off her lips, Maddie was quick to loosen Alex's restraints. She untied the scarves and unlocked the cuffs and poured her hot limbs over Alex's shivering body. Taking advantage of experiencing freedom of motion again, Alex curled her arms around Maddie's neck and drew her close.

"You can whip me any time," she whispered in Maddie's ear.

"I intend to," Maddie replied and bit into her earlobe.

MADDIE

"I don't think I've ever witnessed such smugness in your smile before." Maddie sat across from Isabella on her friend's roof terrace, nibbling on one of the croissants she had brought from The Bean.

"I don't think I've ever had reason to feel this smug."

Isabella leaned back in her chair. "I almost feel as if I got myself a trophy wife."

"I heard that." Nat stepped out on the balcony, her hair still wet from the shower. "But I'll take it as a compliment." She eyed the pastries. "Does *your* trophy wife know you're eating this?" Nat fixed her clear blue eyes on Maddie and accompanied her question with a smirk.

"What she doesn't know, won't hurt her." Maddie took a big bite out of the croissant. "And my calorie burn is way up since she's in my bed every night. It compensates."

"Already keeping secrets from each other." Nat stood behind Isabella and rubbed her shoulders. "Let's see what the shrink has to say about that." She kissed Isabella on top of the head.

"A few secrets are crucial to the success of any relationship." Isabella put her hands on top of Nat's. "I, for instance, have no idea where you were for the better part of last night. And I don't intend to ask."

"See, this is what I have to deal with every day. This emotional manipulation. I know she can't help herself, but still." Nat squeezed Isabella's shoulders and Isabella let her head fall back onto Nat's belly. "And you know full well I may not have spent the better part of the night in your bed, but I was there for the best part." Nat leaned down and planted a kiss on Isabella's nose.

"Mind and word games. This is what my life has become. Oh, how I wish I had landed a hot fitness instructor as my trophy wife. It seems so much less complicated."

Nat curled her fingers around Isabella's neck and mock-strangled her. "I know Alex seems perfect, but she's only human, just like the rest of us." While stepping away from Isabella, Nat grabbed a pastry and sat down in between her and Maddie. "You must have discovered that by now." Nat cast her glance towards Maddie again.

"Well, there is the unfortunate habit of dim sum with the family every other Sunday. As if she'd be disinherited if she dared to miss one Pozzato family meal." It was a struggle every time Alex had to make it to Tai Po before noon on a Sunday. Her parents lived in a house in the country Maddie had not yet been invited to.

"You've been here long enough to know you don't cross a Chinese mother when it comes to yum cha. It's tradition. You don't mess with that."

"For some reason it was never an issue with the company I kept before." Maddie thought about June and her growing belly. She was probably at dim sum as well, Mark's family fawning over their pregnant daughter-in-law.

"Either way, you can't blame Alex. She's being a good daughter." Nat chimed in. "They raised her well."

Maddie nodded, hesitating to broach the next subject, even though it had been bugging her. "There's also the case of the unmentionable ex." She searched Nat's face for a reaction. If anyone had information about Rita, it was her. "I know Rita cheated on her, but that's it. It's not as if I need all the details about their affair, far from it, but I do believe she would benefit from talking about it once in a while."

"Give her some time." Nat's tone was serious. "It'll sort itself out."

"Really? How?" Maddie made eye-contact with Isabella in the hope of getting some support. "If she won't even acknowledge the woman's existence."

"Alex is simply not the kind of person who needs to talk through everything extensively to process. She's not that kind of lesbian. I mean, she is half-Chinese." Nat sounded as if she really needed to convince Maddie of this.

"It's not because they don't easily talk about their feelings that they couldn't benefit from it," Isabella said. "I've been practising in Hong Kong for fifteen years and the only Chinese clients I ever get are the ones born and bred abroad."

"I do hope it doesn't come back to bite her in the ass." Maddie, who had no interest in discussing the mental state of the local population, brought the subject back to Alex. "I wish she'd share more. I can see it in her eyes sometimes, this darkness, this well of emotions not dealt with."

"There's only one solution. Instead of talking about it with us, confront Alex." Isabella extended her hand over the table and reached for Maddie's. "And don't push her."

"She does have some wise things to say now and again." Nat smiled at Isabella. "Then again, she attended university for about ten years so that education had better pay off."

Maddie sagged back in her chair and let the easy banter between Nat and Isabella pass her by. As far as she knew, they didn't have skeletons in their closet like Alex had.

* * *

"Did you tell them about me yet?" Maddie had awaited Alex's return from Tai Po anxiously. After the impromptu chat she'd had with Nat and Isabella she was eager to get something out of her.

Alex walked over to where Maddie was sitting and pushed her down into the sofa cushions. "For now, you're still my dirty, little, whip-cracking secret." She smiled down at Maddie before kissing her.

Maddie wasn't that dead-set on getting Alex's parents' approval, but she decided to use them as a way to instigate the conversation she wanted to have. "Are you afraid I won't stack up against the memory of Rita?"

"What?" Alex pushed herself up, making her triceps bulge in the process. "No."

"I know they thought the world of her." Alex hadn't given her that information, but Nat had mentioned it once, late at night after a dinner including too much wine. "I understand your hesitance."

"You want to meet my parents? Is that what this is about?" Alex crawled off Maddie and sat down on the ottoman next to the sofa, far enough not to touch her accidentally.

"No. I mean, I do one day when you're ready, but we've only just got together." Maddie already felt herself pussyfooting out. She couldn't do it. She didn't have the words to address Alex in a way that would make her open up.

"How about when we've been seeing each other for three months? I'll introduce you officially then, but you will regret it because you'll be spending many a Sunday off the island." Alex managed a smile again and it was all Maddie needed to let the subject go completely. Maddie wasn't in the business of making Alex feel bad. On the contrary, her sole task was to make her feel as good as possible.

"Deal, but you'll have to come back with me to Melbourne in the spring so my family can finally be convinced I'm not a complete romantic disaster." It surprised Maddie she was thinking so long-term. And that she even contemplated introducing Alex to her family, who had only ever seen her with Emma.

"We'll see." Alex offered her hand and Maddie gladly took it. "Let's just enjoy the delicious early stages of this relationship without worrying about family."

A broad smile split Maddie's face in two. "While you were being a family girl, I went online and bought this." Maddie grabbed her iPad from the coffee table and showed Alex a picture of a dolphin-shaped sex toy. "Delivery in two days."

Alex rolled her eyes. "You have a box full of those already. I'm beginning to worry about you."

"This one's waterproof, though. And turbo-charged." Maddie pulled Alex closer and sunk her teeth softly into the flesh of her shoulder.

"I may have to confiscate your credit card before this online shopping gets out of hand." Alex let herself slide onto Maddie. "They have support groups for that, you know. I'll go with you if you can't find it in yourself to go alone."

"Shut up and kiss me already." Maddie pulled Alex's tank top over her head, gasped as she always did at the sight of her flawless torso, and pushed her down into the sofa.

ALEX

Alex clicked the reply button to the e-mail Rita had sent her, then closed the e-mail window altogether. She'd repeated this process five times already. She'd read Rita's e-mail about a hundred times, even though she knew it by heart by now.

Rita confessed to having been a heartless bitch. She'd taken Alex for granted for too long. She'd acted as if nothing could touch her. She'd never forgive herself for hurting Alex the way she did.

But just because Rita was coming to terms with her mistakes, Alex shouldn't. Still, there was that tug. It had started deep inside of her. Not immediately after receiving the e-mail. Anger had come first—a crash of blind rage rushing through Alex's blood. Who did Rita think she was? Casting Alex aside like that and then trying to weasel her way back in with an e-mail. But this was Rita and, try as she might, Alex couldn't ignore her. Not forever. Not when the words blinking on the screen spoke of enduring love and endless regret.

Alex had Maddie now. She could be strong. She found herself in a good position to face Rita. She could have the upper hand in this. And it might be exactly what she needed.

Alex started typing and, despite the hammering of her heart, she knew she was doing the right thing. Not for Rita. Definitely not for Maddie, who Alex had kept in the dark about Rita's message, but for herself. She could face her fear head on. She'd meet Rita, stare her straight in the eyes and tell her to go to hell.

Thursday after my evening class. The Rambler at 9.30 p.m. It was as simple as that. Alex was confronting Rita four months after their brutal break-up. She'd have to pick up some extra classes this week, to burn off the stress.

Apart from when she'd just received the e-mail, the topic of Rita had been left untouched between her and Nat. This was Alex's private battle—and she knew what Nat would say, anyway. Alex had contemplated telling Maddie, but she couldn't see the point. She tried to keep conversation about Rita to a minimum in any circumstance. She didn't want what she had with Maddie to be tainted by tales of what Rita had done to her and how incredibly inadequate it had made her feel. Rita was the past, Maddie the future.

Alex flipped her laptop shut, gathered some clean underwear in her backpack and made her way to Maddie's floor.

* * *

"Let's do the Dragon's Back tomorrow." Alex glanced at her three table companions who were all indulging in too much wine. "It's one of the easier hikes in Hong Kong."

"Don't you have family dim sum?" Maddie, who'd probably drained a bottle all by herself, slipped her hand on Alex's thigh.

"That was last week, babe." Alex remembered how Maddie had tried to corner her. It had only resulted in a half-hearted attempt at trying to make her open up about Rita and Maddie had soon abandoned her efforts when she'd sensed Alex's reluctance. Maybe we can talk about her after Thursday, Alex thought. Maybe I'll be able to deal with it then.

"Easier? You are taking the more advanced age of our companions into consideration, I hope? I've done it a couple of times and it nearly killed me." Nat raised her eyebrows. "Language is my thing and *easy* is not the right word to describe the path running over that mountain."

Alex needed action. As much as her body needed the rest, she couldn't bear the thought of a lazy Sunday afternoon. Exercising was the only activity capable of putting a stop to the endless churning of her brain. Had she made the right decision? What would Rita say? Should she tell Maddie? "Children do it. Pensioners do it. Everyone does it. You all belong to an excellent gym which keeps you in great shape. All that's left to do is go easy on the wine."

Nat reached for the bottle and topped up Alex's glass. Alex let her, she wouldn't drink it and that way it didn't end up in Maddie's glass.

"I've tackled the Dragon's Back many times. Admittedly, it has been a while, but I'd love to do it again. It's a wonderful Sunday afternoon activity in winter." Isabella smiled at Alex. "Good plan." She turned to Nat. "I'll show the ageists how it's done."

"You don't have to prove anything to me, darling." Nat shot Isabella a wink. "I'm well acquainted with your high levels of endurance by now."

"That just leaves me then." Maddie started to slur her words. If she didn't stop drinking soon she would never make it to the top tomorrow. "I'm a Dragon's Back virgin, I'm afraid. In fact, in all the time I've been here I've only been on one hike and that was the one across Lamma Island."

"That's not a hike," Isabella, a seasoned walker, said. "That's a leisurely stroll."

Maddie turned to face Alex. "I trust you only have my best interests at heart."

Alex pondered this statement for a second. She wasn't planning to climb this mountain to benefit Maddie's health. This was a purely selfish activity, set up only to take her mind off Rita. "I'll be with you every step of the way."

The look in Maddie's watery eyes brimmed with love. "I know you will."

MADDIE

The hike was a bad idea. Maddie's temples throbbed, her calves burned and she had a foul taste in her mouth. Yet, the view was almost worth it.

While the others seemed to float upwards along the narrow, steep trail, their feet barely touching the ground at an ungodly pace, Maddie lagged behind more and more. Alex waited for her at regular intervals, but Maddie felt increasingly alone in the staggering landscape of green mountains and indigo sea.

"Bad legs today, Madison?" Isabella asked, a self-righteous smile on her face.

Maddie loved her friend dearly, but she felt so miserable, so out of touch with everything they were enjoying, she limited her reply to a low grunt.

"Clearly your girlfriend hasn't been working you hard enough." Nat put a hand on Isabella's shoulder. "I, on the other hand, am extremely proud of mine."

They both stood there gloating, basking in the improbable love they'd come to share. They truly were the oddest couple ever.

"Come on, babe." Alex shuffled a little closer. "The worst is over now."

"You said that last time we stopped, before this hike turned into actual rock climbing." Maddie had caught her breath and was able to string sentences together again.

Alex grabbed her hand and pulled her up. "Look at this." Alex waved her arm in front of the splendour below them. White-tipped waves crashing to shore and wet-suited surfers trying to catch them. Endless forests in all shades of green stretched away from them. "Aren't you glad you decided to stay in Hong Kong when you see this."

"I didn't stay for this." Maddie curled her arms around Alex's waist. "I stayed for you."

Alex inched closer until their bellies touched, Alex's rock hard abs brushing against Maddie's irregularly heaving abdomen while she recovered from the effort. "I love you."

There was an intensity in the way she said it Maddie hadn't noticed before, an urgency to her words previously hidden—or non-existent.

"I love you too, baby, but I'll love you even more once you've gotten me off this mountain in one piece."

"How much more are we talking about?" Alex nuzzled her lips against Maddie's neck.

"Hey, lovebirds." Nat's voice cut through their tender moment. "If we want to see those surfers up close before dark, we'd better get going."

Maddie's mouth fell open in desperation. The surfers seemed impossibly far away.

"It's mostly downhill." Isabella could always read the distress on Maddie's face. "Before you know it we'll be listening to the roar of the waves with a cold beer in our hands."

"Best not mention any alcoholic beverages." Alex gently squeezed Maddie's neck before letting go off her. "Come on, I'll walk behind you. We'll let them get away from us and enjoy a romantic walk down. Just the two of us."

Butterflies flapped their wings in Maddie's stomach. She searched for Alex's hand and didn't intend to let go of it any time soon. Her body was in ruins after too much wine last night and the unexpectedly steep climb over uneven, treacherous mountain paths, but she had Alex and as long as she had someone as strong and capable as Alex by her side, she would be all right.

Together, they made it down, Nat and Isabella mere dots in the distance whenever the path ran straight long enough. Maddie had already been convinced of her feelings for Alex before she'd climbed the Dragon's Back, but came down the mountain with everything she felt reconfirmed and strengthened.

The disobedient curl that kept leaping free from Alex's pony tail and jumped up and down on her forehead. Her athletic hands on Maddie's back when they crossed a particularly difficult stretch of rocks. The way her abs stood out beneath her top when she twisted her body sideways and the immediate effect it had on Maddie. The sweet words of encouragement she had whispered in her ear on the final short climb to the beach. Despite her hangover, it was a gorgeous day and Maddie felt privileged to spend it with the most beautiful woman she knew—and she got to take her home afterwards as well.

Nat and Isabella had already started on their second bottle of San Miguel by the time Alex and Maddie arrived. Maddie crashed down in a chair, her gaze planted on the horizon, and she wondered what had caused her to experience this level of happiness so suddenly and unexpectedly. Mere weeks ago she was fumbling with a married woman in her office, deciding on whether to stay or not. Now she sat in one of the prettiest spots of Hong Kong, the sun setting behind her, after having climbed a mountain with the woman she loved more than anything.

She looked at Alex and she knew. She laughed away a tear —the sheer force of her smile enough to make it back down —and clinked the neck of her bottle against Alex's. This was love, the real kind, the lasting kind. She'd come a long way to find it, but here she was.

ALEX

Alex tried to swallow the tightness out of her throat. It didn't work. Rita's upper lip still curved deliciously upward and the blue of her eyes shone as crystal clear as ever. Adrenalin sped through her veins as Alex approached the low table where Rita sat, one long leg slung over the other.

"Hey," Alex said and everything that came before just fell away. Tears too strong to be ignored stung her eyelids as she crashed into the chair opposite Rita. "I probably shouldn't have come."

Rita clasped her hands in front of her mouth and pierced more of Alex's resolve with those unblinking eyes. She breathed heavily through her nose and shook her head.

"You have no idea how sorry I am," she said through

spread-out fingers barricading her lips. "I am so sorry."

Alex tried to hold on to thoughts of Maddie, of her radiant smile and softly whispered hellos in the morning, but they seemed to evaporate at the mere sight of Rita. As if Rita was the real deal and Maddie a copy, an expertly made one, but still just a copy of the woman sitting in front of her and tearing her heart to shreds again with a few words.

Alex scrambled for her bag which had fallen to the floor when she sat down and pushed herself up. "This…" She shook her head. "No…" It was all she could muster, all her constricted throat allowed to pass through.

Rita shot up out of her chair and curled her fingers around Alex's wrist, squeezing with gentle firmness—the way she always did. "Please." Her voice trembled. "Stay."

The touch of Rita's skin on hers quickened Alex's pulse, making her heart thump in her temples. Alex looked down at Rita's hand, its fingers so long and perfect. The pleasure they had given her. How they had made her surrender for years on end. Six years and then this. Walking away was not an option.

"Let's go somewhere more private." The emotions coursing through Alex were not meant for public display. There was some serious crying to be done. And shouting at this woman who had taken it all from her.

"I still live around the corner." Rita's fingers lingered around Alex's wrist, but more limp than Alex had ever felt them.

Alex nodded and walked out of the bar. Rita left some bills on the table to pay for her over-priced glass of Sauvignon Blanc. At least she hadn't had the audacity to order a bottle.

The sound of Rita's heels clacking on the pavement echoed through Alex's skull. She couldn't think, only feel. This had to be done. Whatever it was. Whatever would happen. Rita had to repent, despite not being the repenting type by a long shot.

The doorman smiled broadly at Alex. She had lived in this building for three years. She'd made Rita's apartment her own. It had been their home. Alex shot him an apologetic grin.

The elevator ride to the thirty-fifth floor was awkward but swift. Alex had grown up in a city full of tall buildings and had learned to hide her mental state in elevators from a young age. Instead of looking at Rita, she scanned her own reflection in the mirror.

What did that Mandarin teacher have that she didn't? It was the one question that had plagued Alex incessantly after their break-up. Why had she suddenly not been good enough anymore?

Alex's breath hitched in her throat when she entered Rita's apartment. Everything looked exactly the same as on the day she'd left. An ocean of memories flooded her brain. Rita kicking off her heels after a long day at work, her body slackening but her eyes still full of fire. Rita leaning with her back against the balcony window, demanding that Alex strip just by gazing into her eyes. Rita's hot body covering her from the back while she pushed Alex into the cold glass of the windows, naked and on display for anyone whose eyes happened to venture to their lit-up flat.

The tension seemed to drop from Rita's muscles now she found herself on home turf. She untied her hair and let it fall to her shoulders like a soft golden curtain.

"Please, sit." She walked to the wine fridge and pulled out a bottle of Oyster Bay. "Would you like some?"

Alex nodded eagerly. She approached the sofa and couldn't help picturing Rita and Peggy on it. Peggy's naked body splayed out under Rita while she did her thing. Peggy taking Alex's place. Alex sat down on the corner edge, not wanting to associate her body with anything that happened on the grey cushions after her time on them was done.

"Here you go." Rita handed her a glass of wine and pulled an ottoman closer. She sat down and stared Alex straight in the face. "I made a terrible mistake. Not one I can ever make right. I do realise that."

"Why?" Alex mumbled. "Why did you do it?"

Rita took a deep breath. "If only I knew." Her eyes grew moist and her knuckles turned white as she clenched her fingers around the stem of her glass. "Because I'm weak. And foolish. And only half the woman you are."

"I did everything you asked me to." Alex's voice cracked. "Everything."

"I know, baby. I know. I'll never forgive myself for hurting you. Never." Rita wiped the beginning of a tear from her eye.

"I presume you stopped taking Mandarin classes."

"Peggy and I are no longer seeing each other." Rita sat her glass on the coffee table and inched closer. "She had nothing on you. It was a silly infatuation. I certainly never loved her the way I loved you…still love you."

"You loved her enough to cheat on me for weeks." Anger swept through Alex's bones. Months of frustration trembled in her voice. "You were the one for me, Rita. The only one. I've never loved anyone…" Tears took over from words. They streamed down her face and landed with fat thuds in the wine Rita had poured her.

Rita took the glass from her hand and deposited it on the floor. She grabbed Alex's hands and buried them in hers. Warmth spread across Alex's skin and she looked up until her eyes found Rita's.

"I know." Rita's voice broke as her hands crept up Alex's arms. "I'll do whatever it takes."

Alex couldn't speak. After her initial anger over Rita's infidelity had made way for deep sadness, she'd dreamed of Rita saying those words. Now she was sitting in front of her uttering them, her eyes brimming with tears and her nails digging into Alex's biceps, they felt so meaningless and empty.

"Fuck you, Rita," Alex whispered, but it was loud enough to startle her ex-girlfriend. "When you destroy something as pure and powerful as the love we shared, it's gone forever. There is no going back and there is absolutely nothing you can do." Alex shook Rita's hands off her. "You can sit here and shed a little tear and feel all remorseful, but it doesn't change anything. You broke my heart and my trust and I will never feel the same way about you again."

"I don't expect you to. I just want—"

"I don't care about what you want." Alex rose. "And by the way, I'm seeing someone."

Alex cast one more glance at Rita's flabbergasted face before heading for the door and banging it shut behind her. She had to steady herself against the wall while waiting for the elevator and, adrenalin pumping through her blood, prayed Rita wouldn't come after her.

Once inside the safety of the steel lift cabin, she exhaled, taking in the red patches of skin on her face, and thought of Maddie. Sweet Maddie who had rescued her from the post-Rita blues. Alex looked her mirror image in the eye and wondered if Maddie could ever be enough.

MADDIE

The signal beeped in Maddie's ear. She launched the receiver back into its cradle with a loud sigh of frustration. Alex's evening class was finished by now and it wasn't like her to ignore her phone, let alone a call from Maddie. She just wanted to hear Alex's voice for a few minutes while waiting for her ten p.m. conference call with the New York office. She should have gone home and taken it there instead, but by the time she realised her call was only half an hour away, she figured she may as well stay in the office and get some more work done.

It was five to ten and she tried again. Long, taunting beeps rang in her ear. Maybe Alex forgot her mobile in the gym. Or perhaps she had better things to do than answer a call from her girlfriend. That's what they were now—girlfriends. Their affair was not a slow burn. It was full on from the beginning. Both of them desperate to leave mistakes from the past behind and launch themselves into this new romance as if everything depended on it. As if new love could undo former heartbreak.

She watched the clock as it ticked into ten. Forty-five minutes later the elevator spat her out into the bank's ornate lobby. Maddie refused to count the hours she'd spent in her office that day. She didn't have to count to know they were well above average, even the crazy Hong Kong workaholic average.

It was only a five-minute walk to the escalator. Maddie breathed in the mild early December air and contemplated a quick drink at a pub in Soho, but she had a refrigerator full of wine at home and maybe Alex would be around.

She'd given Alex a spare key after two weeks of dating and every time she walked through the door of her flat she hoped to encounter Alex's well-toned form draped over the sofa. Not one for late nights of pub-crawling—or late nights of anything not including a naked Maddie in her arms—Alex was usually there when Maddie arrived home after working late.

She wasn't today.

Maddie poured herself a glass of wine and took a few gulps before heading to the apartment located on the floor below. Maddie didn't have a key to Alex's place. Instead of ringing the bell, she knocked on the door gently.

Nat answered with her hair in a mess, her t-shirt wrinkled and her trousers half zipped open. She looked at Maddie as if she'd seen a ghost.

"Who is it?" Maddie easily recognised Isabella's Scottish drawl coming from the bedroom.

"Do you have any idea where Alex is? I've been trying to reach her all night. Is she here?" Maddie scanned the living room behind Nat for any other signs of life.

"Come in." Nat widened the door and stepped aside. "Your best friend won't be too pleased." She winked at Maddie. "It's well past her bedtime."

Isabella emerged from the bedroom with nothing but a tight red robe covering her body. "Maddie? What's going on?"

"Gosh, I'm sorry." Maddie made for the door again. "I'm worrying about nothing. Alex is probably on her way over as we speak. Do continue whatever it was you were doing." Maddie managed a tight grin.

"I haven't seen her since she left for work this afternoon," Nat said. "She didn't mention any plans for afterwards. Maybe she's in Tai Po?"

"It's not like her to be off the grid like this and she's not answering her phone." Maddie brought a finger to her mouth and started chewing on a nail.

"Come on." Isabella slung an arm over Maddie's shoulder and escorted her to the sofa. "Nat, will you try her mobile, please?"

"Yes, ma'am." Nat shot Isabella a quick wink and snagged her iPhone off the coffee table.

"Hey, Pizza," Nat said into the receiver after two seconds. "Where the hell are you?"

Elation washed over Maddie. At least Alex was all right.

"Maddie's here looking for you. Maybe give her a buzz?" Nat continued as she walked into the kitchen, preventing Maddie from hearing what else she was saying. It took five more minutes before Nat emerged from the kitchen.

"She's fine." Nat dropped her phone on one of the many book shelves. "She says not to worry about her. She'll be home by midnight."

"Where is she?" It was obvious Nat wasn't giving Maddie the full story.

Nat sighed. "I'm sorry, Maddie." She looked at Isabella with a desperate look on her face. "I'm sure she'll explain in the morning. She urged me to ask you not to wait up for her."

"Is she coming over to mine?" Maddie's heart started thundering in her chest. Something was up and she didn't have a clue as to what it could be.

"I don't think so." Nat inched closer and crouched in

front of Maddie. "Look, all I can say is she's facing some demons from her past. She may look perfect on the outside. She may even behave damn near perfect, but we all have our issues. Don't press her on it. Give her some space."

"Is it Rita?" Maddie saw it with great clarity now.

"Yes." Nat nodded briefly. "But no worries—"

"Is she with Rita now?" Anguish tightened Maddie's chest.

"No. I assure you she's not. She just needs some time." Nat stretched herself up. "You know Alex. She'd rather walk it off than burden anyone with her problems."

"It will be all right," Isabella chimed in. "Come on, I'll pour you a glass of wine."

"I'd better go home. I have an early start tomorrow."

Maddie wasn't worried about Alex cheating on her. Nonetheless, jealousy gnawed on her insides because how could she possibly compete with the greatest love of Alex's life? A love so great Alex couldn't bring herself to talk about it.

"If you're sure." Isabella squeezed Maddie's hand. "You're more than welcome to stay."

"If you see her," Maddie faced Nat, "tell her to take all the time she needs." Her stomach knotted together at the thought of Alex being too preoccupied with another woman to return her call. Maddie held her head up high as she exited Nat's flat, but she feared the worst.

ALEX

"Hey." Nat's voice startled Alex as she flicked on the light in the living room at well past one in the morning.

"What are you doing up?" She was grateful to see a friendly face. "Is there no love making to be done tonight?"

"I figured you'd need to talk about it." Nat ruffled the blanket she was covered in to the side to make room for Alex.

"And do you know how old Isabella is? She needs her beauty sleep."

It was still weird to hear Nat talk about someone with such affection in her voice. She'd obviously dozed off while waiting for her. Her hair rioted in all directions and her big blue eyes struggled with the sudden light. Alex crashed down next to Nat and let her head sink to her flatmate's shoulder.

"I feel as if I've opened Pandora's box." Alex took a deep breath before continuing. "The effect she still has on me took me by surprise. What Rita and I had was so all-consuming. I loved her so much." Tears started welling up behind her eyes again. "Of course, she ruined it by getting off with her bloody tutor, but at the end of the day, she's still Rita, you know. My Rita. Seeing her shook me so hard." Alex brushed a teardrop from her cheek. "And she looked gorgeous as ever."

"Maddie knows your disappearing act had something to do with Rita." Nat cleared her throat. "I'm sorry, but I couldn't lie when she asked."

Alex shook her head. "I walked along Bowen Road, all the way to Wan Chai and back thinking about what to do with Maddie. I don't want to hurt her, but I couldn't see her. She called me several times and I couldn't even face speaking to her on the phone. I have no idea what to say to her."

"Tell her the truth. She'll understand."

"I don't even know what the truth is. All I know is that when I saw Rita, everyone else paled in comparison. Maddie included." Alex buried her face in her hands. "God, I feel awful just saying that."

Nat curled an arm around Alex's shoulders. "Seeing Rita again was always going to be hard. Just don't make any hasty decisions."

"It was all too much too soon. Maddie is wonderful and I care for her a great deal, but what was I thinking? That I'd just jump into bed with someone who vaguely reminded me of Rita and everything would be all right? How utterly stupid."

"Is there any part of you that would contemplate giving

Rita another chance?"

"Every part of me not controlled by rational thinking." Alex looked up and turned to face Nat. "Do you think that in our life we can come across one person who touches us so deeply everything changes? Someone we'd forgive the worst crimes. Someone we can't help but fall for over and over again?"

"Oh, Pizza." Nat drew her near and cradled Alex in her arms. "You need to sleep on this. Rita showed her true colours in the end and no one is as perfect as we want them to be." Nat twirled her fingers through Alex's hair. "I witnessed first-hand what Rita Lowe did to you. She does not deserve a second chance from someone as good-natured and awesome like you. She simply doesn't."

"I know." Alex sniffled and rubbed her nose with the back of her hand. "I know she doesn't deserve it."

* * *

After a night of tossing and turning Alex got out of bed at the crack of dawn. When she walked into the kitchen to eat her morning grapefruit, she found Isabella drinking a glass of water.

"Morning." Isabella was dressed in one of Nat's black Blondie t-shirts and a faded pair of Nat's boxer shorts. Without make-up and her hair in a tousled mess, she looked like a different person.

"Sorry for keeping Nat up last night." It dawned on Alex how irritating it was that her best friend and flatmate's girlfriend was her own girlfriend's best friend.

"No worries." Isabella deposited her empty glass in the sink. "I know it's not easy that we're all so up in each other's business." Was she reading Alex's mind? "But I just want to say I've known Maddie for a few years and she's a changed woman. Since she met you something opened up inside of her. She's crazy about you and maybe she's not good at expressing it, but it's written all over her face."

Alex stared at the floor. She was hardly in the mood for

an early morning lecture on her relationship, but she didn't want to offend Nat's girlfriend.

"Point taken." Alex waited for Isabella to leave the kitchen before starting her morning ritual of carving out grapefruit chunks, but Isabella stayed put, resting her brown eyes on Alex.

This must be how she gets people to say things they don't want to talk about. A loaded silence and a stare that seems to see through you, as if she already knows what you're going to say but is waiting for you to connect the dots in your head. How utterly condescending. Alex had always been more of a fan of working things out in the gym instead of talking them through.

"I presume I'll see you in class this evening?" A night of fitful sleep hadn't exactly cleared the fog in Alex's brain, but she knew she needed to talk to Maddie sooner rather than later. She didn't want to disrespect her even more by discussing Rita with anyone else but her.

"You will." Isabella scooted past her, pausing to lay a hand on Alex's forearm briefly. "If you need to talk, you know where to find me."

"In Nat's bed, you mean?" Alex hoped to lighten the mood. It wasn't her style to take her insecurities out on other people, and she knew Isabella meant well.

"She does seem to experience difficulties letting me out." Isabella tapped her on the shoulder and exited the kitchen.

Alex realised a clean break with Maddie—if that's what she ended up needing—was out of the question. She'd have to move out of The Ivy first.

MADDIE

Maddie had barely stepped out of the shower when the chime of the doorbell startled her. It was seven a.m.

It could only be Alex.

A towel draped around her body and her hair dripping wet, she padded to the door and swung it open. Both fear and relief washed over her at the sight of Alex. She looked strung-out, worry visible in the shallow lines of her face and sadness swimming in her dark eyes. But at least she was there.

Maddie wanted to pull her in and hold her close for long moments, but she thought better of it. Alex hadn't used her key. And she hardly looked like the bearer of good news.

"Come in." She had trouble looking Alex in the eye. A persistently optimistic part of her screamed for recognition from somewhere in the back of her mind, but Maddie had known—and caused—enough heartache to know love didn't always win. She was also a firm believer in expecting the worst.

Alex entered the flat without saying anything. Only yesterday morning they had been fine. Maddie had kissed Alex goodbye while she snoozed a while longer in her bed. Maddie hadn't seen Alex since, but the vibe between them couldn't be more different.

"Let me quickly put something on." It felt wrong to receive whatever news Alex was about to deliver so scantily clad. Maddie rushed to her bedroom and slipped into a lying-around pair of jeans and a hoodie. Before heading back into the living room, she took a deep breath, tears already working their way up to her eyes.

"Do you want some tea?" Bringing water to the boil would give Maddie another few minutes of respite. Alex's demeanour was enough of a giveaway. She sat in the couch like a bird with its wings torn out. Defeated and no sign of hope in her eyes.

"No." Alex shook her head. "Please, sit down for a minute."

Maddie chose the arm chair across from Alex. What on earth had happened in the last twenty-four hours? Alex was a mere shadow of the cheerful bundle of energy she usually was. Her hair was uncombed and even her muscles—always so divine-looking—seemed less toned.

"I'm sorry about going AWOL last night." Alex breathed in deeply, as if calming her nerves. It didn't stop her hands from shaking. She looked up and closed her eyes for an instant. "Rita contacted me about a week ago. I tried to ignore it, but…I couldn't. I had to see her. I should have told you, I know that, but I had no idea it would be like this."

Maddie let her body sag into the soft cushions of the chair. She braced herself for what was coming next.

"When I found out about her and Peggy, I was in pieces. And then you came along and it was simply wonderful. I happily fell in love with you because it allowed me to ignore all the pain she had caused me. I used you to feel good about myself again. To my surprise, it worked." Alex looked away. "Until last night." She swallowed and bit her lip. "There's no easy way to say this."

Maddie's entire body started trembling, agony rattling her. She was forty but she hadn't been on the receiving end of a break-up often. This one was about to knock her sideways.

"Are you going back to her?" Her voice sounded icy, exactly the way she wanted it to sound.

"Heavens no." Alex shook her head. "Never." She slid to the edge of her seat. "I guess I just need some time. I have all these emotions coming at me, things I haven't dealt with. Issues I pushed aside the second you came along."

"But you still love her."

Alex sighed and gave a curt nod of the head. "I don't want us to split up. Not like this. You mean too much to me. I just…" Alex massaged her forehead with her fingertips. "Aargh, this is exactly the kind of lesbian I never wanted to be. The one who overcomplicates things and doesn't seem to be able to make up her mind." She looked up again. "I don't want to string you along and I want to be honest with you. Seeing Rita was a punch in the gut. Like the universe asking me what the hell I was playing at."

"Let me stop you right there." Maddie had enough of

Alex going around in circles. "From where I'm sitting, it's really simple." Her heart thundered in her chest. "Either you want to be with me or you don't. There is no in between."

"That's what I'm trying to say. It's not so simple. It's—"

Maddie cut her off again. "It is to me. You're not over your ex. You're not ready for this relationship. I get it." Maddie tried hard to swallow back the onslaught of tears prickling her eyelids. "Don't forget to return your key."

"It doesn't have to be like this. We can talk about it."

"No, we can't. There's nothing left to say." Maddie fidgeted with her fingers to keep them from shaking too much. "I'd like you to go now, please." She shot Alex one last glare.

"I don't have my key on me. I'll give it to Isabella." Alex rose from the sofa and the thought of her leaving, of her exiting the flat for good, caused Maddie's stomach to contract painfully.

Maddie looked the other way, out of the window with the spectacular view. She didn't watch as Alex made her way to the door and closed it behind her with the gentlest of thuds. She waited until she heard the bell of the elevator before bursting into tears and burying her face in her hands, soaking the hoodie—which turned out to belong to Alex—and staring into the darkness of her palms for a long time.

When she pushed herself out of the armchair after time seemed to have stood still for hours, she knew she was done with Hong Kong. She had tried and failed. She wasn't enough for Alex, that sweet, kind-hearted girl who wouldn't hurt a fly, but who had just ripped her heart to pieces.

ALEX

"I should probably move out." Alex sat with her knees tucked into her chest on a chair across from Nat's desk.

"Has seeing Rita fried your brain, Pizza? Because all of a

sudden you don't seem capable of making rational decisions anymore." Nat looked shaken. Her skin was pale and her eyelids sagged over her blue eyes.

"All I was asking for was some time to figure things out —"

"You told a woman who loves you that you love someone else, Alex. No one wants to hear that. No one."

"I was being honest."

"Yeah well, sometimes a little white lie goes a long way if it keeps you from breaking someone's heart." Nat pinched the bridge of her nose. "I told you not to make any rash decisions, and what do you do first thing in the morning? Before the crack of fucking dawn…and for what? For that two-timing bitch who hurt you so much you couldn't get out of bed for days? Do you remember? Because I certainly do."

Alex rocked back and forth in her chair, hoping it would lull her into oblivion. She wasn't expecting a pat on the back, but a little compassion would have been nice. Isabella had been right. They had all become too entangled.

"It's not as if I'm going back to her. I will never forget what Rita did and I will most likely never forgive her, but stop reducing her to just that. We were together for six years and they were the six happiest years of my life."

"I know, Pizza, I know." Nat got up out of her chair. "But that's over now. There was no need to sacrifice a perfectly good thing just for the memory of it." She walked towards Alex and planted her hands on her shoulders. "I wish I could shake the righteousness out of you sometimes. It would make everyone's life a lot easier." Nat opened her arms and pressed Alex's head against her belly. "You did what you had to do, but I believe you made a terrible mistake."

"I can't just ignore how I feel. That wouldn't be right." Alex buried her nose in Nat's crumpled t-shirt.

"And heaven forbid something feels not right in the perfect world of Alessandra Pozzato."

"When has my life ever been perfect?"

"That's just it, Pizza. Life is never perfect, but you always try to be. It's about time you gave that up and started slumming with the rest of us."

Alex freed herself from Nat's hug. "Do you want to go somewhere? Just for a few days. Phuket or Samui? Somewhere as close to perfect as possible."

"You can run, but you can't hide, Pizza. And if you have any feelings for Maddie at all, I strongly urge you to make it right as soon as possible."

* * *

Ever since they'd met, Maddie had made it a point to make it to Alex's Friday evening seven-thirty body combat class. Often barging in late, elbowing her way to the front—a dangerous thing to do in a room full of people punching the air—with a wide smile etched across her face. It was how they started their weekend, together and all the happier for it.

It was odd not to see her focused face, to not be able to shoot Maddie a quick wink in between tracks and dream about how her blue-grey eyes would stare into her own later, after a shower and a quick meal. Isabella and Nat kicked side to side and the fact they were there made Maddie's absence sting even more.

Alex kept glancing at the door, hoping, in vain, for one of Maddie's late arrivals. For a sign she'd not completely given up on her—on them. But what could she possibly have expected? That Maddie would just sit back and take it? That she would understand that Alex needed some time on her own to heal from the kick in the stomach seeing Rita again had delivered? Maybe she had made a mistake, but what other choice did she have? She could hardly crawl into bed with Maddie while her head was filled to the brim with memories of Rita.

On automatic pilot, Alex made it through class. Nat and Isabella waited for her outside the studio. They walked to the locker room in silence because there wasn't much that could be said.

Tears rushed to Alex's eyes when she hit the shower. Maddie always took the cubicle across from her, leaving the door ajar—against all gym regulations. Obviously Maddie had construed Alex's state of distress this morning as a sign she didn't love her enough. At the time, Maddie's assessment might not even have been that far off because Alex had barely held it together. She'd gone to Maddie's without thinking anything through, her mind in shambles and her heart in ruins. But whatever it was she had meant to say, it certainly wasn't that she suddenly didn't love Maddie anymore.

"Do you want to grab some dinner?" Nat sat on a leather bench in the lobby and looked up from her phone. "Or we can skip that and go straight for drinks?"

"I'm teaching in the morning." Alex sunk down next to her. "And I'm not very hungry."

"Says Miss Goody Two Shoes who's always ready to lynch me when I dare to miss a meal." Nat raised her eyebrows. "I'm not taking no for an answer. Let's pick up a deliciously high-calorie pepperoni pizza. And before you say anything, not one of those organic ones you fancy so much. It's Friday evening. Live a little."

"I don't want to be the third wheel, Nat." Alex nodded in Isabella's direction, who was pacing around caught up in a phone conversation.

Nat sighed before speaking. "If you ever say something like that again, I'll de-friend you. And not just on Facebook." She elbowed Alex in the stomach. "Come on."

Nat gestured at Isabella, signalling they were ready to leave. Isabella held up a finger, asking for a little bit more time.

"I'll wait for you outside." Alex headed for the glass doors that slid open as she approached.

Rita stood slanted against a concrete pillar, her hair pulled back in a high ponytail and her eyes blazing as ever. Alex dropped her gym bag and brought two fingers to her mouth.

MADDIE

Maddie hopped off the escalator and rounded the corner of the platform closest to Shape. She hadn't hurried to Alex's class, not wanting to upset her by making Alex teach her for a full hour. Instead, she'd opted for a more casual encounter afterwards.

Alex was worth fighting for.

As the day had progressed the thought had settled into her mind more vigorously with every passing minute. She was kind and smart and funny and breathtakingly beautiful. And Maddie's reaction this morning had been a tad too dramatic. She'd gone into protective mode, shutting out every other possible outcome than banning Alex from her life.

She'd been wrong.

Maddie would wait until Alex disentangled herself from the remnants of her relationship with Rita. Not being the passive onlooking type though, Maddie had done some research on Rita. Sure, she was pretty, but, at least in the pictures Maddie had come across on the internet, not the knock-out stunner Maddie had expected her to be. She wasn't even as high up at her bank as Maddie was at Crawford & Charles. Rita may have had the advantage of a history with Alex, but she had the serious disadvantage of having broken her heart. Maddie could take her.

Her actions this morning had been born from pure hurt and the ever-present desire to take the upper hand in any situation. If Alex wanted to cool things between them, Maddie would save her the trouble and make the decision for her. It's what she did. The person she had become after five years of relationship nothingness. But she'd underestimated the effect Alex had had on her in the short weeks they'd been dating. She didn't want to lose her to her own pig-headedness. She didn't want to lose her without a fight.

Alex just exited the building as Maddie arrived. Through the glass door she saw Isabella speaking on the phone. Nat pointed at her watch while making eyes at her.

Something made Alex stop dead in her tracks. She stood there gobsmacked. Had she seen Maddie approach from the side? Her eyes were aimed in front of her though. Maddie took a few more steps and caught the reason for the stupefied look on Alex's face.

Rita looked better in person, more regal and commanding. But Maddie wasn't interested in spying on Rita Lowe. She needed to see how Alex reacted to her after the initial shock wore off. From the way her jaw slacked, it was clear Alex hadn't been expecting her.

Maddie stopped and hid in the shadows near the escalator, opposite the gym building. Dozens of people hurried past and she could easily stay out of view. She shuffled close enough to be able to hear whatever conversation might ensue, but Alex didn't look quite ready to start talking yet.

Rita straightened her posture and took a step toward Alex. She just waved and smiled, not saying anything. As if putting herself on display—as if merely being there—would be enough to sway Alex into…Into what?

Alex didn't appear swayed in the least, her lips pressed together and her eyes narrowed to slits.

"Before you say anything," Rita started, while invading Alex's space a little more. "I haven't come here to argue, nor to beg for your forgiveness. I wanted to give you this."

Rita took hold of Alex's wrist and twisted her palm upwards. With her other hand she let something fall into it. Maddie was standing too far away to see what it was.

"I thought you might like it back."

Alex stared into her palm as if the most precious treasure in the world had landed in her hand. Maddie was itching to find out what it was, but she opted to stay in hiding and study Alex a bit longer.

"Yeah." It was the first word Alex uttered and it came out

cracked and quivering.

"Call me if you want to talk." Rita stroked Alex's lower arm with the back of her hand for a brief moment. "Anytime."

Alex didn't reply, but looked shaken. As Rita turned on her heels, Nat and Isabella exited the gym.

Maddie hesitated a split second too long and before she could emerge from the shadows, the three of them had set off in the other direction.

Maddie's plan had come undone in front of her eyes. This wasn't the gentle reconnection she had hoped for. It should have been her standing there waiting for Alex instead of Rita. It should have been her causing that array of emotions to creep along Alex's face. She'd lost this battle and she didn't know how to gear up for another one.

She'd been ready for a fight, but what if this was a war impossible to win?

ALEX

To any bystander not in the know—anyone apart from Alex and Rita—the rock Alex cradled in her hand was just an insignificant grey piece of matter. To Alex it was a reminder of the best day of her life.

When Alex had met Rita more than six years ago on a junk trip, she'd fallen hard and fast for the confident, long-legged blonde with the cool blue eyes. Alex had boarded the boat as a carefree twenty-something eager for a relaxed good time on her day off. She had disembarked eight hours later as a hormonal lovesick mess, reduced to monosyllabic replies to any questions asked, enthralled by Rita and her loud, room-filling personality.

They'd swum out to the shore together, Alex showing off her form and Rita—surprisingly—keeping up, and gotten caught up in a tipsy pseudo-philosophical conversation about a piece of rock stranded on the beach. Unbeknownst to Alex, Rita had smuggled the rock into her bathing suit and presented it to her a few weeks later, on the night it had finally happened.

Alex believed she didn't stand a chance with the likes of Rita. Surely she could have any woman she wanted. They probably lined up for her, like all good Chinese people do when something delicious is on offer. She'd barely even tried, apart from hanging out whenever she could with the crowd that had introduced them.

"Remember this?" Rita had asked, while digging the piece of rock out of her coat pocket. "I'll certainly never forget."

It had been the prelude to their first night together and they'd been insanely happy for the next six years. Even Alex's mother, who was notoriously hard to please, had taken a shine to the posh banker with her expensive pant suits and impeccable manners.

And then, all of a sudden, Rita wanted to take Mandarin classes, an initiative Alex had encouraged. She'd never have guessed it would be the end of them.

"Pizza's getting cold, Pizza." Nat rapped her knuckles against Alex's bedroom door. "What are you doing in there, anyway?"

Alex inhaled deeply, cast one last glance at the rock, and flung it into a corner of the room. She got up from the bed and opened the door.

"I'm ready for that drink now."

* * *

"I have the ultimate question for you." They sat slouched in the sofa, shoulder to shoulder. Isabella was long gone and Nat had introduced Alex to the harder stuff. They'd shared more than half a bottle of Scotch and, despite the incessant spinning of her head, Alex felt free of worry for the first time since seeing Rita again. "If you were to go into your bedroom now and dig up your vibrator…"

"My what?" She nudged Nat in the side. "I don't have a vibrator."

"Sure. Whatever." Nat pinched her in the thigh. "You get naked, get in the mood for one of your one-minute rides."

"Wha—"

"I told you before, Pizza. These walls are thin. Flatmates don't have secrets in this building." Nat turned to her, a lopsided grin on her face, her eyes watery with the effects of alcohol. "Anyway, what I want to know is…who will you be thinking of?"

Alex burst out laughing. "The noises I had to hear coming from your bedroom. The least you can do is show me the courtesy of not mentioning my unmentionables."

"Never mind that. Answer the question." Nat placed her hands on Alex's knees. She'd stopped pushing her bangs out of her eyes and her face was half-covered with hair.

"What kind of a question is that?" Alex held on to Nat's arm in order not to fall flat on her back. The booze seemed to interfere with her core strength. "It's too intimate."

"I'm not asking you to go on television and broadcast it. You don't even have to tell me, if you're really going to be so prissy about it. Just think about it."

Alex leaned forward and buried her face in her hands. "Oh god, I don't know."

"Make an effort. This is important." Nat slapped her on the thighs. "Come on. In vino veritas."

"Scotch is a bit stronger than wine. I think I'm way past any truth at this point." Alex looked up and brushed a curl off her forehead. "I can't believe I have to teach a nine a.m. class tomorrow."

"I got you drunk, I'll come to your class as moral support. Now, focus. Who's it going to be?"

Nat couldn't possibly be as trashed as her. She was used to drinking hard liquor. The strongest Alex managed was a G&T, which had nothing on the way this stuff burned in her throat. Nat was serious.

"I'll give you an answer in the morning." Alex checked the wall clock. It was two a.m. She'd taught classes with mild hangovers before, but tomorrow would kill her. "I have to go to bed."

"You can go to bed as soon as you make a decision. It's not rocket science, Pizza. Just follow this." Nat tapped her fingers to her chest. "And that, I guess." She pinched her eyebrows together and pointed her thumb between Alex's legs. "You will have forgotten all about this in the morning. I promise."

Alex let her head fall onto her shoulders and sighed. She stared at the ceiling, at where Maddie lived and she knew.

"Maddie. I'd be thinking of Maddie."

"Thank god for that." Nat pulled her close for a hug. "You'd be crazy not to."

"What have I done?" Panic gripped her, crashing into her from all sides. "I have to go see her." Alex pulled herself free from Nat's embrace and tried to get up. Instead she slipped out of the sofa, head first, onto the carpet.

She lay there helplessly, her feet tangled up in sofa cushions, her shoulders crushed into the carpet and her balance non-existent.

"Oh, Pizza." Nat rose and huddled over her. "Come on, I'll put you to bed." She extended her hand, but Alex didn't have the strength left to grab it.

"I must go and apologise." Alex's eyes fluttered from the ceiling above her to Nat's arm. "Before it's too late."

Nat crouched down and slipped her arm under Alex's back. "There's plenty of time for that in the morning. Believe me, you don't want Maddie to see you like this."

"I have to work in the morning." Alex finally managed to grab hold of Nat's other arm. Nat's weight shifted and, losing her balance, she tumbled on top of Alex.

"Hey, I'm taken," Nat said, before succumbing to a fit of giggles. Alex laughed with her, their bellies shaking against each other. "Remind me to never get you drunk again, Pizza."

MADDIE

Maddie stood in front of her wardrobe, hesitating whether to put on her yoga pants or not. She was baffled by the amount of tank tops piling up on her shelves, all belonging to Alex. The prospect of seeing Alex's shoulder line—a sight as addictive as anything—tipped her over the edge. She pulled her fitness clothes out of the closet and, heart already pounding out of control in her chest, slipped into them.

She had plenty of time for a coffee at The Bean before Alex's nine a.m. body balance class. She ordered a double espresso, eager for the caffeine to pump some energy into her body. After tossing and turning the better part of the night away, Maddie had decided she had some fight left in her. If anyone was worth it, it was Alessandra Pozzato.

While briefly looking up from the stream of work e-mails flooding the inbox of her phone, Maddie spotted two familiar figures sliding down the escalator. Her pulse quickened at the prospect of Nat and Alex stopping at The Bean for a coffee, but their faces slipped out of vision and the door of the coffee house remained shut for the next few minutes.

Nerves tore through Maddie's body as she made her way to Shape. She'd lingered in The Bean long enough to miss Alex in the locker room. She wanted to look at her in silence before having to speak to her. She wanted to see how she'd react to Maddie's presence in class. Maddie didn't want to risk Rita turning up afterwards again, with another relic from their past —which is what Maddie figured Rita had planted in Alex's hand the night before. She didn't want to miss her chance this time.

Alex was already running through her obligatory introduction lines when Maddie entered the studio. She found a spot in the back before daring to face the front.

Alex's words halted for the briefest of moments as she

acknowledged Maddie's presence. She followed up with a small smile before addressing her attention back to the group.

Maddie had never seen circles so dark curving underneath Alex's eyes. Her voice sounded gravelly and her movements appeared far less fluid than usual. Either these were signs of heartache, or she was suffering from a severe hangover. Maybe a combination of both.

All Maddie wanted to do was rush to the front, cradle Alex in her arms and tell her she'd give her all the time in the world. She'd wait. Then again, waiting until the end of class to talk to her already proved quite the challenge. At least she could shamelessly gawk at Alex, who, no matter how destroyed she looked, was always a sight for sore eyes.

She wore a white tank top as usual and, when pushing up from cobra into downward dog, her biceps still bulged obscenely. This is my woman, Maddie thought. For as long as she could remember, she'd never allowed herself to think something like that. She believed such thoughts to be quite ludicrous actually, but here she was. This was love and, for the first time in her life, Maddie was not running away.

"Give yourself a round of applause." Alex sounded relieved when she spoke the traditional last words of every class. "It's not always easy on Saturday morning." She shot the group a weary smile before rubbing her temples. Maddie disposed of her mat outside the studio and positioned herself at the exit while nodding at a few regulars.

She swallowed the tightness out of her throat as Alex and Nat approached.

"I have to run," Nat said, for once choosing to be diplomatic. She slapped Alex on the shoulder briefly and smiled at Maddie.

"Hey," Alex started as soon as the crowd around them thinned.

"Hi." Maddie felt like a teenager, standing around awkwardly and having no clue where to begin to say all the things she had to say. "You look like you could use a strong cup of coffee."

"Only small sips of water for me today." Alex puffed some air through her nostrils. "Nat and I had a bit of a bender last night and I have no idea how I made it through class."

"And this was only the first one of the day." Maddie inadvertently brought her hand to Alex's shoulder, but stopped herself a split second before it touched skin.

"Tell me about it." Alex's eyes followed the path of Maddie's now idle hand. "I must admit I was surprised to see you."

"Can we talk?" Maddie dropped her hand.

"Yes." Alex took a deep breath. "That would be good."

Ten minutes later they sat across from each other in The Bean, both still in work-out clothes, Maddie sipping another espresso and Alex trying her luck with a lemon tea.

"I've never been so ready for the weekend to begin." Alex stretched her arms above her head, accentuating her shoulder muscles.

"I'm sorry for overreacting." Maddie cut straight to the chase because she had no idea how to go about it any other way. "I was hurt. Well, mainly my ego was hurt and I thought if I beat you to the punch…if I broke up with you, that would somehow make me feel better. It didn't."

Alex shook her head. "Your reaction was completely comprehensible. I should have handled the situation with more delicacy." She grimaced and put a hand on her belly. "This tea is not working for me."

"I want you to know I will wait for you. As long as it takes." Maddie's hands trembled as she lifted her cup from its saucer.

Alex shook her head again and fear rushed through Maddie's blood. "Rita was a big part of my life for a long time. Seeing her again rendered me temporarily insane, I'm afraid. But it's no excuse for my behaviour. We are…" Alex hesitated. "We were in a relationship and I had no right to treat you like that, nor to behave as if the world was about to come to an end just because I laid eyes on my ex."

"I saw her last night. Outside the gym after body combat. I saw the two of you together. I didn't mean to spy…I had come to see you, but she was there when—"

"I had no idea she'd be there." Alex cut her off, wincing at the memory. "She's getting out the big guns now, but the bigger her gestures, the less they mean to me." Alex leaned forward. She paused before continuing. "I don't want her, Maddie. I want you."

Maddie bit her bottom lip and had trouble keeping her gaze on Alex.

"If you'll still have me, of course." Insecurity tugged at Alex's voice. "After the way I behaved…"

"What are you doing later today." Bursts of joy popped in Maddie's veins.

"Mentally preparing for my next class and afterwards I'm going to have to take a nap." Alex smiled sheepishly.

"Come nap at my flat, I'll prepare lunch." Maddie realised her enthusiasm was getting the better of her. "I'm sorry, I'm jumping the gun the way I usually do."

"How about dinner?" Alex grinned and another weight lifted off Maddie's shoulders. "I may be up for some of your spaghetti carbonara by then."

Maddie smirked. "You mean a replay of our first date?"

"I'd love that, but you shouldn't overdress this time around."

"Deal." Maddie's heart jumped in her chest.

Later, after Alex had made her way back to the gym for her final class of the week—a chaste peck on the cheek as goodbye—Maddie lingered in The Bean and wondered if it really would be that easy. Probably not, but at least things were looking up.

ALEX

Alex peered at her reflection in the mirror. The worst of the headache had died down, but her eyes drooped and her shoulders hunched, no matter how many times she corrected her posture. More than that, she was mentally and physically exhausted. And now she had a date to prepare for.

"Never again, Pozzato," she told her mirror image and applied the emergency eye balm Nat had given her. "Only to be used in extreme circumstances," Nat had said. A fresh start with Maddie qualified as just that.

She'd slept for three hours in the afternoon, after finding Rita's rock in the corner of her bedroom and stashing it as far away as possible in her unused sock drawer. Fatigue had taken her and had given her mind no chance to dwell on past and present loves. She'd tumbled into a dreamless sleep and had woken up feeling slightly better, but not exactly looking like someone who was about to reenact a sexy first date.

"Don't make the same mistake again," she whispered to herself. The only way going back to Maddie now would be different than when she had launched herself blindly into their affair a few weeks before, would be if she was honest with herself. Rita was alive and kicking, living her life on the same stretch of over-populated land as Alex was, and she was gunning for a reunion. Ignoring Rita's existence had been the easiest way to deal with the painful collapse of their relationship, but now it was time to re-acknowledge she had an ex running around out there. An ex who had caused her a great deal of pain, but who had also provided years of happiness. These were the facts. Now all that remained was to find a way to deal with them.

"You're not alone, Pizza." Alex channelled Nat's advice in her head. "You have me and Maddie and I also happen to know a really good shrink." Alex managed a smile. Her face still looked ghastly and her body felt as if all life had been drained from it, but at least she had hope. She shot herself a wink in the mirror and went on her way to meet Maddie.

* * *

"How are you feeling?" Maddie's eyes brimmed with compassion as she held the door open.

"Shattered." Alex barely made it into the apartment before her throat tightened and a flood of tears welled up behind her eyes. She pushed her back into the door for support and pulled Maddie close. "Oh damn," she said, her voice muffled by Maddie's shoulder. Alex let the tears flow out, all of them, while Maddie wrapped her body around her.

"It's all right." Maddie patted her hair and rubbed her neck.

Alex knew, as ruined and confused as she felt in that moment, Maddie was right. It was okay for her to cry on Maddie's shoulder. She didn't have to strive for perfection in everything she did every hour of every day. She could come home to Maddie and display some insecurities.

"Great start to our date," Alex said after the biggest wave of tears had subsided. "Can we try again?"

"How about we go straight to the massage part?" Maddie gently freed herself from their embrace and searched for Alex's eyes. A crooked grin split her lips.

Alex remembered the shoulder ache she'd had on their first date and Maddie's swift offer to massage some oil into it. "I'm too tired to protest, not that I want to." Alex lifted up her tank top to brush the last tears from her face.

"Do you want to eat first?" Maddie asked.

Alex shook her head and headed for the sofa.

"What are the chances of you falling asleep while my hands perform their magic on your shapely body?" Maddie asked while cracking her fingers ostentatiously.

"I'd say ninety to ninety-five percent, but only because you're such an expert at it."

"Then please allow me to invite you into my boudoir so I

don't have to do my back in when I transport you afterwards."

"Your pillow talk has certainly improved." Alex sat down in the sofa. "Speaking of which, maybe we should talk first."

Maddie approached the sofa and perched next to Alex. "You're exhausted and I don't care what we do, as long as you're here with me."

"But you cooked and—"

"It doesn't matter." Maddie slanted her body forwards until her forehead touched Alex's. "I'm just happy you're here."

Alex lifted up her hand and found Maddie's neck. Gently, she pushed Maddie upward and stared into her eyes. "I love you."

Maddie's eyes grew moist and she wrapped her fingers around Alex's hand. She brought it to her mouth and pressed a soft kiss on its palm. When Maddie's eyes found Alex's again, a full-blown tear dangled from an eyelash, ready to tumble down.

Alex pulled her closer and kissed Maddie on the cheekbone, on the spot where the teardrop had just landed.

"I love you too," Maddie said.

It only took a split second for their lips to find each other. They'd kissed many times before, but this lip-lock was different. It was a reaffirmation of their connection. It was the beginning of them as a couple that could weather many a storm.

As divine as kissing Maddie felt, the fatigue and the fact she hadn't eaten all day started to catch up with Alex. A bout of light-headedness caused her to retreat from the warmth of Maddie's mouth.

Maddie's eyes sparkled with desire and her words came clipped and lustful. "Are you all right?"

"I've had better days. The stuff Nat poured me was nasty." Alex let herself fall against the armrest.

"Come on, let's get you to bed." Maddie rose and extended her hand.

"You do realise I'll be out of it so much tonight, you'll be able to do whatever you want with me." Alex let Maddie pull her up. Maddie slung her arm around her waist and guided her to the bedroom.

"As if I need you to be out of it for that," Maddie whispered in her ear. Chills spread across Alex's flesh.

Maddie undressed her slowly, starting by pulling Alex's tank top over her head. She halted her actions to gawk at Alex's abs.

"I'm going to need some alone time with those very soon."

Alex smiled in response and let Maddie take off her bra. Her jeans soon followed until she stood in front of Maddie wearing only a pair of bright red boy shorts.

Maddie hesitated. Alex thought she'd already displayed a huge amount of self-control, undressing her like that without the prospect of some extensive fondling to follow. Bringing her hands to her side, Alex tugged her shorts off and tossed them into a corner of the room. "I'm ready for my massage now."

"I'll get the lotion." Maddie's voice was a low whisper and instead of heading for the bathroom where she kept the massage oil, she stood there a few moments longer, breathlessly taking in Alex's naked body.

Alex broke the spell and crashed down on the bed. As soon as her body made contact, she felt herself sink into the mattress. Whatever was on Maddie's mind, it would have to wait until she'd had a good night's sleep and had shed the wretched remnants of this hangover. She settled on her belly and spread her arms and legs wide while waiting for Maddie to return.

MADDIE

Maddie squirted some oil into her hand and warmed it

between her palms. Alex looked as good as ready to doze off, but Maddie had other plans. Alex should know better by now than to offer her naked body on a silver platter like this and not be faced with consequences. Lust drummed in Maddie's veins at the sight of Alex's smooth shoulders, toned back, and perfectly arched bottom. What was a reconciliation without make up sex anyway? She'd taken her clothes off while Alex was already planted firmly on her belly, her head buried in the pillows. She'd start the massage with her hands, but planned to use other body parts to finish.

"Aah," Alex moaned at the first contact of Maddie's hand with the skin of her shoulders. Maddie let her fingers slide over them gently, as if reacquainting herself with Alex's flesh. Had it really only been three days since she was last in her bed? It felt more like three weeks, what with the emotional toll it had taken on Maddie. For the first time in her life, at the ripe age of forty, she had felt as if she'd stood to lose it all. Because of another woman.

"That feels so good." Alex's voice was hoarse and muffled by the pillows, but still sent a pang of lust up Maddie's core.

"And I've only just begun." Maddie leaned her upper body over Alex, making sure her hard nipples brushed the skin of her back. She dug her fingers into Alex's shoulders and rubbed them with gusto. She felt Alex relax under her hands. It wasn't total submission yet, but that could wait until later.

With the side of her hands she rubbed along Alex's spine, causing her to groan underneath her. Had she really expected to fall asleep with Maddie all over her? From the bottom of Alex's back, Maddie made her way back up again, kneading the muscles she encountered as expertly as she could. She repeated the process until Alex alternated between purring and gasping for air. Then she zoned in on Alex's behind.

Alex's shoulders were Maddie's favourite body part to feast her eyes on, but she couldn't get enough of stroking that perfect behind, immaculately shaped from hours spent on the spin bike.

Maddie pressed her thumbs deep into the muscles of Alex's bum, starting on the sides, but soon drifting more towards the middle, tapering down to that delicious curve where the bottom meets the thigh.

Maddie was so floored by the sensual image of Alex's behind covered in glistening oil she had to clear her throat before she could speak. "Spread your legs for me, babe."

Despite the limpness of her body, Alex immediately obliged.

Before allowing her hands to slip between Alex's upper thighs, Maddie spent some time on Alex's legs, alternating kneading motions with a light scratching of her nails over Alex's skin, which had turned completely to gooseflesh. She pushed herself up on all fours and hovered over Alex. Her nipples traced lines in the lotion clinging to the skin of Alex's back. Maddie pulled herself up until her mouth was at Alex's ear.

"Do you want me to stop?" Maddie smiled at the reference to their first date, the one this evening was supposed to be a replay of. In reality, tonight's events couldn't be further removed from the first evening they'd spent in her flat, innocently flirting and kissing.

"God no." Alex's breath hitched and her reply came out as a lustful whisper.

Maddie slithered her body back down and let one nipple explore between the cheeks of Alex's behind until she had enough of guiding her nipples over Alex's skin. It was time for her hands to take over again.

She positioned herself next to Alex, leaning on one elbow, her breasts pushing into Alex's side. Slowly, she inched her fingers over Alex's buttocks down between her legs. A small wet spot had already formed on the sheet beneath Alex's pink glistening pussy. With the tip of her index finger, Maddie sampled the degree of wetness pooling between Alex's upper thighs. Maddie couldn't recall her ever being this moist and she became acutely aware of a throbbing sensation between her own legs. Although she had planned to pleasure Alex while she lazily half-snoozed on her belly, she was suddenly overcome by an unstoppable desire to see Alex's face.

"Can you turn over, please?" Maddie didn't wait for Alex's reply and snaked a hand under her belly, while the other pushed on her hipbone.

Alex didn't need much coaxing. The earlier signs of sheer exhaustion on her face had been replaced by eyes glinting with lust and lips parted with want. Maddie once more had her beliefs confirmed that there was only one cure for a vile hangover and she was administering it right now.

As soon as Alex had spun on her back, she pulled Maddie into her for a long, deep kiss. She buried her hands in Maddie's hair and locked her elbows behind her neck as if never wanting to let go of her again.

Maddie let her lips wander over to Alex's ear. "I need to have you now." Alex replied with a nod of her chin against Maddie's neck.

Trailing her lips down over Alex's breasts, briefly stopping to nip at the rock hard buds of her nipples, Maddie found what she was looking for. Alex's pussy lips shimmering with wetness and puffy with desire. She locked eyes with Alex, who had thrown her arms upwards and arched her back, her naked breasts protruding and her stiff nipples piercing the air. Gazing into the blackness of Alex's glassy stare, she traced a finger along her inner thighs before circling it around the rim of Alex's entrance.

Alex responded by arching her back further and pushing herself closer to Maddie's hand. She moved one arm from the pillow to where Maddie's other hand dug into the mattress to keep her balance, and curled her fingers around Maddie's wrist.

Maddie's finger entered and Alex blinked her eyes shut for the instant it took Maddie to go deep. Maddie retracted and immediately added another finger, sliding through Alex's wetness. She looked at her fingers as they slicked in and out of

Alex, flesh against flesh, wetness pooling everywhere, the sound of skin meeting Alex's moistness mingling with her low-pitched groans.

Maddie needed to be closer. Without interrupting the motion of her hand, and the rhythm that seemed to be bringing Alex to a climax in record time, she pushed herself up until her face was at the same height as Alex's.

"You are so gorgeous. So sexy. So everything," she said into Alex's half-open mouth, her words barely audible over Alex's shrieks.

Alex wrapped her hands around Maddie's neck and pulled her in for a kiss. She pushed her tongue deep into Maddie's mouth, grunting and groaning while meeting the thrusts of Maddie's fingers with her pelvis.

Maddie couldn't recall having ever seen Alex lose herself so much. She was just a body now, a body filled with love and lust and a need for Maddie so great she, at last, lost all sense of decorum. At least that's what it felt like to Maddie and it made her so hot, made her want Alex so much more, she couldn't stop herself from rubbing her clit against Alex's muscly thigh.

"Oh yes," Alex moaned and shoved her entire body into Maddie's fingers, staying suspended in the air while her orgasm trembled through her flesh. "Oh god, yes." She fell back into the mattress with a deep sigh.

Maddie felt possessed with need. She couldn't wait until gentle pleasantries and post-orgasmic kisses had been exchanged. She needed Alex inside her now. She pushed herself up and straddled Alex's slender form. She took hold of Alex's right hand and brought it to her aching pussy.

"Fuck me, babe. I..." Maddie couldn't finish her sentence because Alex had already entered her.

Maddie met Alex halfway and bucked down on her while her hands rested alongside Alex's face, her eyes staring down at the woman who made her feel things with an abandon completely foreign to her.

The climax creeping up on Maddie was one born from

pure need. It wasn't a slow build. It wasn't the result of a string of sensual movements colliding into an inevitable explosion inside her. It was Alex taking her, claiming her as hers again. It was the physical expression of their new beginning. It was love and it was need and it was heaven.

Maddie panted heavily through the waves crashing into her from everywhere. From Alex's eyes looking up at her and Alex's left hand scratching her back and Alex's right hand filling her with everything she had. Sweat dripped out of Alex's hair and it was so quintessentially her, muscles rippling under her skin while sweat trickled along, shoulders broad and curls dancing around her face.

"I love you," she groaned as she crashed down on Alex's supple body, the orgasm momentarily incapacitating her.

"And I love you," Alex said. She slid her fingers out of Maddie gently and held her in her arms for long heavenly minutes, maybe hours. Maddie couldn't be sure. Time seemed to have stopped and frozen them in that moment of perfect unification. It was just them against the rest of the world: predatory exes and overcrowded cities, ruthless bankers and too much work, problematic pasts and scorned lovers. It was just them and it was how it was meant to be.

ALEX

Alex woke before Maddie and stared at the sleeping form beside her while her stomach rumbled. She'd missed all meals the day before. Then again, that hadn't even been the most unusual part of the day.

Despite their similarities in looks and certain common personality traits, Maddie slept differently than Rita. She allowed her mouth to drop open slightly and she liked to edge towards the middle of the bed, whereas Rita seemed controlled even in dreams. Even when sleeping she looked as if playing a part in a commercial for Egyptian cotton sheets, her hair tied up neatly and a black silk mask covering her eyes. Towards the end of their affair, she let Alex spoon her, but only for the first ten minutes of the night. Then she shook her off, claiming she was too warm or she couldn't breathe, depending on how dramatic she felt.

Maddie lay on her back, her straight blond hair splayed all over the pillow, the duvet only covering her body from the waist down. Alex hoisted herself up on one elbow and let a hand drift over Maddie's chest. Her breasts were bigger than Rita's. Alex had noticed them the first time she'd met Maddie in body combat class, when she'd made the group do jumping jacks for thirty seconds to raise their heartbeat. The bigger chested women always stood out in moments like that. She smiled at the memory.

Alex hadn't suffered many hangovers in her life, but yesterday's had been epic. To wake up without that relentless thud in her temples and that queasy feeling in her stomach seemed like a miracle, but here she was, feeling more than fine.

"Please tell me it's Sunday." Maddie opened her eyes and arched her back while stretching out her limbs.

Alex nodded while letting her drifting hand disappear under the covers. She traced two fingers over Maddie's lower abdomen.

"Does this morning assault on my privates mean we're back together?" Maddie caught Alex's fingers in her palm and held her gaze.

"If you'll still have me now that you know I'm damaged goods." Alex held her breath.

"As if that was ever up to me." Maddie pushed Alex's hand down into her pubic hair. "And anyway, I'll still want you when your spectacular abs have turned to flab and your hair has gone grey."

Maddie was right. The choice had been up to Alex and she had chosen.

"How dare you suggest I'll someday live without a six

pack. I might as well be dead." Alex dipped one finger between Maddie's legs and wondered if the woman was ever not wet and ready to go when she was in her company.

"Music to my ears, babe." Maddie's voice shifted to ragged whispers as Alex started circling a finger around her clit. She threw her head back into the pillows and let go of Alex's hand. "Let me feel them."

Maddie brought her hand to Alex's belly and scratched her skin lightly before digging her nails in. In reaction, Alex pushed a finger inside Maddie.

"Mmm," Maddie moaned and snuck her hand up to Alex's chest until it cupped her breast.

Alex moved her finger and being inside Maddie moistened her thighs. Heat pulsed between her legs. It wasn't enough anymore to just feel Maddie's hand on her breast. She needed more. As if she had to make up for fleeing.

Slowly, she let her finger slip out of Maddie. She kissed Maddie below the belly button before pushing herself up, twisting on her knees until her back faced Maddie, and spread her legs to straddle her.

Alex had barely found her balance when she felt Maddie's nails dig into the skin of her behind.

"Sunday brunch," Maddie said, "my favourite meal of the week."

Alex bent her elbows and crouched down over Maddie's sex. Before she had a chance to even plant a kiss on it, she felt Maddie's lips on her, sucking her into her mouth. Alex returned the favour. Her tongue trailed over Maddie's upside-down pussy, a film of Maddie's wetness clinging to her chin.

Maddie didn't waste any time inserting a finger inside of Alex, which made it hard for Alex to focus on her own activities. It was never easy to be in charge in Maddie's bed. One trait she definitely had in common with Rita. Alex wouldn't want it any other way. Maddie's finger twisted deep from the start and Alex bucked her hips back, wanting to take in as much of Maddie as she could.

Alex curved her arms over Maddie's thighs so her hands had free reign over Maddie's pussy. With one hand she exposed Maddie's clit. The other one she positioned at the entrance of Maddie's pussy. While her tongue danced over Maddie's clit, Alex slid two fingers inside of Maddie.

Tasting and feeling Maddie the way she was doing, so intimate and intoxicating, while Maddie was doing the exact same thing to her, was a potent stimulant. Alex felt heat gather between her legs and she moaned into Maddie's pussy as she licked her clit.

She felt herself soar to climactic heights within seconds, Maddie's wetness in her face and her fingers in her pussy. Maddie was using just fingers now and they felt full and lush inside of Alex.

Alex thrust down harder and tried not to lose her focus, letting her fingers disappear into Maddie and lavishing the attention of her tongue on Maddie's clit.

Maddie's other hand sailed to Alex's abs, her nails digging deep into Alex's muscles again. It was enough to set Alex off. She halted her movements while Maddie's fingers dug deep. The exquisite pain of Maddie's fingernails on her abs blended with the contractions of her pussy walls around the fingers of Maddie's other hand. Alex's mouth was on Maddie's pussy lips, but she was too lost in the moment to do anything. She just groaned and squirmed and let the release wash over her.

Maddie knew Alex's body well enough by now and finished her off with three deep thrusts before retracting her fingers and brushing the back of her other hand tenderly over Alex's belly.

"Oh fuck," Alex sighed, her body lying spent and spread-eagled across Maddie's.

Maddie tapped her bottom playfully. "Hop off, Lothario."

"But I haven't fin—"

"We'll take care of that in a minute. Not that it isn't a pleasure to look at, but I'd rather see your face right now instead of your behind."

A blush creeping along her cheeks, Alex crawled off Maddie, turned around, and crashed down next to her.

Maddie gathered Alex in her arms. "I like the way you think," she whispered in Alex's ear.

"I'm sorry I couldn't hold it any longer." Alex buried her face in Maddie's hair.

"It's funny how your stamina in bed is exactly the opposite of your stamina in class."

"It's hardly a matter of endurance. It's you. You so easily reduce me to a puddle of wetness and want. I take no responsibility for it."

"I wouldn't want you to." Maddie slipped out from under Alex's grasp and looked down at her. "I'm flattered I have such an effect on you."

"Enough about me." Alex drew Maddie in for a kiss, their first of the day, and embraced her for long minutes. "Let's focus on you."

"What did you have in mind?" Maddie shot her a broad smile.

Alex looked around. "I presume hand cuffs are out of the question?"

Maddie nodded and winked.

"I'll pick up where I left off earlier then." Alex pushed Maddie down again, her hand trailing down along Maddie's belly.

"Sounds just about perfect to me." Maddie pulled Alex close for a kiss while Alex slipped a finger inside the heat between her legs.

MADDIE

Maddie followed Alex into the shower cubicle. It was Wednesday night after Alex's last class of the day and all she'd been able to think about for the past hour was Alex's body slammed against the tiled wall of the shower.

"What are you doing?" Alex planted her hands on her hips. Quite the sight when she was completely naked. "Get out of here."

Maddie inched closer and covered Alex's hands with hers. She knew full well Alex didn't mess around with displays of affection at work. She'd wink at Maddie during class, but even that gesture had grown less frequent as their affair had progressed.

"I'd like to stay."

Alex shook Maddie's hands off her. "No way," she whispered. "I can get fired for this."

"I know it's not your speciality, but you'll have to be extra quiet then." Maddie turned on the tab and manoeuvred Alex against the wall.

Alex took a deep breath and put her hands on Maddie's shoulders. "I know you used to get off on office sex, but I thought you were past that now."

"Ouch." Water splashed around them and Alex's hair started to cling to her forehead in delicious wet strands. Maddie backed off.

Alex's black eyes shot daggers at Maddie. She wasn't kidding.

"Get out of my cubicle and make sure no one sees you." Her voice was low and gravelly. She looked a little bit turned on. Or maybe it was an angry side of her Maddie hadn't yet had the pleasure to encounter.

"Okay. I'm going." Maddie gave Alex her cool sexy stare and for the first time ever it didn't seem to have any effect. Dejected, she stuck her head out of the door, made sure no one was around and ducked into the shower cubicle across from Alex.

Angry Alex was hot, especially without clothes and with water raining down her body. Maddie imagined it was Alex who rubbed the soap into her skin and washed her hair, not gently, but with firm movements supported by strong muscles.

She couldn't wait to get home.

When they towelled off and got dressed in the communal area, Alex turned her back to Maddie. Maddie could only imagine the brooding fury in her eyes as she watched Alex's muscles flex while she slipped into her clothes.

On their way out, Alex still hadn't said a word. It wasn't until the door of the gym was firmly shut behind them that Alex blew a fuse.

"Don't you ever put me in that position again," she hissed, loud enough for Maddie to hear but hushed enough to not provide passers-by with unexpected entertainment. "This is my job. There are rules and I stick to them. I believe in ethical—" Alex halted mid-rant. Her mouth fell open and her expression changed into one Maddie had only seen once before.

Maddie spun on her heels and stared straight into Rita Lowe's face.

"Trouble in paradise?" Rita's voice was clear and sultry. It was odd to stand so close to her, facing off really.

Alex regained composure much quicker than last time. Maybe the mood she'd been in before had something to do with it. Maddie had never seen her so feisty. Hands balled into fists and lips drawn tight.

"I realise my teaching schedule is freely available online, but I don't take kindly to stalking." She took a step closer to Maddie, whose heart thumped frantically in her chest. "Whatever it is you have to say, Rita. Or whatever prop from our past you want to give me that you rendered meaningless the day you started fucking Peggy, I'm not interested." Alex grabbed Maddie's hand. "I told you I'm seeing someone." Her fingers trembled against Maddie's palm. "This is Maddie, my girlfriend." Alex huddled closer and Maddie flung a protective arm around her shoulder.

"Nice to meet you, Rita." Maddie painted the most friendly fake smile on her lips she could muster and extended her free hand.

"And you." Rita shook her hand with a firm grip. "I'd best be on my way." A forced grin played on her face. She nodded at Alex and walked up the platform leading to the escalator.

Maddie's heart jumped in her chest. Alex couldn't have chosen her in a more obvious way. She faced her and dragged her into her arms.

"Are you all right?"

Alex circled her arms around Maddie's middle. "You'll take any excuse to hug me in front of my work place." She nuzzled her nose into Maddie's neck.

"I'm sorry about earlier. I was out of line."

"You're such a nymphomaniac. I can't take you anywhere."

"I'm only a maniac for you, babe." Maddie loosened herself from their embrace. "And you have no idea how happy you just made me."

"Shunning my stalking, manipulative, cheating ex in front of you, you mean? That was the easy part." A crooked smile tugged at the corners of Alex's mouth. Maddie knew she was acting much tougher than she felt. She'd sensed the incontrollable tremor in Alex's fingers when she'd addressed Rita. She'd heard the uneasiness beneath the steel in her voice.

"Oh yeah?" Maddie didn't know if she should push for more of a conversation on the topic or not.

"The hard part will be getting you in those cuffs later on, to punish you for your lewd behaviour."

"It's best to set the record straight from the start, babe. It's never going to happen."

"Have you met these?" Alex flexed her biceps and guided Maddie's hand toward the impressive bulge forming underneath her jacket sleeve.

"Best get me home now before I have to resort to inappropriate actions in the vicinity of the gym again." Maddie curled her hand around Alex's arm at bicep height and coaxed her towards the escalator.

"I do have other ways of punishing you. I hope you realise that." Alex's face was all cheekiness. Her dark eyes lighting up and body relaxing. "The weather should be ideal for a leisurely stroll along the Dragon's Back this weekend. What do you think?"

"I'll take the hand cuffs."

ALEX

"Maddie and I bumped into Rita last night." Alex and Nat sat across from each other at Munchies. Two girls at a table nearby had been looking at Nat longingly for the twenty minutes they'd been there. Nat had been staring back a bit too much for Alex's comfort.

"What?" This got Nat's full attention. "An ultimate lesbian drama moment. Tell me all about it."

"I told her to bugger off."

"Who? Maddie or Rita?" A huge smile split Nat's face. "Just kidding, Pizza."

Alex mock-smiled. "Not even remotely funny, Orange." Alex took stock of the girls. They looked about seventeen, but were probably in their mid-twenties. They seemed like the exact type Nat would have gone for before things heated up between her and Isabella. "And what are you doing making eyes at those girls?"

"Lighten up. Isabella and I are not exclusive, you know."

Alex's eyebrows shot up. "Does Isabella know that?"

"What do you mean? I know you're of the more prudish variety, but isn't that implied at the beginning of any courtship?" Nat openly ogled the girls now and Alex stiffened at the sound of their giggles cutting through the air.

"No. Of course it's not." Alex leaned over the table. "Are you saying you've been seeing other people?" Alex hesitated for a second. "Since you and Isabella got together?"

"I haven't been going out of my way to meet them. Isabella keeps me pretty occupied." Nat met Alex halfway across the table. "And satisfied, I must add. But sometimes, when one is out and about, things…happen."

"What sort of things?" Alex couldn't believe it. Maybe she'd been living under a rock of late, what with Rita resurfacing and the intensifying of her relationship with Maddie, but she'd assumed Nat and Isabella were a done deal from the beginning. She'd certainly never suspected Nat was still up to her old tricks.

"No need to make a big deal out of it, Pizza."

The smug smile on Nat's face drove Alex crazy. She could deal with Nat the philanderer when she'd been single, but she couldn't accept that kind of behaviour now she was with Isabella.

"If you're cheating on Isabella, I swear to you, I'll never speak to you again." Alex realised she'd recently fallen victim to over-complicating the matters of the heart in her own life, but this was just ludicrous.

"I'm not cheating on her. We simply haven't set the boundaries of our relationship yet. It's only been a few weeks and I'm not sure if I'll ever choose monogamy again."

Alex was at a loss for words. She knew the person sitting in front of her inside and out, but she'd never expected this. She'd always believed Nat's loose ways were a means to waste time until the right woman came along.

Then it hit her.

She looked into Nat's bright blue eyes and realised her best friend was scared out of her mind. Nathalie Orange was afraid Isabella would break her heart the way Claire had done and she was reacting in typical Nat fashion.

"I know it's scary. All these new crazy feelings crashing down on you and the insecurity accompanying them, but there are other ways to deal with them."

"Like regular exercise, you mean? Alessandra Pozzato's cure for everything." Nat went on the defence. Alex knew she'd hit the nail on the head.

"Please, talk to Isabella about this before you ruin something really good."

"Don't worry about it, Pizza. Isabella and I are fine. I like her, a lot. Despite the fact she's fifty and, by the odd chance we're still together in ten years, she'll be sixty by the time I'm in my mid-forties. That's a woman's prime, you know." Nat eased back into her chair, her eyes darting to the table with the girls. "Look at them. The very image of youth. Not a laughter line visible on their face and all they do is giggle."

"You speak as if you're about to start menopause. That's very dramatic, even for you." Alex eyed the girls. They did nothing for her.

"Drama is my job." Nat sighed. "And I've come to know too much about menopause for someone my age."

Alex dug her wallet out of her bag and put some bills on the table. "Come on. I'm getting you out of here before you do something you'll regret." She extended her hand and Nat took it. She made Alex work for it and didn't cooperate when she dragged her out of her chair.

"How many?" Alex asked when they were on their way back home.

"How many what?" Nat's face was the picture of innocence, as if she didn't know what Alex meant.

Alex stopped to look her in the eye. "How many girls since you started dating Isabella?"

"Does it matter?" Nat shrugged.

"It should." Alex suddenly felt like someone's mother. "I know you Nat. I know why you do what you do. I've also never seen your eyes so vibrant and your demeanour so gentle as when you're with her. Do this for yourself."

"I won't fuck it up. I promise. I just need some time to get used to the idea of getting seriously involved with someone again."

"Okay." Alex slapped Nat on the behind. "Now get your ass home so I can lock you in your office until dinner time."

"No wonder Maddie spanks you. You're insufferable sometimes." Nat leapt out of Alex's way before she could slap her again. Alex smiled and followed her flatmate home.

MADDIE

Maddie and Isabella shared a taxi to Copyright, the book store hosting the launch of Nat's first translated book in Chinese. Isabella looked out of the window, a sparse smile on her face.

"You must be excited for her," Maddie said. "Hell, even I'm excited."

"Sure. It's all very thrilling." Isabella didn't turn to Maddie when she spoke.

"What's wrong?" Maddie hadn't heard of any trouble. She did sometimes wonder if the fact that she was Isabella's best friend kept Alex from sharing certain information about Nat with her. But that was Alex's business and she couldn't blame her if she did.

Isabella sighed. "It's not that I had expected her to be, but…she's not faithful. And now that her books are being published in Chinese, she'll get even more offers she won't be able to refuse." She fidgeted with her hands in her lap. "It's as if everyone in this city wants a piece of Nathalie Orange and all I get are leftovers. I'm not sure I can live with that."

"But…" Maddie was stumped for words. "You guys seem so happy."

"We are. That's what makes it so frustrating." Isabella finally faced Maddie. "I don't know if she expects me to know or if she thinks I'm stupid. Either way, it hasn't been a topic of conversation yet."

"Are you sure?" Maddie had heard all about Nat's three-year stay in Trampville, but she'd thought that had ended once she'd gotten into bed with Isabella.

Isabella nodded. "Of course I'm sure. It's not as if she

goes to great lengths to hide it. She just won't talk about it. When we're together it's this frenzy of sex and lust and hormones and, frankly, I find myself unable to bring it up. And yes, I know how ridiculous that sounds coming from my mouth."

The taxi driver sighed as if the weight of the world rested on his shoulders because he was stuck in cross-harbour traffic.

"What will you do?" Maddie imagined Alex cheating on her and winced at the idea.

"She claims she moved to Hong Kong because of the anonymity, but I see how she revels in the attention she gets. She loves the spotlight, no matter what she says. And she's grown so accustomed to a certain lifestyle. I'm not entirely sure I fit into her plans."

"But you're in love with her." Maddie moved a little closer to Isabella, as if proximity could make it right.

"That I am." Isabella sucked her bottom lip into her mouth.

After a long minute of silence in which Maddie had no idea what to say, Isabella took a deep breath and continued.

"I'm quite sure she doesn't deliberately want to hurt me. I'm smart enough to figure out her reasons and I do know she's in love with me too. There's no way she'd be with me otherwise, but the differences between us are so huge."

Traffic started moving again and the car picked up speed. Maddie checked her watch. They'd make it in time. She needed that glass of champagne waiting for her.

"I'll fight for her, but I'm not convinced we're meant to be."

It was odd to see a woman dressed to the nines look so defeated. Isabella always scrubbed up nicely, but no matter the state of their relationship, she'd outdone herself for Nat's big do. Her lips were painted a crimson red, accentuating their sensual curve. Her long brown hair was pinned to the top of her head in an elaborate display of hair origami. She wore a maroon tight-fitted dress with low back cleavage not a lot of fifty-year-old women could pull off and the heels of her Jimmy Choo's were at least six inches long. Nat needed her head examined for not wanting to share her bed every night with a woman so gorgeous and sophisticated.

"I'm sure she'll see the error of her ways soon. How can she not?" Maddie shot Isabella an encouraging smile. "She's not blind is she?"

"She is sometimes. She's also young and successful and all she has to do is bat her eyes at a girl and the poor thing is as good as hers."

"But you're a catch." Maddie pressed her hands on Isabella's finicky fingers. "And don't you forget it."

The cab pulled up in front of the giant bookstore located on the ground floor of another of Hong Kong's high rises.

Maddie spotted Nat and Alex near a table in the back, surrounded by a throng of girls. She got Isabella's point.

"Let's knock'em dead." She gently elbowed Isabella in the side and started sashaying her way through the crowd.

Even Alex had dressed up for the occasion. She looked sensational in her skin-tight black jeans and knee-length boots. A boat-neck top exposed her collarbones, which made up for the fact that her delicious arms were covered by the sleeves of a beige blazer.

Maddie couldn't help but notice how Nat's gaze shifted from her posse of admirers to her approaching girlfriend. No doubt Isabella had dressed to impress, and it was working. It was her way of saying to Nat that she could take an army of her girls.

"You look fantastic." Maddie kissed Alex on the mouth. Her hair was down and cascaded to her shoulders and Maddie wanted to take her home already. She had plans for those boots.

Even Alex couldn't keep her eyes off Isabella. She wolf-whistled and winked at Nat, who had a huge smile plastered on her face. If Isabella hadn't just told her about their issues, Maddie would have been none the wiser. Isabella certainly looked the part of the breathtaking partner of a celebrated author.

"Did you know about their problems?" She whispered in Alex's ear. "About Nat's infidelity."

"It recently came to my attention."

"At least *we* are all right now." She found Alex's hand and curled her fingers around it.

"We most definitely are." Alex's smile was joyful and free of worry.

A waiter approached and offered them a glass of champagne. The four of them faced each other and clinked rims. The party was about to begin.

CLOSE ENOUGH

ISABELLA

Isabella did not have a good feeling about this. She cradled the bag with two of Nat's favourite egg sandwiches from The Bean in one hand and stabbed the elevator button with the other. She'd stayed at the after-party at Volt following Nat's book launch until two a.m. before giving in to fatigue and, frankly, the overwhelming feeling that Nat didn't want her there. She'd ended up going home alone, leaving Nat with a slew of giggling admirers.

She had wanted to be the bigger person, a mature woman immune to bouts of jealousy. She had wanted to act her age—a wise almost fifty—but she'd had enough. And it had hurt like hell. Still, she felt as if she had to make up for it now.

She pushed the button for the forty-second floor while her heart thundered in her chest. Knowing Nat, she'd probably ignore the fact that Isabella fled her party, shoot her a crooked smile and gather her in her arms. Nat was really good at pretending things never happened. Isabella was starting to get the hang of it as well, despite it not being a quality she wanted to possess. No matter Nat's state of undress or the seductiveness of her glance, Isabella had to stand her ground. They had to talk.

She rang the bell, but nothing happened. Immediately, Isabella suspected that Nat hadn't come home. It was almost noon. That must have been quite a night. Anguish tightened

Isabella's chest. She pressed the buzzer again and its piercing ding-dong caused her stomach to contract. Isabella turned on her heels and made for the elevator. Just as she pushed the button, the door to Nat's flat flew open.

"Where's the fire?" Nat looked like death warmed up. Her complexion was so pale it nearly blended in with the white walls of the hallway. She wore nothing but a long t-shirt barely covering her privates. If she was happy to see Isabella at all, there was no trace of that on her face.

"I brought you lunch." Isabella stepped closer and the smell of digesting booze hit her nostrils. She handed the bag of sandwiches to Nat, who accepted it with a look of bewilderment in her eyes.

They stood there for a few seconds like half-strangers, not a whiff of romance between them. Isabella couldn't help but wonder what the hell she was doing with the likes of Nat.

"Thanks." Nat shifted her weight from one bare foot to the other. "I'd invite you in, but the place is a mess. Why don't I come up later—"

The sound of footsteps behind her startled Nat. Isabella peered inside, believing it was Alex. Nat shut the door behind her as much as possible without locking herself out, but Isabella had seen enough. The woman inside Nat's flat was Asian, but it certainly wasn't Alex.

Anger flashed through Isabella's bones. She inched closer to Nat, ignored the stale smell on her breath, and stared her straight in the eyes. "If you don't want this to work, it won't." She spun on her heels and marched toward the elevator bank. She jabbed the button frantically. Of course both elevators had to make their way up from the ground floor.

"Wait." Nat pulled the t-shirt down as she followed Isabella, but it was too short to hide anything. Isabella could hardly stand to look at her. Did she really love this person? Was this what her life had become?

"Don't bother." She shot Nat an icy glare. "I know what you're going to say and I'm not interested."

Thankful to live in a new building with speedy elevators, Isabella ignored Nat's defeated face and slipped inside the steel cabin as soon as its doors opened. As the doors slid shut, Nat slipped out of view.

Isabella blamed herself mostly. Nat had turned to her in her darkest moments and what had Isabella done? She had given in. While Nat wasn't a client and, technically as well as ethically, Isabella had done nothing wrong, this whole outcome had been so predictable.

It's not as if Isabella didn't know that Nat was doing the very thing she'd just witnessed. It's not as if, in the weeks they'd been seeing each other, Isabella hadn't counted the ways in which their affair was doomed.

She entered her flat and glanced at the clock. Her only appointment today was at five p.m. so she had plenty of time to compose herself. And beat herself up about what had just happened.

NAT

The first thing Nat did after Isabella left was kick Cindy out. She couldn't stand to be around her corny smile and Hello Kitty ways one second longer. After taking a shower, she stared at the egg sandwiches Isabella had brought her as if they held the answers to all her prayers.

She knew she'd gone too far. She'd hurt the one person who had truly understood her, the one woman who'd had the nerve to call her on her bullshit. Excuses and half-assed explanations wouldn't work, but maybe a massive and long overdue mea culpa would. Either way, losing Isabella was not an option.

Nat made her way up to the penthouse and, heart hammering furiously in her throat, rang Isabella's bell. Her heart nearly stopped when she heard Isabella's heels approach, the click-clacking sound making her palms sweat and her blood pressure spike.

Isabella opened the door without saying anything. She spread it wide and walked to the sofa, where she sat down and waited for Nat to enter. She always looked so well put together, her make-up applied immaculately, her hair brushed to perfection and her skirts expensive.

Despite the shower and the clean jeans and t-shirt she'd put on, Nat felt scruffy, dirty even.

Nat closed the door and chose an armchair across from Isabella. She couldn't look her in the eye just yet. What would she say? I'm sorry? And how could that ever be enough?

"I'm sorry," she said, "that you had to see that."

"Tell me something, please. Because I'm dying to know." All compassion had drained from Isabella's voice. The compassion Nat had craved so much. "I waited for you last night, for hours I stood by your side, which should have made it pretty clear that I wanted to end the night with you."

"I know. I—" Nat pleaded.

"Let me finish, please." Isabella crossed one leg over the other. "How long did it take you before you went home with that girl?"

"I don't remember, really. But that's not the point." Nat squirmed in her seat.

Isabella shook her head. "I know we are very different and I'm fully aware that some things have become second nature to you. I also know that you are scared out of your mind because of how you feel about me, but I won't be disrespected like that. No matter your motivations."

"If you want us to be exclusive, we can talk about that." Nat felt like a right douche-bag for saying that. Frankly, she had no idea what to say. It was so much easier to spend the night with a girl who barely spoke her language and didn't have the words to question her integrity.

"Exclusive?" Isabella puffed some air through her nostrils. "Give me a break." She uncrossed her legs and leaned her elbows on her knees. "Do you think I've been running around with other women since we started dating?" She stared Nat straight in the face. "Do you?"

"No." All Nat could do was shake her head.

"Let me break this down for you." Isabella sighed, but still wore her poker face. Nat had hoped to see a little bit more devastation. "This thing between us has absolutely no way of working. You're not ready by a long shot and I should never have confused my desire to help you with…" She paused. "With whatever it is I'm feeling for you." She glared at Nat and she looked achingly beautiful. "And in case you're wondering… Yes, you hurt me. And that's what we'll end up doing to each other if we don't end this now."

"Can I say something?" Hearing the word *end* stirred something in Nat's gut. "I'm well aware of my flaws and I fully realise I'm not an easy person to be with. I'm not making excuses for what I did and I'm sorry that I hurt and disrespected you. I really am." Nat hesitated. "But, damn it, we are good together and I won't give up on you so easily." Nat debated getting out of her chair and moving closer so she could at least touch Isabella, but thought better of it. "You didn't confuse your desire to help me with feelings for me. What happens when we are together is not confusion, Isabella. It's real and it's beautiful and it's the best thing that ever happened to me."

Isabella leaned back in the sofa. She swallowed hard. "Words, words, words. I know you get paid a lot of money to string them together in sentences on paper, but honestly, at this point, after what I've just seen, after I waited for hours for you to come home with me, they don't mean anything to me." Isabella's voice shot up. "I don't need any more words from you. Sure, we have good chemistry. We're good in bed together, but how dare you use that as an example when you just spent the night with someone else?" She half-shouted the last sentence.

Nat knew there was nothing else she could say. Isabella

was right. The only way she could prove her love was by showing Isabella how she felt.

"I should never have let it come this far. That was my mistake." Isabella fiddled with the hem of her skirt. "Yours was to take me for granted a little bit too much." She fixed her gaze on Nat. "I'd like you to go now. There's nothing left to say."

"I'll go." Nat rose. "But this is not over, and you know it." She made her way to the door, heart racing and legs wobbly. Before leaving she cast one more glance at Isabella, whose face had gone red with fury. "There's no way I'm letting you go."

Nat sounded much more confident than she felt. She had no idea how to go about winning Isabella back, but she'd make it up as she went along. It was what she always did.

ISABELLA

Isabella watched the door Nat had walked out of. Part of her was curious to see what kind of fight Nat would put up, but mostly she felt too deflated to believe anything Nat had just said.

Nat had never made her any promises. They had certainly not rushed into their affair the way Maddie and Alex had—everything all at once. They'd both kept a certain distance. Isabella figured Nat's need for frequent nights by herself came from a place of self-preservation and fear. Isabella just deemed it normal. It wasn't even that she had expected Nat to be faithful from the get-go. It was more the glaring impossibility of it all.

Two people can feel attracted to each other and still make each other's life miserable. Isabella had seen it occur often enough. She'd spent hours listening to tales of misunderstood gestures and dashed expectations, because some people only want what they can't have. Isabella refused to be one of them. She dug her phone out of her purse and called Maddie, hoping she'd still be on her lunch break. Maddie picked up after one ring.

"Hey stranger, what was it like to party with the young all night?"

"Horrible." Isabella remembered feeling her age while she waited for Nat to wrap up one small talk session after the other. "It's over."

Silence on the other end of the line. Isabella waited for her words to register with Maddie.

"But… What?" Maddie's eloquence was the next thing to bite the dust that day.

"Nat obviously thought it much more exciting to take home Cindy from The Bean instead of me. At least I think it was her. I didn't really get a good look at her latest conquest when I brought her ladyship sandwiches for lunch."

"Jesus Christ." Silence again. "Are you all right?"

"What was I thinking, Maddie? Really? Where was my mind when I decided to hop into bed with Nathalie Orange? I've made mistakes before, but this was simply ludicrous." Isabella wasn't expecting answers. She was mostly just scolding herself. "But hey, I had my eye-opening experience and, trust me, I'm not making the same mistake again."

"What do you want to do tonight? Go out or kill a few bottles of Bordeaux at home?"

"Nothing too heavy. I'm seeing two clients before noon tomorrow." Isabella sighed. "And don't you have your regular Friday night personal training session? Now that you and Alex are all hunky-dory again?"

"Alex will understand. She will kill Nat for this, by the way. She doesn't raise her voice often, but there's nothing that gets under her skin more than infidelity. Cancel tomorrow's clients. I'm serious. And I'll bring a bottle of your favourite Scotch. We're going on a bender."

"I guess this qualifies as an emergency." Isabella wasn't

sure if focusing on other people's problems would make her feel better or not. "Do send my apologies to Alex for snatching you away from her."

"Don't worry about that. She'll be too busy giving Nat a piece of her mind."

Isabella couldn't help but feel sorry for Nat. Alex didn't understand her the way she did. Isabella believed no one really did, but it was this kind of thinking that had landed her into Nat's bed in the first place. She ended the call with Maddie and rescheduled her Saturday appointments.

* * *

Isabella and Maddie sat overlooking the glowing lights of Victoria harbour from Isabella's terrace. Isabella didn't know about Maddie, but she hadn't been this wasted since the nineties.

"The sex was spectacular." She banged her empty glass onto the wooden table. "I mean, not just good, or fantastic, but unbelievably spectacular."

Maddie's mouth fell open, more in mock amazement than anything else. "Well, she's had a lot of practice."

Isabella was gone far enough to laugh hysterically at Maddie's remark.

"Listen to me, Maddie." Isabella tried to slant her body over the table in a conspiratory manner, but she just banged her chest against the edge. She ignored the pain flaring through her flesh. Nothing really hurt when you had half a bottle of Scotch diluting your blood. "Have you ever come so hard, it feels like a fountain of wetness gushes out of you?"

Maddie pondered this for a moment, before arching her eyebrows up. "You mean, you know, what's it called?"

Isabella nodded. "Yeah, exactly that." She leaned back against her chair, lost in a sea of drunken, but incredibly hot memories. "She's the only one who has ever done that to me." Isabella glanced at Maddie's perplexed face. "I had to buy extra sheets. They were drenched every other night."

Maddie started convulsing with laughter. Isabella gladly

joined her, until she couldn't distinguish the tears born from laughter from the ones born from pain, frustration and disappointment.

"I've never…" Maddie sipped from her glass of Scotch. "I mean, that has never happened to me, nor to anyone who ended up in my bed." She searched for Isabella's eyes. "What's it like?"

Isabella wiped the tears from her eyes. "The first time it happened I was so shocked." She chuckled at the memory. "Of course, Nat was all cool and relaxed about it. Acting as if it was the most normal thing in the world. You know what she's like."

"Too cool for old-timers like us." Maddie clinked her glass against Isabella's.

"But once I got over the initial embarrassment of, well, spraying my wetness around, it was the most amazing feeling I've ever had. No kidding." Isabella refilled her glass. She was sure she was blushing, but it was dark and they were both plastered and it didn't matter. "On top of that, it was total surrender. I'll be fifty soon and I've seen a thing or two in my life. Then this skinny-jeaned hipster in her thirties comes along and makes me squirt all over her face. It's a very humbling experience." Isabella grabbed Maddie's hand over the table. "This is between us though, okay? Please, don't tell Alex about this."

Maddie raised two fingers. "I swear." She hesitated to ask the next question. "What's the secret? I mean, how did she… you know."

Isabella clasped her hands together behind the back of her head. "I have absolutely no idea. And I forbid you to ask the expert."

They sat in silence for a few minutes. Isabella guessed Maddie was trying to figure out the best way to turn this new information into a treat for Alex.

"What are you going to do?" Maddie asked. "Have you closed the door on you and Nat forever?"

"I believe she hasn't left me much choice." It hurt when she said it. Not because of the forthcoming absence of spectacular sex. Not even because Nat had slept with Cindy, and probably a few others since she started seeing Isabella. But because Isabella had glimpsed the good-natured, funny and kind, but ultimately helpless person hiding beneath Nathalie Orange's brazen veneer.

NAT

Nat dragged herself to body combat class. She was tired, hungover and sad, but she figured it was the only place where she could corner Alex without getting too much of a mouthful. With lacklustre punches and half executed kicks, she made it to the end of Alex's Friday night session. She sat wiping her brow on a bench outside the studio, when Alex approached.

Alex sank down next to her and sighed. "Oh, Nat. I really should have locked you in your room."

"You could have tried, Pizza. I'd still have found a way to sneak a girl in. Really, you mustn't blame yourself." Nat shot Alex a weary grin. "Let's go home so you can yell at me for a few hours."

Alex put a hand on Nat's thigh. "Don't take this as my approval of your lewd, scandalous behaviour, roomie, but I think a talking-to is the last thing you need right now."

"You really are a changed woman. I'm surprised we're still on speaking terms, to be honest." Nat curled her fingers around Alex's hand.

"I'm not the one who got hurt. From what Maddie told me Isabella is livid, but I know that the person suffering most from the consequences of your actions is you, Nat. You don't need a scolding. You need a plan of action." Alex rose and pulled Nat up. "Come on, we need to get you your woman back."

Nat stood speechless for a while before following Alex to the locker room. "Excuse me, lady in white tank top, who are you and what have you done to my self-righteous flatmate?"

"For some reason, more than three years after Claire left you, you still feel the need to sabotage anything good that comes your way. But I have eyes in my head and I know love when I see it. You're crazy about Isabella and it looks like you need a little help aligning your actions to your feelings."

A happy end-of-the-week buzz hung in the changing room. Several women in various states of undress greeted Alex, a few winked at Nat. She focused on getting her sweaty clothes off and hurried to the shower. She'd never expected Alex to cut her this much slack. She certainly didn't feel as if she deserved it.

Nat cringed when they passed The Bean on their way home. "Another place I can never set foot in again."

"Oh please, if that were an issue, you wouldn't be able to go anywhere in this town anymore." Alex slapped her on the shoulder. "Hey, there's an idea."

"Very funny." Nat thought about what Alex had said earlier. "Do you really think I can win her back?"

Alex turned towards her. "Yes, I do. I mean, it's not as if you've been trying like mad to keep her so far."

"Touché." Nat hooked her arm through Alex's.

"I know you're not a big fan of them, but we will need some rules." They fell in step together. Nat felt blessed to have someone as level-headed as Alex by her side. "No more girls." Alex squeezed her arm. "Please, repeat after me."

Nat giggled and held up two fingers. "From here on out, my goods belong to one woman only."

"Goods? Really?" Alex shook her head. "You're such a romantic."

"And that banker on the forty-third floor is one lucky chick to have scored someone like you." Nat squeezed Alex's bicep.

"You should probably lay off the bottle for a while as well, as it tends to screw up your judgment."

"No girls, no booze... sounds like something an esteemed doctor prescribed not too long ago."

"Exactly, what better way to get her back than to play by her rules?"

"If only it were that simple." Nat remembered the expression on Isabella's face. "She was angrier than I've ever seen her, but more than that, she looked extremely disappointed. Disgusted even."

They reached the entrance of The Ivy and waited for the elevator in silence. The lobby of a posh building was not a place to discuss winning back one's lesbian lover.

"Here's an idea," Alex said as soon as they entered their flat. "Maddie's at Isabella's and they're both hammered. Why don't we go up there. She might be more pliable while intoxicated."

"Are you nuts?" Nat's heart pounded beneath her ribcage. "She kicked me out of there just a few hours ago."

"Of course she did. She just spotted a half-naked barista thirty years her junior in your flat. What else was she going to do?" Alex put her hands on Nat's shoulders. "Just stop by for a few minutes, show her you're serious about getting her back. At least, she'll know you're not out on the town somewhere enjoying the attention of another girl."

Words, words, words. Isabella's outbreak still rang clearly in Nat's ear. "Can I at least have a drink before we go up?"

Alex pouted her lips and brought her hands to her sides.

"Okay, okay." Nat held her palms up. "The third rule is following the other two rules. Fair enough."

"Do you have anything you can give her? Something meaningful?"

"This is why I need you, Pizza. I would never think of something like that."

"Oh, I know. You'd just barge in, slap on a crooked smile and hope for the best. Those times have passed. This is serious. Make an effort."

"All right, oh highly appraised Romantic Guru." Nat looked around the flat. What could she possibly give to Isabella? It certainly couldn't be a bottle of Scotch. Or a strap-on. She scanned the book shelves. Of course. "Hold on a second."

Nat dashed to her office, flipped up the lid of her laptop and opened the document she'd been working on last. After printing five pages of a work in progress no one had laid eyes on yet, she checked herself in the hallway mirror, and went to see Isabella, Alex by her side.

ISABELLA

Isabella had reached the melancholy stage of drunkenness and wondered what Nat would be up to. Although still furious with her, it was hard to shake the memory of her scent—and the dexterity of her fingers. Would she be out and about? Off into the Hong Kong night looking for prey, for someone to forget the day with?

"Shall we open another bottle?" Isabella glanced at Maddie, who hung slumped in her chair. It probably wasn't a good idea.

"Only if it's a bottle of water." Maddie's speech slurred. "I believe I've had enough."

"I'll get one." Isabella hoisted herself out of her chair and the world started spinning. Slowly, she made her way inside. Just as she entered the kitchen, the bell rang.

Isabella had expected Alex to turn up. She hadn't counted on Nat materialising in her doorway.

"Drunk girlfriend pick-up service," Alex said and made her way past Isabella into the flat.

"She's outside," Isabella mumbled, her eyes fixed on Nat. She looked effortlessly gorgeous in a tight pair of jeans and a too small t-shirt with a picture of a young Michael Jackson stencilled on.

"I know I'm the last person you want to see and I mean no disrespect," Nat started. Her skin glowed and her eyes sparkled. Who was this person standing in front of her, having hijacked Nat's body? "I wanted to give you this."

Isabella steadied herself against the wall and eyed the small pile of papers in Nat's hand. She was afraid to speak, unsure of what would come out of her mouth in the state she was in.

Nat stretched out her arm and handed Isabella the stack of papers. Isabella wasn't wearing her glasses, and even if she had been, her vision would be too blurred to make out what was written on them. Instead of saying anything, she moved out of the way, gesturing for Nat to enter.

"I'm going to take this mess home." Alex appeared with Maddie leaning on her arm. "Make sure to drink plenty of water before you go to bed." She fixed her gaze on both Nat and Isabella before exiting the flat.

Suddenly, Isabella found herself alone with Nat.

"Why don't you sit down?" Nat took charge. "I'll get you some water."

Isabella watched her dart into the kitchen. Dizziness and alcohol-induced lack of judgement suppressed the rage that had been with her all day. She realised she was still clutching the papers Nat had given her between rigid fingers. She disposed of them on the coffee table and sank down in the sofa. When she leaned her head against the backrest for balance, the world started spinning again.

"I got you some painkillers as well." Nat emerged from the kitchen with a big glass of water and two white pills. "Drink up."

So many things were wrong with this picture. How did this happen? How did Nat end up here while Isabella was in such a state? Isabella swallowed the pills and gulped down the water.

"Would you like me to go?" Nat crouched down next to her. "Or do you need a hand getting into bed?"

"I'm not that wasted." The words came out much colder than Isabella had anticipated, much colder than how she was feeling.

Nat shot up and immediately Isabella missed the friendly stare of her blue eyes. She dug her hands in the pockets of her jeans and glanced around. Clearly Nat didn't have a clue what she was doing here either.

"Hey." All rational thought left Isabella. She was tired and hurt and had had enough of harsh words and disappointed facial expressions. She extended her hand. "Come here."

Nat slipped her fingers around Isabella's and her touch sent a jolt of electricity through Isabella's bones. Isabella pulled her close until Nat fell down on the sofa next to her.

"Don't get your hopes up," she said as she pressed her lips against the back of Nat's hand. "Because this doesn't mean anything."

One more time, Isabella thought. *Just one more time.* Then her mind went blank.

She frantically tugged at Nat's t-shirt and tore off her bra. If she was doing this—and oh how she wanted to—she'd make sure not to display too much of the silly, crazy affection she had for this girl. No tenderness and no time for niceties.

Nat's eyes blazed with fire. Her mouth came down hard on Isabella's lips as she unbuttoned her blouse. She yanked it off, threw it on the floor and pushed Isabella down on the sofa.

"Just one thing," Nat panted in between shallow breaths. "I know I don't deserve you and I also know I have a funny way of showing it, but I'm crazy about you."

"Show me now." Isabella stared up into Nat's eyes. Ideally, she'd be on top, but half a bottle of Scotch and Nat's dominant bedroom habits were a bit too much to contend with.

"I will." Nat fixed her glare on Isabella while she zipped

her out of her skirt. Isabella's panties soon followed and there she was, lying naked beneath the lover she'd only just kicked to the curb.

"Take off your pants," Isabella commanded.

A small smile played around Nat's lips. She shook her head. The ongoing fight for top was half the reason why sex between them was always so devastatingly good. Isabella fully realised she didn't stand a chance tonight. Surrendering was her only option.

Isabella's head spun out of control when Nat closed her lips around her nipple. She didn't suck gently. Her teeth grazed along the ridge as goosebumps spread over Isabella's skin. Isabella buried her hands in Nat's hair and pulled her head towards her mouth. Their lips met and Isabella wondered how she would ever live without these sensations delivered by someone with whom she should be so out of touch but who felt so right for her.

When someone is about to slip their finger inside of you it hardly matters that they're more than a decade younger. When someone has you panting at their fingertips just because of the bright blue stare of their eyes, their emotional maturity is not really a factor.

Isabella knew she was smitten. She'd known it all along. She wasn't the forgive-and-forget kind though. She'd meant what she'd said earlier. Neither one of them should get their hopes up too high, but first, before she allowed the cold, hard facts to reign again, she had a climax to receive.

Nat's fingers traced down, halting at her breasts to twist her nipples into hard peaks, trailing south before skating through Isabella's wetness. The intensity of their kiss amped up the lower Nat's hand ventured—more teeth than tongue already. Nat slid two fingers inside and it felt as if the entire day fell away from Isabella. As if none of it had happened. Nat started with slow thrusts, but already Isabella felt herself tumble through the cushions of the sofa, felt her mind wander off to that no man's land of pure pleasure.

Nat curled her fingers inside, faster and faster, while she sucked Isabella's bottom lip into her mouth. She bit down hard and slipped in deep and Isabella's blood pounded in her veins.

"Oh fuck," she moaned into Nat's mouth, spurring her on to increase her speed.

Head spinning and muscles trembling, Isabella cried out. "You," she screamed. "You always do this."

NAT

Nat bit back a tear. She looked down at Isabella in her wrecked, pleasured state and she realised what she had lost.

"I'm in no condition to reciprocate, I'm afraid," Isabella mumbled as she drew Nat near.

Nat allowed her body to sink into Isabella's. She drank in her scent of liquor and magnolias. She had no idea what to say.

"You can't stay." Isabella held onto Nat, her actions not following the meaning of her words.

Nat nodded against Isabella's neck. "I know." She didn't move, didn't want to move. They lay wrapped up in each other for minutes and Nat wasn't sure if this was the last goodbye or perhaps a cautious new beginning.

"Don't fall asleep on top of me," Isabella whispered in Nat's ear and giggled.

Nat pushed herself up and exclaimed the words to their private joke. "You've topped me enough for one day." The smile on Isabella's face acted as a warm balm to her heart. "Come on, I'll put you to bed." Isabella was still naked beneath her, skin smooth and muscles soft.

"I think I'm old enough to take care of that myself." Isabella reached for a blanket she kept tucked away behind the sofa, ushering Nat off of her in the process.

Nat scanned the room for the whereabouts of her t-shirt. She found it flung over a corner of the coffee table, next to the short story she'd brought Isabella. While Isabella wrapped herself chastely in the blanket, Nat slipped into her t-shirt and, with the disappearance of naked body parts, the atmosphere in Isabella's flat changed dramatically—all reminders of what had just happened erased.

"Do you need anything before I go?" Nat asked. She wanted to add, "more water," but the look on Isabella's face made the words freeze in her throat. As if the day's events had just caught up with her again, Isabella's glance turned to ice. She huddled in the corner of the sofa and curtly shook her head.

"I'm sorry," Nat said one last time before making her way to the door. "See you around."

* * *

Days went by without a word from Isabella. Nat sat in The Bean for hours, ignoring Cindy's shy glance, staring out of the window, at the escalator zooming past, waiting for Isabella's regal posture to glide by. Whenever she hung out in the lobby of The Ivy, always finding a reason to linger about longer than necessary, her mouth went dry with anticipation, but Isabella never showed.

She didn't turn up for any of Alex's classes and both Maddie and Alex claimed not to have heard from Isabella in a while. Nat suspected Maddie to be under strict orders not to divulge any information.

After a week of Isabella nothingness, Nat couldn't take it anymore. She called Isabella's secretary, gave a false name and booked an appointment for the next day.

Isabella's office was located around the corner of The Ivy, catering mainly to overpaid expats and their spouses living in the Mid-Levels. Nat's heart hammered in her throat as she pushed open the door. She'd never been there and the fact she'd never met Isabella's assistant worked in her favour.

A petite Chinese woman manned the desk. The badge pinned to her collar read Charlotte. Charlotte was all reassuring smiles and gave Nat an extensive first-timer questionnaire to fill in. Everything she wrote down was a lie.

"Can I pay in advance?" She asked when she returned the clipboard to Charlotte. "I have an important appointment scheduled after this and I will have to run." She figured if she'd already paid for Isabella's time, she'd be less likely to get thrown out.

"Of course, Miss..." Charlotte checked the papers Nat had filled in. "Evans. Just a minute."

Nat scanned her surroundings while Charlotte billed her for time with her ex-girlfriend. The reception slash waiting area was decorated in a completely different style than Isabella's home. The armchairs were big and plush, inviting you to sink into their warm brown cushions. A large shag carpet adorned the floor and the walls were covered with a dozen golden-framed Hong Kong sea and mountain views.

"That'll be three thousand, please," Charlotte said without scorn.

Nat forked over the money with a smile and settled in one of the chairs, waiting her turn.

At exactly five minutes before eleven the door of Isabella's office swung open. A perky blonde with big green eyes exited, Isabella's hand resting on her shoulder. While the blonde made her way to the reception desk, Charlotte handed Isabella the clipboard holding a Miss Caroline Evans's information.

"See you next week, Kelly," she said to the blonde, before eyeing the papers in her hands and approaching the arm chair Nat occupied.

"Miss Ev—" Nat's fake name didn't make it off Isabella's lips. Her eyes narrowed while most colour drained from her face.

"Doctor Douglas." Nat rose and extended her hand. "Pleasure."

Isabella shook her hand briefly and stepped aside to invite Nat into her office. She didn't turn around immediately after closing the door, as if contemplating a counter move.

"I suppose asking what the hell you are doing in my office would be a stupid question?" Isabella motioned for Nat to take a seat in one of two low chairs positioned across from each other. A small round table stood in between.

"Did no one ever tell you there's no such thing as a stupid question?" Nat was glad she at least had the element of surprise on her side.

They sat down and faced each other.

ISABELLA

Isabella quickly regained composure. "Give me one good reason to not ask you to leave this instant?" She leaned back and slung one leg over the other.

"I'll give you two, Doc." Nat appeared to be her confident self again. "One: I've paid three thousand honkies for your time." She raised her eyebrows and tilted her head. "And secondly, I poured my soul into that story I gave you and I'm still waiting for a critique."

Isabella couldn't help but smile. "Don't you belong to a writers group for that?"

"An extra opinion never hurts. Especially because I was writing slightly out of my genre and comfort zone." Nat's cocksure facade started to crack.

The story Nat had given her on the night they'd last seen each other was a scorching, sensual tale of a younger and an older woman falling madly in love. It wasn't difficult to see where Nat had gotten her inspiration.

"Since when are you dabbling in non-fiction?" Isabella had read the story multiple times and each time it had left her a sobbing mess.

"It's as much fiction as any of my other stuff, unless, of course, you want to change the outcome of current events." Nat's blue eyes glared at Isabella.

"I do agree there is a fictional element to it, seeing as the younger character is much more honourable than the person I presume she is based on." Isabella didn't waiver under Nat's unflinching glance.

"I thought it would be obvious from the undertone of the story that it's not a question of honour." Nat sucked her bottom lip into her mouth before continuing. "Or maybe you just didn't get it."

"Nathalie Orange, always up for a quick repartee." Isabella felt anger flare through her bones again, because, from where she was sitting, it was Nat who clearly didn't get it. "But when will she learn that actions ring so much truer than words?"

"I'm sitting here in front of you. That required an action."

Isabella could tell Nat was getting antsy. She probably wasn't used to her games not having the desired effect on people. "That's hardly the kind of action I'm referring to."

"If I could undo what I did, don't you think I would?" Nat's voice grew small.

Isabella shook her head. "No, I honestly don't think you would."

Nat's features narrowed, hurt visible in the drawn lines of her face. Isabella shuffled forward in her chair.

"I know why you do what you do. I know being with these girls makes you feel safe. And it's pretty obvious being with me takes you so much out of your comfort zone, all you want is to retreat into your safe haven. Be my guest, Nat. Just don't expect any encouragement from me." Nat's posture deflated and the ice in Isabella's chest started melting. "Hey, you're a paying client." Isabella turned her palms upwards. "You should get your money's worth."

"All I'm asking for is a second chance." Nat was a mere shadow of the woman who had walked into Isabella's office fifteen minutes ago.

As much as Isabella wanted to say yes, she knew it would

be a mistake. She had her own heart to take into consideration as well. "No." Isabella suppressed the urge to crouch next to Nat and put a comforting hand on her knee while she explained her categoric refusal. "It's not that I don't appreciate the effort you've made to come here, but it's not that simple. Nothing has changed. For all I know, as soon as you leave this building, you're up to your old tricks again. I waited beside you for hours that night of your book party, well past a woman my age's bedtime, and even that didn't stop you." The distance between them gaped wider with every passing second. "You're not ready for the kind of relationship I want."

A minute of silence passed. Isabella waited for Nat to regain composure and say something.

"What can I do?" Nat's voice hesitated between defeated and arrogant. "Because, obviously, I don't have a clue."

"You've been in successful long-term relationships before. Why is it so hard for you now?"

Isabella watched the transformation take place in front of her eyes. The vulnerability Nat had just displayed morphed into a false sense of confidence and the *Nat Swag* was back. "Hell if I know, Doc." Nat stood up. "But all this psycho babble is driving me insane."

Isabella checked her watch. Part of her wanted Nat to stay, but she knew it wouldn't lead anywhere. The Nat standing in front of her now was the one who chased young girls and drank her pain away with too many glasses of Scotch. "We have some time left."

"That's all right. I won't ask for a refund." Nat headed for the door. "Why don't you buy yourself a bottle of nice champagne and toast to your obvious superiority."

Isabella watched Nat exit. There was no middle ground for a psycho-analyst and a person who bolted at the slightest hint of confrontation. And that was the least of their differences.

NAT

"You have to come, Orange. Even if it's just for one drink." Alex leaned against the door of Nat's office.

"There's no such thing as one drink in this town, Pizza." Nat slanted against the backrest of her office chair. "And I don't like spending my free time with people who believe they're too good for me."

"You know you're driving me crazy, right?" Alex walked towards her and swivelled the chair so Nat faced her. "It's Maddie's birthday and I want you to be there. Don't be so stubborn." She yanked Nat up by the arms. "Off to the bathroom you go." Alex positioned herself behind Nat and pushed her out of her office in the direction of the bathroom.

"Just don't expect me to play nice with Miss Upper Crust."

"Believe me, the only expectation I have is for you to show up and at least look merry." Alex shoved Nat into the bathroom and closed the door.

Nat studied her image in the mirror. She hadn't gotten much sleep since her last face off with Isabella last week. She'd been both dreading and looking forward to tonight. Of course, Isabella would be at Maddie's party. Nat had long decided against the idea of finding a date, simply to spite Isabella, because she knew full well there was truth to her words. So much truth, in fact, they still stung every time Nat relived the twenty minutes she had spent in Isabella's client chair.

* * *

The Cube was the sort of stuck-up banker bar Nat avoided at all costs. She stood out amongst the designer suits in her skinny jeans and leather jacket. As soon as she and Alex arrived, a pert hostess shoved a glass of champagne in her hands. Nat knocked it back in a few greedy gulps.

They found Maddie at the bar, surrounded by a couple

of suits who Nat suspected to be her colleagues. Isabella was nowhere to be seen.

"She's going to love your present." Alex coaxed Nat forward.

"Happy birthday, neighbour." Nat kissed Maddie on the cheek and threw in a quick, firm hug. She handed her the present wrapped in Hello Kitty paper.

Maddie made light work of the wrapping. "Hiking shoes… how extremely considerate." She drew her lips into a wide smile.

"With these babies on your feet, you'll slay the Dragon's Back in no time. Hungover or not." Nat gave her neighbour another hug and grabbed a glass of champagne from a passing waiter's tray.

"I expect you by my side." Maddie winked at Nat. "I don't like to suffer on my own." Maddie cast her glance next to Nat's head. "Isabella has arrived. Please, keep it civil." She leaned into Nat's ear. "She's hurting much more than she would ever let on."

Nat turned around and watched Isabella make her way through the crowd. She wore a simple black dress and looked excruciatingly beautiful. The dress hugged her figure flawlessly and made the red of her lipstick pop. Isabella merely nodded at Nat as she walked past her to embrace her best friend.

The four of them hadn't stood so closely together since Nat's book launch party—the night it had all gone wrong. When Isabella had first arrived, taking Nat's breath away with how dashing she looked, Nat had felt on top of the world. They had celebrated together, enjoying the champagne and the elation of nights like that. Nat had felt it clearly. A surge of adrenalin every time Isabella shot her a wink. A galloping in her chest at the mere hint of a smile. She was head over heels in love with this woman and she had no idea what to do. The whole setting was a dead ringer for her life with Claire. Book party. Success. Love. A happiness so overwhelming she couldn't ever imagine life being any other way—until Claire had dumped her.

Isabella had been right on the money when she'd said Nat wasn't ready for the kind of relationship she was looking for. But if she wasn't ready now—if she didn't kick herself into being ready—when would she ever be?

Nat was afraid of being happy. She was afraid of loving one person who could so easily tell her it was all over. Instead of following her heart and going home with Isabella, she had, once again, given in to fear and drowned it in a bottle of Scotch. It wasn't happiness, but it hurt so much less than a broken heart. Ending up in bed with Cindy was just an afterthought, a habit that was hard to break. It had nothing on a night with Isabella, it didn't even come close.

"We must go hiking this weekend," Maddie said. Her one eye was a bit smaller than her other—a telltale sign of tipsiness according to Alex. "Look what Nat gave me." She pointed at the shoebox behind her on the bar.

"I'll take you up on that, honey," Alex said, "and there will be no weaselling out."

"I appreciate you all being here tonight, but more than anything, for my birthday, I'd like for the four of us to hang out again without awkwardness. I want all four of us to go on that hike this weekend."

Alex stepped in. "It looks like someone skipped dinner and can't handle her liquor." She curled her arm around Maddie's shoulder. "You're only getting away with it because it's your birthday."

"Let's do it," Nat said. "This Sunday. The four of us and The Dragon's Back."

The other three looked at her as if she'd been the only one who'd stood in the way of that happening.

"We're all adults here. It should be doable."

Isabella shot her a small smile. Nat's heart jumped in her chest.

ISABELLA

"That was big of you," Isabella said. She and Nat leaned their backs against the bar. They hadn't spoken since Nat had fled her office. "Are you sure you want to spend an afternoon with the superior likes of me?"

"If you can put up with someone as fickle as me." Nat turned to her. "I don't see why not."

A smile came to Isabella's face. "Maybe self-deprecating humour will save us in the end."

Nat shook her head. "If that were a possibility, I would have been saved years ago."

Isabella rubbed her fingers over her chin. "I really did like your story." She searched for Nat's eyes. "Whenever I read it, it never fails to bring a tear to my eye."

"An ironic tear or a real one?" Nat shuffled her feet.

"In all my life I've never heard of an ironic tear." Isabella inched closer. "Where do you come up with these things?"

"I was just wondering if you were having a laugh." Nat chewed the inside of her lip.

Not caring what sort of signal it would send, Isabella put a hand on her shoulder. "I was unkind last time we talked about it. I'm sorry. It's beautiful and…" She hesitated. "I'm honoured to have served as inspiration for it. Really." Isabella let her hand slide down Nat's arm.

Nat didn't reply.

"I do presume Miriam is based on me?" Isabella managed a tight smile. Suddenly, her stomach was in knots.

"I've been thinking about what you said. About me not being ready for the sort of relationship you want." She brushed a strand of black hair out of her eyes. "You were absolutely right." Her eyes darkened. "This fling we had, it was crazy. We're too different and we want other things from life. I realise that now."

Isabella was taken aback by what she was hearing. She didn't immediately know how to react.

"I hope we can be friends again soon, Doc. I really do."

Was this Nat wanting to have the final say? Was it a ploy to rattle Isabella's cage? Or was it plain old retreating into familiar patterns again? Isabella could hardly diagnose the situation objectively.

"Yes. I'd like that." Isabella didn't want to be friends with Nat. She had no desire to witness her decadent path to self-destruction first-hand. "But let's give it some time."

"I believe we have until Sunday."

Isabella raised her eyebrows.

Nat pointed at the hiking shoes she had given Maddie. "Dragon's Back, remember?"

"Right." Isabella straightened the strap of her purse over her shoulder. "I'd better get going." The sight of Nat tilted against the bar, her hair in its usual mess and her eyes bright and blue, quickened her pulse. She didn't feel like leaving Nat behind. She certainly didn't feel like going home alone, but it's not as if she had options. "Bye." She slanted forward and kissed Nat gently on the cheek, letting her lips linger an instant too long.

As she edged away, Nat grabbed her by the fingers, stroking them against her palm for a second. Isabella thought her heart would burst out of her chest. When she turned to say goodbye to Maddie and Alex, her eyes were moist with tears.

* * *

"I thought we could do part of the Wilson Trail," Alex said. "It's quite steep, but not that long and the views are stunning."

Maddie groaned next to her. "I'm over forty now, babe. Go easy on me."

"And me," Nat chimed in. "Rough night at the office." She sniffed her coffee. "I'm only here because I promised Pizza and you know how she holds a grudge. It doesn't make for comfortable living when your flatmate isn't speaking to you." She eyed Isabella, who had to stop her mouth from falling open. How could Nat go from remorsefully apologetic and wanting a second chance to this person who didn't seem to care one way or another so quickly?

"Let me guess," Isabella went on the offensive, "girls and liquor aplenty?"

Maddie and Alex exchanged a look of despair.

"You think you know me so well, Doc." She fixed her eyes on Isabella. "But when I said office I actually meant office. I was up all night writing. I'm turning that story I gave you into either a hefty novella or maybe even a full-length novel."

"So you really are crossing over into romance." The hike had not begun yet, but Isabella's heart was already pounding in her throat. "How daring."

"Who said anything about romance?" Nat deposited her empty cup on the table between them. "It's about love, of course, but romance has nothing to do with it."

"Okay, ladies. Keep such discussions for on the trail please." Alex clapped her hands ostentatiously. "Let's go."

Nat shot Isabella an undecipherable smile before getting up and slinging an arm over Alex's shoulder.

* * *

"Oh my god," Isabella exclaimed. "I really thought I had seen it all." Sweat dripped out of her hair and every muscle in her legs burned, but the view below her was staggering. Hong Kong stretched out panoramically in front of her. The tall buildings of the island to the left and the old airport to the right. In between a clear blue sky and green slopes tumbling down.

"See, now this is romantic," Nat said. "You and me on top of this hill with this view. I'm fairly certain babies have been made here."

Isabella giggled. A natural endorphin high pushed all negative feelings to the back of her brain. Alex and Maddie hadn't reached the top yet and it was just the two of them. She inched closer to Nat, willing to forget and eager to touch.

NAT

Nat heard Isabella creep up on her. Her body heat radiated onto the bare skin of her neck and arms and she had to rely on all the will power inside of her to not turn around and kiss Isabella.

Earlier, she had only pretended to not be enthusiastic about the hike. The real reason why she'd been up all night was because she was too excited to sleep. The words she had written were all sappy and dripped with the kind of mushy romance Nat usually shied away from. It was pathetic, really, the way she had allowed herself to fall for this woman, especially after Isabella had spoken the magic word *No. No, you can't have a second chance.*

Nat was sure Isabella was a fine psychiatrist, but she obviously hadn't figured out that saying no to Nathalie Orange had the same effect as waving a red cloth at a bull. After she'd licked her wounds, she'd come up with the most effective plan in the book: playing hard to get. Judging from Isabella's facial expressions at Maddie's party, it was working like a charm. Isabella's body was so close Nat could practically feel her heart beat.

"Jesus Christ," Maddie panted behind them, doubling over with her hands on her knees.

Nat turned around, away from the view, and nearly bumped into Isabella.

"Sit down for a second, babe." Alex grabbed Maddie's hand and led her to a giant rock off the trail. "I do admit, it's a bit tougher than I remember."

Nat smiled at Isabella, whose cheeks had flushed a telling red.

"Look at me," Isabella said, "this climb was so strenuous my head must look as if it's about to explode."

"It must be the romance in the view," Nat teased. She didn't think it possible, but Isabella's complexion turned a deeper crimson.

"Everyone over forty," Alex commanded, "take five, please." She gestured at Isabella to sit next to Maddie on the rock. Alex dug into her backpack and distributed bottles of water.

Nat waited until the blush had left Isabella's cheeks to crouch beside her. "Everything all right there, friend?" She knew she was pushing it, but she couldn't help herself. After all that had happened, seeing Isabella squirm was simply too entertaining.

"Peachy." Isabella brushed a drop of sweat off her forehead and looked Nat straight in the eye. "I'd like to see you do this in fifteen years."

* * *

Maddie and Isabella decided to tackle the steep descent at their own pace, resulting in an almost race downhill between Alex and Nat.

"Do you really think you can beat me?" Alex asked. "I keep fit for a living."

"I happen to have a lot of pent-up energy at my disposal." Nat hopped down the rocky stairs with an ease that surprised her.

"So I've noticed." Alex effortlessly kept up. She was right. Nat would never be able to shake her off. "Are you getting your flirt on with Isabella again?"

"Nope," Nat lied. "Just trying to keep it friendly."

"Exactly how friendly?" They'd reached a flat patch and walked side by side. The bushes along the path were human-sized and the sun made long shadows of their shapes.

"She made it perfectly clear we're done and, after what I did, I have to respect that. If she wants to take things further again, she'll have to make the first move."

"Yeah right." Alex elbowed Nat in the side. "As if that's the Orange style."

"I'm a changed woman, Pizza." Nat nodded at Alex, as if she had to convince herself as well. "I swear."

"What does that mean, though? No more girls? No more wandering the Hong Kong streets at night looking for prey?"

"Jesus," Nat chuckled. "What image do you have of me?"

"The one you want me to have."

Dried leaves cracked under their feet.

"I know it sounds crazy, but since we've broken up I've had absolutely no desire to hook up with anyone else." Nat shrugged. "It's only when we're together and... I don't know... I feel the heat, so to speak, I have this urge to destroy it."

"Have you told Isabella this?" Alex's voice was soft, almost a whisper, as if the question begged a solemn tone.

"Of course not." Nat's heart sank. "I don't want her to go off me completely."

Alex sighed but didn't say anything.

"What?" Nat asked. "Spit it out, I know you're dying to say it."

"Okay." Alex stopped and faced Nat. "It's so like you to play games, to flirt, to hide behind sarcastic comments, but have you ever contemplated just telling her the truth? It might make matters less complicated."

"That's just not the Orange style, is it?" Nat looked away, but all she saw were green bushes and an endless path stretching out in front of her.

"This is me, Nat. You don't have to put on a front for me." Alex grabbed her by the arms. "And, truth be told, it's not as if none of us know what the real deal is. We're basically just waiting for *your* penny to drop."

"What the hell are you talking about?" Nat tried to shake Alex's hands off her, but Alex was much stronger than her.

"Here's what's going to happen." Alex's fingers dug into Nat's biceps. "We're going to wait for them to catch up. I'll let you and Isabella get a head start before Maddie and I continue down the hill. You are going to tell Isabella what you just told me and end this ridiculous farce once and for all."

"You have no idea—"

"Have I ever not wanted what was best for you?"

Nat looked down at her dusty shoes.

"Look at me, Nat. Don't give me all this bullshit about the two of you not being right for each other. It's not because you make an odd couple that you don't belong together. You're crazy about her and she's totally smitten with you. All that needs to happen is for you to stop being so bloody difficult."

"Do you think I enjoy being how I am? That I take pleasure in destroying the one really good thing that happened to me in years?" Nat spit out the words. Alex didn't budge.

"Pleasure? No. Refuge? Oh, yes. Man up, Nat. I'm not asking you to go off to war or do something really horrible. This is love, and yes, sometimes you have to take chances, but when it works, it's the most beautiful thing in the world. This can work. I have no doubt in my mind it can."

"How long have you been working on this speech, Pizza? Because, honestly…"

"Nu-uh." Alex brought her face mere inches away from Nat's, her dark eyes staring Nat down. "I'm not having any of that. I am your best friend and I'm not letting you get away with ruining this."

"What's going on here?" They hadn't heard Maddie and Isabella turn the bend. "Lovers' tiff?" Isabella asked.

ISABELLA

Isabella scanned Nat's face. She looked as if, despite the clear blue sky, thunderclouds were gathering over her head.

"She's all yours on the last stretch down," Alex said. "I've said my piece." She walked over to Maddie and grabbed her hand. "Come on, babe, I want to show you something over there."

It wasn't the smoothest of moves, but once again, Isabella found herself alone with Nat on a mountain path. It wasn't hard to guess what the quarrel between Alex and Nat had been about.

"Shall we go on?" Isabella kept her voice as neutral as possible.

Nat nodded, a sullen expression on her face. She reminded Isabella of a petulant child sometimes, especially when things weren't going her way. They started walking in silence, the only sound their footsteps on gravel.

"Do you want to talk about it?" Isabella asked, not sure if she could bear another minute of quiet between them.

Nat balled her fists in the pockets of her jeans. She was not the type to wear sweat pants when venturing outside. "If all of you claim to know me so well, then why should I bother explaining myself?"

This was going to be a long walk down.

"What needs to be explained?" Isabella played it cool.

Nat stopped and faced Isabella. "Don't take me for a fool."

"Okay." Isabella took hold of Nat's wrist and guided her to a concrete step off the path. "Sit down, please."

Nat crashed down, a storm raging in her eyes. Isabella sat down next to her. "I'm listening." She patted Nat's knee. "I still owe you some therapy time, anyway."

Nat took a deep breath. "Has it occurred to anyone that I simply don't know how to say this?"

"Take your time." Isabella was well acquainted with all the stalling techniques. She hadn't expected this conversation to take place on the slope of a mountain, but it was as good a place as any. At least Nat couldn't dash off again as soon as she felt trapped by what was going on in her head.

"Nat," Isabella turned to her so she could get a good look at her face. "I realise this is very hard for you." She made sure all traces of irony had left her voice. "But this is important. You need to confront it by saying it."

Nat stared into her eyes. She swallowed, opened her mouth to speak, but nothing came out. Then, out of the blue, she grabbed Isabella's head, pulled her close and pressed her lips lightly against Isabella's. When she pulled back and opened her eyes, a tear dangled from a hooded eyelid.

Immediately, heat exploded in Isabella's bones. She wanted nothing more than another one of those kisses, but she knew she had to keep a clear head. It was now or never.

"There," Nat whispered, "I said it."

A smile formed on Isabella's lips. "Nice try." She took hold of Nat's hands, brushing her thumbs over Nat's fingers. "Try again."

"You really are the most patient woman I know." Nat squeezed Isabella's hands. "Why do you put up with my shit?"

Instead of replying with a non-direct, *You know why*, and falling back into that old trap of not disclosing her feelings, Isabella opted for the direct approach. "Because," she leaned forward until her lips reached Nat's ear, "I'm in love with you."

Her heart raced and her pulse quickened. She hadn't planned on saying it, but sometimes, certain emotions just find their way out.

"I..." Nat started. Her mouth rested close to Isabella's ear. The sound of approaching footsteps seemed to startle her before she could finish her sentence. Maddie and Alex had caught up with them. They waved and went on their way. Isabella waited until they had rounded the next bend to speak.

"I believe you were about to say something?" She felt her muscles go soft and her stomach twist. Nat didn't have the advantage of hiding her eyes anymore. They faced each other, their fingers interlaced and palms sweating.

"I'm in love with you too." Nat sighed. "I've been in love with you for weeks, but my feelings for you are hardly the issue."

"So what is the issue?" This conversation could have so

many outcomes. Nat was so jittery, she could storm off at any moment. It was what she usually did when they approached the heart of the matter.

"It's me. It's always me." Nat's fingers nearly squeezed all life out of Isabella's. "I suck at relationships. When someone comes too close, I do my very best to chase them away, even though that's the last thing I want."

"What *do* you want?" Isabella experienced some trouble keeping her voice steady.

"That's very simple." The blue sky reflected in Nat's eyes. "I want you."

It was one of the more romantic moments of Isabella's life. Still, it didn't solve any problems. "Then what's keeping you from being with me?"

"This paralysing fear inside of me that, once I let myself go all in, you'll break my heart."

At last, Isabella thought, the words have found a way out. It was a start. "I understand your hesitance, but you can't deny yourself happiness because of fear."

"Yeah, well, that's easier said than done." Nat pulled her fingers from Isabella's grasp. "I was ludicrously happy once. Ecstatic with my life. A one-woman girl, ready to pop the question... the works. And then it all came crashing down."

"Obviously, time hasn't done a very good job at healing your wounds." Isabella shuffled closer, needing to feel Nat's heat on her skin. "But, believe it or not, what you've experienced is pretty universal. We all go through it at some point in our lives. Look at Alex, for instance, and how well she's doing now."

"Alex is different. She was born for good things. She's an optimist. I'm the opposite."

"Alex is in love, just like you. Instead of letting fear take over, she allows herself to be happy. Love involves risk, otherwise it wouldn't be worth it." Isabella brought her hand to her chest. "Will you take a risk for me?"

"I wish I knew how." Nat chewed the inside of her

cheek.

"How about one day at a time?"

NAT

"I can't make any promises." Nat hated herself for saying that. "I know what I'm like."

Isabella didn't flinch. "I'm not asking you to." If she moved any closer, she'd be on Nat's lap soon. "But I want you to talk to me instead of running away into the night."

"I know that talking about feelings is how you make your living, but—"

"There you go again." Isabella cut her off. "We really have to do something about that mouth of yours."

"What? I'm not allowed to speak my mind?" Nat realised she was going on the defensive again. It was so easy.

"Sure you are, as long as you speak from the heart instead of this place of distress and panic."

Nat was ready to admit they were sharing a profound moment, but she was well aware change was not accomplished in moments like this. It was made at decision time. Since Claire, Nat had always made the wrong decision.

"Here's what's going to happen." She rose from the concrete step and straddled Isabella's knees. "I'm going to kiss you." She leaned in and let her lips hover over Isabella's mouth before slipping in her tongue. The soft peck soon intensified, weeks of longing compressed in that instant and Nat had trouble pulling away. "I forgot what I was going to say next." She hoisted Isabella up by her arms and hugged her tight.

"We have a pretty steep descent ahead of us," Isabella mumbled against the skin of Nat's neck. "You have plenty of time to remember."

After they made their way down the most difficult steps in silence, too out of breath to speak, Nat said, "I remember what I was going to say."

Drops of sweat pearled on Isabella's forehead when she looked at Nat expectantly. "What's that?"

"I'll race you to the end point for the privilege of top tonight."

Isabella laughed out loud. "Do try." She sped past Nat, but they both knew she could never win.

* * *

"The problem with me is that I have no idea how to take things slowly." Nat speared a morsel of steak on her fork. "I want to jump your bones right now." They'd showered and changed and decided to continue their talk over some much needed food in a nearby steak house.

"Trust me, there's nothing I want more right now either, but food is an even baser need than sex." Nat didn't know how Isabella scrubbed up so well after an afternoon of intense activity. She wore a starched white blouse, open at the throat, and a dark yellow necklace setting off her brown eyes. Her face didn't show any signs of exertion.

"I'm glad that, at least, we both agree on how this day will end." A moist heat already glowed between Nat's legs.

"Physical attraction was never the problem between us." Isabella curled her red-nailed fingers around the stem of her wine glass.

Nat's throat went dry. She kept her eyes on Isabella while she chewed her food slowly. Attending to the needs of her growling stomach suddenly seemed less urgent.

"We should have gone on a hike sooner. It seems to work wonders for clearing the air."

Isabella painted on a coy smile. "We both know the hike had much less to do with it than the talking-to Alex gave you."

"True. For an uptight wanna-be saint, she makes a really good friend." Nat reciprocated Isabella's smile. "I do love her dearly."

"You should be grateful to her." Isabella laid her fork down. Was she starting to lose her appetite as well?

"Why?" Nat had found her confidence again. "You as good as made a move on me at the top of the hill. Breathing down my neck like that."

"Temporary moment of weakness." Isabella took a sip of her wine. "I duly confess." She sat her glass back down and rested her eyes solemnly on Nat. "So, what's your game plan, hot shot? How do you intend to make this work." The big reunion in the bedroom would have to wait until Nat passed this test.

"Like you said. One day at a time."

"Oh, and suddenly it's that easy?" Isabella shoved her half-empty plate of food to the side and leaned over the table. "I take this very seriously."

Nat loved it when Isabella got serious—but usually for all the wrong reasons. "I won't pretend to have any quick answers," she tried. "But I asked you for a second chance and if you're willing to give me one, I will rise to the occasion."

"I am giving you a second chance because, obviously, I don't have any other choice." She shot Nat a small grin. "What with being smitten and all."

Nat's heart leapt in her chest.

"I can't give you any guarantees. No one can. But I promise to treat you with the respect you deserve." Nat never felt comfortable when the conversation turned too emotional. "Does that mean we're exclusive?"

Isabella plucked her napkin from her lap, rolled it in a ball and flung it at Nat.

Nat caught it in one hand. "I'll take that as a yes."

Isabella raised her hand to call for the waiter. "Let's get out of here."

"Yes please." Butterflies worked their magic in Nat's stomach. "I hope you haven't forgotten about the prize I won this afternoon."

ISABELLA

On the short walk home, Isabella let her fingers slip around Nat's hand. The path of their affair had not run very smoothly thus far, but it was clear they both wanted it to succeed. For now, a leap of faith would have to do.

Hand in hand, they strolled to The Ivy. Spencer shot them a wide smile when they entered the lobby. They rode the elevator in silence, as if both recognising the solemnity of the moment. After Isabella unlocked her front door, Nat grabbed both her hands and stroked them gently.

"I never meant to hurt you." A moist film coated her eyes.

"I know." Isabella freed her hands and trailed her fingers along Nat's bare arms. She wasn't one for dressing up and wore a bright yellow t-shirt with the word *available* printed on in big white letters. Isabella understood a lot of things, but she failed to grasp Nat's sense of style. The skinny jeans and quirky tops suited her though, despite the fact that at almost thirty-five, she should have outgrown them. Isabella was certain Nat didn't give a damn and she loved her more for it. "Let's get this atrocity off you," she joked, before slowly hoisting the t-shirt over Nat's head.

"I'll have to get rid of that one." Nat held the t-shirt in her hand for a brief moment. "As I appear to have become unavailable." She tossed it to the floor.

"You're all mine now." Isabella pulled Nat closer and stared into her eyes before leaning in to kiss her. "A million girls are weeping."

"Enough talk, Doc." Nat's lips stretched into a smile against hers. Her hands disappeared in Isabella's hair as she drew her near.

The first kiss rushed through Isabella, reaching every cell of her body. She would never have guessed she'd fall for a thirty-something, slightly lost, ironic t-shirt wearing girl—but fallen she had.

Nat's lips tasted of wine and sunshine—the sunshine they'd picked up on that pivotal hike earlier in the day. Isabella's panties grew damp as their kiss intensified. Everything about Nat was soft. There was no urgency in her kiss and the usual firmness in her grasp was absent. She traced the tips of her fingers lightly over Isabella's back, as if not wanting to claim anything too quickly, making her shiver.

"Come on." Isabella tore her lips away from Nat's and dragged her in the direction of the bedroom. They stood in front of the bed and Nat started to unbutton Isabella's blouse. Nat was surely a very skilled lover, but she never showed much restraint. The languid speed at which she undressed Isabella, and how it stood in stark contrast to how she usually did it— rushed and insistent—made Isabella's skin tingle.

Nat guided the blouse over Isabella's shoulders and followed up with a soft peck above her sternum. Her hands meandered to Isabella's back, where they unclasped her bra. The eager look Nat shot Isabella's bare breasts made her breath hitch in her throat. Nat brushed the meaty part of her thumbs over Isabella's nipples and they stood to attention immediately, crinkling up under her able touch.

While her hands cupped Isabella's breasts, thumbs still fondling, Nat nuzzled the delicate skin of Isabella's neck. The soft nibbles of her lips transformed Isabella's skin into a field of goosebumps. Nat's hands trailed down, to the button of Isabella's jeans, while her lips kept working on her neck, occasionally travelling up to her ear. With a quick flip, the button came undone and Nat lowered the zipper. Slowly, she let a finger slide under the waistband of Isabella's panties. Not far, but enough to cause Isabella's clit to throb with desire.

When Nat lifted her head away from Isabella's neck, her eyes shone with a slow, simmering lust. She coaxed Isabella down onto the bed and kneeled in front of her to remove her trousers. She quickly stepped out of her own jeans and straddled Isabella on the bed.

While Nat hovered on all fours, Isabella took the opportunity to undo her bra. Nat pushed herself up briefly so the garment could slip off her arms. She bent at the elbows and found Isabella's ear again.

"I love you," she said, and the crack in her voice moistened Isabella's eyes.

Isabella locked Nat's neck between her arms and held her tight. "Me too," she said, her voice a breathy whisper.

Nat traced a path of moist kisses from Isabella's ear to her mouth. She dropped her body down on Isabella and covered her in flesh, while her tongue skated along Isabella's lips. Their nipples connected and heat spread through Isabella's muscles. Nat's thigh landed between her legs and her knee pushed into her groin.

"Mmm," Isabella moaned. "I want you so much."

Nat moved the action of her mouth down, leaving a wet trail of kisses in its wake. When she closed her lips around Isabella's stiff nipples, Isabella felt her heart pulse in her clit. The softness of Nat's skin on hers, the gentle but insistent push of her knee between Isabella's legs and the sensation of Nat's tongue dancing over the hard peaks of her nipples blended into an avalanche of pleasure soaring through Isabella's body.

Nat's lips trailed down, leaving a moist path in their wake. Each new stretch of Isabella's skin her mouth touched, turned into gooseflesh. She travelled lower and let her tongue slide just above the waistband of Isabella's panties. Isabella's clit pounded hard beneath the fabric and a wet heat pooled between her upper thighs.

Nat repositioned and dragged her nails over Isabella's skin while she slid her panties off her. Instinctively, Isabella spread wide, welcoming the fresh breath of air hitting her drenched pussy lips. Nat kneeled between Isabella's legs and locked eyes with her. Her gaze was unflinching and determined and set Isabella's blood on fire. Nat slipped her fingers under Isabella's backside and dug them into her flesh. She kept her gaze fixed on Isabella for an instant longer and with such intensity, Isabella could have sworn she felt her heart flutter.

Just the sight of Nat lowering her head in the direction of her throbbing pussy lips was enough for another trickle of juice to drip down Isabella's inner thighs. Nat's lips landed with a gentle smack, the softness of them sending sparks up Isabella's spine. Soon her lips were replaced with tongue, the tip of it circling Isabella's swollen clit.

The emotions of the day and the stimulation of the moment would soon have her tipping over the edge. It all collided in Isabella's brain as a huge burst of pleasure. On any other day, Isabella knew Nat would have made her wait for it, but today was different in so many respects and Nat traced her fingertip around the rim of Isabella's pussy much faster than she had anticipated.

Then she was inside, two fingers curling and twisting, touching Isabella in the spot that made her lose all control. Nat's tongue flicked over her clit, her fingers zoned in and all the slowness Nat had practiced earlier now seemed to have transformed into a focused, highly accurate mission to make Isabella come as hard as possible. It was working.

Isabella grabbed hold of the pillows next to her head, needing to hold on to something. A thrilling warmth ran deep under her skin, invading her muscles, taking over. Nat hit the spot repeatedly and white noise crackled in Isabella's brain. Everything intensified, her entire body pulsed and her flesh seemed to turn to hot liquid.

Her climax shot through her in glorious convulsions, not stopping with the clenching and unclenching of her pussy walls around Nat's fingers, but culminating in a spray of warm liquid running out of her.

NAT

For all her years of experience and all the women who had come at her hands, Nat had never had this effect on anyone. Another something that made Isabella so unique. Previously, she had acted all casual about it, trying to hold on to a few last scraps of cool, but now tears were about to add to the sea of wetness dripping from her face.

"You're on sheet changing duty," Isabella said. "I'm so spent and drenched and middle-aged, I can't lift another finger."

"Really?" Nat wiped a few drops off her chin before pushing herself up to face Isabella. "You're playing the age card?"

"What other perks are there to dating someone as young and with such loose morals as you?"

Nat smiled and kissed Isabella on the nose. "I do wonder if it's an age thing."

"What?" Isabella's expression didn't give anything away, but Nat knew better.

"I was always told the older, the dry—" Nat felt a pillow smack against the back of her head.

"You're ruining my post-orgasmic moment of glory." Isabella pulled her close and planted a kiss on the top of her head. "Shut up already."

"Let's just sleep in the other room."

"You go ahead," Isabella whispered in Nat's ear. "I'll bring the necessary equipment."

Isabella's words sent a shiver up Nat's spine. Their fight for top was turning more and more into a mere verbal game. Nat loved it when Isabella strapped it on for her, but she wasn't the type to say it out loud.

"But I won the race, Doc." She bit into the skin of Isabella's neck.

"Don't tell me you don't want it." Isabella's voice dipped into that lower, sexier register and Nat realised now would be a good time to stop arguing. She lifted her head and looked into Isabella's eyes. Their affair was not an easy one by a long shot, but Nat promised herself she would try.

She made her way to the guest room and tugged off her panties on the way. Just thinking about what stood to happen next made her pussy tingle. Isabella took her time but, as far as Nat was concerned, she could take all the time in the world. Nat stretched out on the bed, her pale skin contrasting with the dark colour of the sheets. The air caressed her nipples and anticipation beat in her veins, sending blood to her hardening clit. Nat had no idea who she had to thank for being allowed into Isabella's life and bed again. She certainly didn't deserve to be here. She'd take Alex out for organic pizza to thank her. She —

All thoughts ceased when Isabella walked into the bedroom, dressed in nothing but a sizeable blue dildo strapped to her pelvis. She held a translucent bottle of lube in her right hand and deposited it on the bedside table. Whichever ones of Isabella's relatives came to visit next, surely they wouldn't want to know what was about to transpire in the room they'd be staying in.

Desire shot through Nat's body, her blood pumping with lust. This reversal of everything she had hinged her life on still caught her by surprise. No wonder she fought it so hard. Change did not come easily to Nathalie Orange. This woman was worth it though. She was worth everything.

Isabella draped her body next to Nat's, glueing her cool skin to the goosebumps running up Nat's flesh. "Before we do this," Isabella said while trailing her fingertips over Nat's belly. "You need to make me a promise."

Excellent timing, Nat thought, but her throat was too constricted to speak. She nodded.

"I don't need you to promise me you'll stop chasing girls. I don't need some silly promise of exclusivity either." Isabella dipped a finger into Nat's belly button. "All I need is for you to promise me that you'll allow yourself to be happy. This mindless Hello-Kitty-girl-limbo you've created for yourself is not happiness."

Nat realised they had a lot of talking to do, but she did question Isabella's timing. In her experience, matters of the heart should not be discussed when one party had a silicone cock strapped to their waist while the other's mouth went dry at the thought of it entering her. Then again, Nat was hardly an expert at discussing matters of the heart.

"I promise." Nat would have promised to grow her hair long and only wear skirts for the rest of her life at that point.

"Don't make promises you can't keep." Isabella's finger travelled upward, approaching the swell of Nat's breasts. "There are no more second chances. This is it."

Fear mixed with the passion brewing in the pit of Nat's stomach. She always tried to steer her emotions far away from any sexual encounter. She started to get a vague inkling of what Isabella was trying to achieve.

Isabella rolled Nat's nipple under the palm of her hand. Nat was not in a position to run away. She didn't want to run away. Isabella's hands on her was all she needed while her words pinched at the hardness around her heart.

"I promise you now and I will promise you again tomorrow and every day after that." Nat hardly recognised her own voice. It came out strangled and tinted by a passion she usually tried to avoid.

"Good." Isabella closed her hand over Nat's breast, catching a nipple between her fingers, and squeezed hard.

ISABELLA

To Isabella, few things were more exciting than having the leather straps of a harness biting into the flesh of her thighs.

Before walking into the room where Nat waited for her, she had taken a few deep breaths to calm her lust. She needed to reintroduce Nat to allowing her heart to connect with what was happening between her legs. Isabella had seen glimpses of it crossing Nat's face when she came—something she didn't suspect Nat did a lot of when she took a nameless girl home. But it had to be said out loud before Isabella delivered the climax of Nat's life—there was no doubt in her mind she would.

Nat's nipple hardened between her fingers and the feel of it sent a jolt up Isabella's pussy. This was going to be one long glorious night of reconnecting.

Isabella slid her body on top of Nat's. The dildo stood rigid between her legs, making her feel in command. Her lips found the tender skin of Nat's neck and Isabella nibbled a path down to the deep hollow between her collar bones. She kissed it gently, aware of how sensitive Nat was in that spot. Nat moaned beneath her, her body spasming with lust.

Pushing herself up on all fours, silicone dangling from her centre, Isabella let her nipples dance over Nat's body. She shifted her weight back until her behind rested on bent legs and she sat surveying Nat. Half-lidded blue eyes revealing only pure need. Hair so dark it blended it in with the black sheets. Porcelain skin stretching over defined muscles. Nat's body was slender and firm and, despite her reputation and her brash mouth, she looked so vulnerable in Isabella's bed. Isabella could stare at her like this for hours.

"Fuck me," Nat growled. She didn't just say it. Her voice was drenched in despair and she dug her heels into Isabella's thighs.

Isabella narrowed her eyes and licked her lips. She'd fuck her all right.

Nat's pussy glistened with desire and Isabella salivated at the thought of plunging her huge toy between those pink, puffy lips. She ran a fingertip over Nat's slit, moisture sucking it in. She made a little detour circling a nail around Nat's clit, but soon two of her fingers were buried deep inside of Nat. Isabella could never get enough of the sight of her fingers parting Nat, of Nat's pussy opening up for her, of Nat's pelvis bucking up, asking for more.

Isabella withdrew after a few strokes. Tonight was about so much more than fingers. She spread Nat's wetness on the dildo until it glistened. No need for extra lube. Leading with her knees, she shuffled forward until the tip of the toy grazed Nat's entrance. Instantly, Nat slid closer. Her self-proclaimed top persona always crumbled at this stage.

As divine as it felt to watch her own fingers disappear inside of Nat, there was nothing like slipping the big, silicone cock into her for that first thrust. It inspired a sense of power and responsibility inside of Isabella. It transformed her into someone with only one goal in that moment—to make Nat scream with pleasure.

Nat's eyes widened a little as Isabella inched deeper. A blush crept up her cheeks and Nat dug her nails into Isabella's triceps.

Isabella bucked her hips and started fucking Nat in a slow, controlled manner. There was no longer anything controlled about Nat. Her mouth drooped open and her breath came out ragged. Ecstasy glinted in her eyes. The sort of abandon you can't just display in front of anyone. Picking up the pace, her hands resting next to Nat's ears, her mouth hovering over Nat's lips, Isabella pushed in deeper. Long, burrowing strokes starting from her core, connecting her with Nat.

"Jesus," Nat moaned. She threw her arms back over her head, her fists burying themselves in the pillows.

Isabella bent her elbows so her breasts slapped against Nat's with every thrust, her nipples growing harder until they became stiff peaks denting Nat's flesh. A sensation of pure bliss danced through Isabella's bones. Despite her fifteen-year-long marriage to Graham, she'd shared intimate moments with quite a few women during the first fifty years of her life, but it was never as all-consuming as this. She couldn't explain nor rationalise how she felt about Nat and that's how she knew it was the real deal. That's how she knew Nathalie Orange was worth fighting for.

Isabella delivered a few more deep strokes before slowly retreating. "Turn around," she said to Nat's bewildered face.

Nat raised her eyebrows but didn't say anything.

"Come on." Isabella patted her on the side of the butt. "On all fours."

Nat hitched her legs up and spun around. She presented her backside to Isabella and jolts of lust thundered up Isabella's pussy. Before taking position with the dildo, Isabella let a finger wander over Nat's swollen pussy lips. Wetness trickled down her legs and her body shuddered with the need to be satisfied again. Isabella gripped Nat's thighs and with one movement, plunged back into Nat. The angle seemed to please her.

"Oh fuck," she moaned and crashed through her elbows, her shoulders meeting the pillow. "Oh god."

Isabella found her rhythm and pounded into Nat from behind. Nat took the whole length of the toy. It slammed into her deeper with every thrust until Isabella felt her pelvis make contact with the skin of Nat's sweaty behind.

Isabella folded her body over Nat's back and curled one arm around her waist. Her rock hard nipples pushed into Nat's back as her finger found Nat's soaking wet clit. She rocked her hips back and forth in small but deep motions. Her finger flicked over Nat's clit, barely grazing it, but enough to coax louder moans out of Nat with every touch.

"Oh yes, yes." The ecstatic cry came from the pillow in which Nat's face was buried. "Yes." The last one was the scream Isabella had been waiting for. It filled the room and Isabella's heart burst with joy.

She slipped out of Nat, who let herself collapse onto the bed, and quickly undid the straps of the harness, discarding the toy as if it hadn't just given them this pleasure. Isabella poured her limbs over Nat's back and buried her nose in Nat's damp hair.

"You scream so good, baby." She scratched her fingernails over Nat's outstretched arms. "I'm so hot for you right now."

She felt Nat's body convulse with giggles beneath her.

NAT

Nat knew she'd have to give up the act soon. With Isabella, she was as much a dildo-wielding top as she was a well-behaved girlfriend to be relied upon at all times. She could work on the latter though. Isabella slid off her and pressed her hot skin against Nat's side. Nat turned to face her.

"I don't know what it is about you and that blue thing." Nat pushed a strand of brown hair away from Isabella's forehead. "Or when and how you learned to do that... but, Jesus Christ in heaven, you're good at it."

Isabella smiled and the curve of her lips ignited a fire deep inside of Nat. It was a smile tinted with deep satisfaction, spreading joy all over her face. "I bet you'd never have thought it would take a lady on the verge of midlife crisis to fuck you into submission."

Nat chuckled and shook her head. She cupped the back of Isabella's head in the palm of her hand and drew her near. "Thank you for your patience with me. Anyone younger would never have understood."

Isabella's lips brushed against hers, soft and loving. When they withdrew from the kiss, Nat studied the glimmer in Isabella's hazel eyes and the gentle curve of her upper lip and she knew she could wake up to that face for a very long time to come.

"Don't mention it," Isabella shrugged. "I'm wise enough for the both of us." The tiny crow's feet bracketing her eyes crinkled upward as she laughed.

"Next week a reporter from the SCMP is doing a profile on me." Nat tried to inch closer to Isabella but their bodies were already glued together. "I'd like you to be there for the interview."

Isabella arched her thin eyebrows up. "And announce to the Hong Kong population you're off the one-night-stand market?"

"Something like that." Nat ran her fingers along Isabella's back. "I'm sick and tired of running away from what I feel."

"Well," Isabella pecked Nat on the cheek, "that's the closest I'll ever come to letting someone ask for my hand in marriage ever again."

"Does that mean yes?"

"I wouldn't miss it." Isabella tilted her head back and stared into Nat's eyes. "But what happened to one day at a time?"

"Try as I might." Nat eased her body on top of Isabella's. "I'm not that kind of girl."

"I've heard that before. It concerned other types of behaviour, but still." Isabella nodded her head in the direction of the discarded dildo and harness. A smug grin tugged at the corners of her mouth.

"What can I say?" Nat nuzzled her nose against Isabella's neck and found her ear. "I love it when you fuck me." She felt Isabella's muscles tense underneath her. "And I'm not ashamed to say that, for you only, I'm a big fat bottom."

"Well then," Isabella pushed Nat up by her shoulders, "on your back you go." She toppled Nat off of her and, before Nat had a chance to protest or say anything, she straddled her, her pussy inches away from Nat's chin. "Time to use your tongue for other purposes than all this endless talk coming out of your mouth." Isabella grinned down at her. She inched closer and let the palms of her hand fall against the wall for support.

Nat pressed her hands against Isabella's butt cheeks and

pulled her close. She smelled of silicone and orgasms and her scent transported Nat back to a few minutes ago, when she lay face down, her head buried into the pillows, while Isabella fucked her from behind.

She ran her tongue along the length of Isabella's slit, tasting her musky wetness, while pressing her nose into the tiny curls above her clit. With her hands she parted Isabella's cheeks and let her fingers dip down, delving deep into Isabella's flesh. Looking up between the swell of Isabella's breasts, she witnessed Isabella chewing her bottom lip while throwing her head back.

She dug her fingertips deeper into the skin of Isabella's bottom while thrusting her tongue high up into Isabella's pussy. Isabella arched her back in response, pushing her pelvis more into Nat's face. Nat's tongue probed inside of Isabella, lapping up her sweet juices and licking around the rim of her pussy. She avoided Isabella's clit for now, wanting to drive her crazy a little bit longer first. She let the tip of her tongue slither between Isabella's folds, while her fingers explored Isabella's backside more. One finger inched closer to Isabella's pussy lips, while the other more daring one circled the delicate rosebud between Isabella's butt cheeks.

"More," Isabella groaned.

"More of what," Nat wanted to ask, but her mouth was full of Isabella and hardly free to form sentences. Nat sucked Isabella's lips into her mouth and briefly let her tongue flick over her clit. It felt engorged against her.

"Yes," Isabella cried out in response, but Nat held back. Instead of focusing on Isabella's clit, she inserted the tip of her finger into her pussy while licking around it. Her other finger pressed against Isabella's back entrance a little harder, not deep, barely slipping in, just enough to make its presence known and apply some delicious pressure.

Isabella's knees started shaking underneath Nat's arm pits. Nat trailed her tongue in a wide circle around Isabella's clit, both fingers gently probing. It stood in stark contrast to the pounding Nat had received earlier, but then again, as Nat had come to realise, they were two vastly different people.

"Please." Isabella's voice was hoarse, a mere whimper splintering against the wall she used for support. "Oh god, please."

Nat unleashed a frenzy of flicks on Isabella's clit. Isabella bucked closer, shoving Nat's head hard into the pillows. Nat stiffened her fingers and let them both delve a little bit deeper while her tongue twirled around Isabella's clit.

Isabella's entire body trembled as her orgasm convulsed through her. Her legs chained Nat's head to the bed as a stream of juice leaked out of her pussy into Nat's mouth. Nat withdrew her fingers and traced them up Isabella's sides, waiting until Isabella was ready to release her from her leg grip.

"I could have died down there," she said, when Isabella crashed on top her.

Isabella chuckled. "Can you think of a better way to go?"

ISABELLA

Isabella woke up in her guest room in an empty bed. Instantly, a cold fist clenched around her heart. Had Nat done a runner already? She listened for sounds in the apartment, but heard nothing but the incessant hum of traffic outside. She allowed her body to sink deeper into the mattress, her muscles sore and her skin sticky after a night of hardly any sleep and a lot of after dark activity.

Refusing to think the worst, she tried to remember if Nat had said anything about an early morning appointment, but all they had talked about, when their mouths were not busy tending to the needs of various body parts, was how to leave the ruins of their early relationship behind and move on.

Isabella had believed every word Nat had said. Not only

because she desperately wanted to, but also, and even more so, because she knew that if they were to stand a chance, she had to trust her—no matter what. Is this how her trust had been repaid? By bolting out before the crack of dawn?

What time was it anyway? Isabella didn't have a clock in her guest room, only a bed with a set of dirty sheets. She crawled out from under the duvet and tip-toed to the bathroom. From the hallway she noticed Nat's bright yellow t-shirt in a puddle on the floor. If Nat wasn't wearing her t-shirt and she wasn't in the apartment, where was she?

The rasping of keys in the lock startled Isabella. She quickly wrapped a robe around her and hurried out of the bathroom. Nat walked in with a huge smile on her face. Isabella recognised one of her blouses hanging loosely from Nat's frame. Nat carried in a shopping bag and deposited it on the table.

"Breakfast in ten." Nat's eyes shimmered with something unknown to Isabella, something she'd only briefly—fleetingly—seen a flicker of before.

Isabella glanced at the wall clock and was horrified to learn it was eleven a.m. She brought a hand to her mouth.

"I believe I missed my eleven o'clock appointment." She looked around for her phone. Why hadn't her assistant called her?

"Not to worry, Doc. I still had Charlotte's number." Nat winked. "And I rang her to ask if she could cancel your clients this morning. I told her it was a medical emergency."

Isabella's jaw sagged. Before she could say anything, Nat interjected, "You were out like a light. Seriously, I tried to wake you at nine, but I figured you needed the rest." She smiled smugly while lifting a carton of eggs out of the shopping bag. "I made an executive decision. I hope you don't mind."

Isabella minded a little bit. Nat had no business giving instructions to her assistant, but she couldn't be angry with the person standing in front of her when all she wanted to do was kiss her and repeat every single action that had made last night so exquisite. Truth be told, Isabella was secretly happy with the extra hours of sleep she'd gotten. And at least Nat was still there, looking the picture of domestic bliss while emptying the contents of the shopping bag into Isabella's fridge.

"I'm famished." Isabella headed into Nat's direction. "Best get your eggs on, chef."

"Let me take this off first." Nat started to unbutton the blouse she was wearing. "I'm a very messy cook." She let the silk fabric slide off her and tossed it on the nearest chair. No sign of a bra.

"A naked private chef. At last, my prayers have been answered." Isabella curled her arms around Nat's waist and drew her close.

"Shower. Now," Nat whispered in her ear.

Isabella slid her hands under the waistband of Nat's jeans and learned she wasn't wearing any panties either. She nipped at Nat's neck with her lips, instant heat coursing through her body.

"If you want to make it to your office at all today, you'd better get a move on." Nat tried to sound stern, but the mock harshness was already slipping from her voice.

"There's always time for this." Isabella unzipped Nat's jeans and tugged them off her. Overcome by a bout of extreme lust, she pushed Nat against the nearest wall and spread her legs with her knee.

The eggs could wait.

* * *

After Isabella's last client of the day had left, she wondered if she wasn't the one who needed her head examined. She was about to reach for her phone and call Maddie when Charlotte snuck her head through the gap in the door.

"There's someone here to see you. She doesn't have an appointment, but she's been here before and she claims it's an emergency."

Isabella hid the smile about to form on her lips. This was exactly the kind of trick Nat would play. "Show her in,

Charlotte. You can go home now."

Charlotte turned around and invited *Miss Evans* into Isabella's office by opening the door wide. Nat wore a tight pair of black jeans, a pair of pointed leather men's shoes and an orange t-shirt saying *Taken*.

"I believe you still owe me about thirty minutes of your professional time, Doctor Douglas."

Isabella leaned back in her chair and shook her head. "If I recall correctly, you ordered me to treat myself to some excellent champagne with what was left of my fee."

Nat closed the door behind her and sat down in the chair opposite Isabella. "Did you?"

"I had no reason to celebrate. Not even my obvious superiority." The t-shirt strained around Nat's shoulders and Isabella wondered why she always bought clothes one size too small. It must be a generational thing.

"My word choice can be dramatic sometimes. It comes with the job." Nat folded her hands over her belly and eased into the seat.

"What did you want to talk about?" Already, lust tore through Isabella's flesh. They'd have to get out of her office soon because Isabella had no intention of giving into her desire here. She'd never be able to focus on anything ever again when working.

"My situation has changed somewhat since we last spoke." Nat curled her lips into a small smile. "I've reacquainted myself with the most amazing woman. A really classy bird. I'm desperate for it to work, but well, I seem to have a tendency to fuck things up."

"Could you clarify what you mean by *a really classy bird*, please?" Isabella kept her face as expressionless as possible. Not an easy feat when her heart started thumping frantically and all she wanted to do was rip that silly t-shirt off of Nat.

NAT

Nat noticed Isabella staring at her chest. She hadn't stopped by Isabella's office for a quickie. In her own way, she had wanted to make an attempt at having a genuine conversation in an environment not inviting sex. But Isabella's office suddenly seemed very sexy.

"Someone so posh she should, objectively speaking, be out of my league."

"Do appearances mean so much to you?" Isabella licked her lips briefly and Nat felt heat rise from her center.

"Do I look as if I care about appearances?" Nat pointed both her thumbs at her body. "She's very different from me, and honestly, I'm scared witless. Scared I'll do the wrong thing again. Scared I'll do something that is quite normal in the world I live in, but very alien to her."

"Can you be a bit more specific?"

Nat had trouble finding the right words. Isabella wore her hair up, exposing her long, lean neck. Her pale blue blouse was open at the throat and Nat couldn't keep her eyes off the hollow of her neck that deepened every time she tilted her head. Her brown eyes sparkled and scanned Nat's face and body in a way that, if Nat were to get up, would surely make her knees buckle.

"I guess what I'm asking is how I can make my intentions known, in case I lose it again?"

"Maybe you're asking the wrong question." Isabella leaned forward. She was still a few feet away from Nat, but just the thought of her coming closer made Nat squirm in her seat. "Maybe you should ask yourself how you can make sure you don't lose it again."

"You're good, Doc." Nat slanted her body forward as well. "Worth every penny of that ludicrous fee."

"Tell me, Miss Evans." Isabella uncrossed her legs. "Do

you have a tendency to steer conversations into a deflecting, humorous direction once they start getting serious?"

"Only when I feel as if I have no clue what I'm talking about anymore."

Isabella nodded her head. "I think it's time for another one of our infamous deals." She painted the beginning of a smile on her face. "Why don't you write it down for me? And I'll let you off the hook for now."

"I may need a bit more incentive than that." Nat rose from her chair. She extended her hand, which was shaking a bit too much for her comfort, and waited for Isabella to take it. She hoisted Isabella up and coaxed her towards the door. Nat was quick to slam Isabella against it before Isabella turned the tables on her again. She made sure the door was locked before hitching up Isabella's skirt.

Her hand dived straight into Isabella's panties. Nat was not surprised to find her soaking wet. She slid one finger into Isabella slowly while gazing into her eyes.

"Come for me and it's a deal."

"Mmm," Isabella moaned. Her eyes glinted with lust and she pressed herself onto Nat's finger.

Nat added another finger and slowly, almost teasingly, fucked Isabella against her office door. With her other hand, she undid the buttons to Isabella's blouse and lifted her breasts out of her bra. The exposure to the conditioned air creased her nipples into stiff buds immediately. As she withdrew her fingers from Isabella's pussy to refocus their action on her clit, she pinched one nipple hard between her thumb and index finger, twisting it for more effect.

Isabella came shivering against her, cursing like a sailor.

"Fuck," she said, after Nat had removed her hand from her panties and left Isabella to get properly dressed again. "This is my office, god damn it. This is no place for shenanigans like this."

"A deal's a deal, Doc." Nat unlocked the door. "I'd better get home and start writing."

Isabella shot Nat a smile that wrapped her heart in a warmth so glorious and thrilling, Nat skipped all the way to The Ivy.

She headed straight for her office, pulled a sheet of paper out of the printer and started writing.

Isabella,

I am an irresponsible, hedonistic, spoiled brat. This doesn't mean I don't think well of myself, but when people continuously tell you how wonderful and great you are for years on end, at one point, a certain amount of entitledness settles into you. This is not an excuse, more of an explanation.

I am also a wounded, frightened, and for a large part, emotionally unavailable bottom who thinks she is a top—just another way of fooling myself. I have treated you in an appalling manner because of this, something I will regret for the rest of my life.

We are an unlikely pair, but, I guess that ever since I got my heart broken three years ago—and I became convinced love was forever out of the question for me—I've been waiting for someone like you to come along. Not someone who could save me from myself (what does that even mean?), but someone who could hold up a mirror to my face and make me look for such a long time, I couldn't hide anymore.

You are that person.

No matter what happens between us, I will always be grateful to you for opening my eyes and making me see there is so much more to life than the pathetic little world I had created for myself.

As much as I believed to be set in my ways, the comfort my (let's call it frivolous) behaviour brings me pales in comparison to what you bring to the table. The sparkle in your eyes when we greet. That bossy grin when you pin me down and know that, once again, you have won. Waking up next to you and not wanting to run away for the first time in years.

In the short time I have known you, you have broken me down and given me the opportunity to build myself back up. You've changed me. Already.

The fact that you have given me a second chance after I hurt you so much (and so recklessly), speaks to the greatness of your heart. Before I met you, when I couldn't sleep and tried to conjure up the perfect woman, someone like you never popped up on the catwalk in my mind. I had to meet you to find you. I had to fight you to find you. Now that I have, I couldn't be happier. I couldn't be more me—something I haven't been in a long time.

I can't promise I'll be perfect, but I promise I will try.

Love,

Nathalie (Orange)

Nat usually didn't show people first drafts, but this one had bled straight from her heart. She shoved it in an envelope, licked it shut the old-fashioned way and dropped it in Isabella's mailbox in the lobby downstairs.

Then, she waited.

ISABELLA

Isabella grinned at the huge cake in front of her shaped in the form of a voluptuous bosom. It had Nathalie Orange written all over it—she probably had them modelled after her own.

"Why did you let her do this?" Isabella faced Alex. "Such vulgarity to mark such a milestone in my life."

"Do you honestly believe I hold any authority over Nat?" Alex slapped Isabella on the shoulder. "I'm so glad you've taken her off my hands. Obviously, you're so much better at dealing with her than I am."

"Stop gossiping about me," Nat interjected. "I'm standing right here." She was dressed in a tight-fitted, low-cut tuxedo, her hair gelled back and her swag on fire. "And baby, if turning fifty doesn't earn you the right to blow out candles sticking from marzipan nipples, then nothing ever will." Nat's arms curled around Isabella's waist and Isabella allowed her body to slide against Nat's. She could hardly wait for the celebrations to end so she could tug that tux off of Nat's frame.

"You need to give Nat some credit for handling the fact she's weeks away from shacking up with a fifty-year-old so well." Maddie joined the conversation.

"Hey, it's not because you're stealing my flatmate that I need to get the U-Haul out as well." Nat tightened her grip around Isabella's waist. Their relationship had not progressed as quickly as Maddie and Alex's, but it was definitely going in the right direction.

"I told her she can't move in before she gets rid of at least half of those ridiculous t-shirts she wears." Isabella squeezed Nat's arms.

"What am I doing with this woman who doesn't appreciate a splash of colour in her life?" Nat asked.

Isabella spun around under Nat's embrace and looked her in the eye. "Their colour is hardly the problem, darling." Nat's blue eyes sparkled.

"Enough bickering already. I want a piece of this boob cake," Alex said.

"You always do, babe." Maddie slung her arm over Alex's shoulder and all four of them chuckled.

"It's my cake, so I'll do the honours." Isabella pecked Nat on the lips and struggled free from her embrace. She divided the cake in four large pieces of half boob and distributed them amongst her three favourite people.

"We need an Irish coffee to go with these." Nat headed towards Isabella's liquor cabinet. "The lady must not stay sober on her fiftieth."

* * *

An hour and two strong Irish coffees later all four of them sat watching the sun set from Isabella's roof terrace.

"What a year," Isabella said. "Remember my forty-ninth, Maddie? We sat here on this terrace feeling very sorry for ourselves."

"We both hadn't had any in months and even a few

bottles of champagne didn't bring out our festive spirit." Maddie sipped from her coffee and pulled a face. She'd never be the whiskey drinking type, not even accompanied by coffee.

"I think my exact words were, 'if things don't change soon I'll be as dry as the Gobi desert by the time I'm fifty.'" Isabella glanced at Nat, who sat grinning stupidly.

"Well, I do hope you will all show your gratitude to me for the rest of your now very moist lives." Alex, as always dressed in a tank top, folded her hands behind her neck.

"You? You're not responsible for this, Pizza." Nat swept her hand through the air over the table. "This is all my doing."

"As always, delusions of grandeur," Alex said. "You had nothing to do with it."

Isabella enjoyed the banter between Nat and Alex. She knew what Alex meant to Nat, and despite trying very hard not to show it, how sad she was to see Alex leaving her flat.

"I moved in here," Alex continued, "and that started it all."

Nat shook her head. "If it hadn't been for me, you'd never have gone near Maddie. You were petrified."

"Allow me to remind you that if it hadn't been for me, you'd have pushed Isabella right out of your life just because you were frozen with fear."

Isabella locked eyes with Maddie and shot her a smile. They might have been sitting in the same spot as last year, but everything else had changed dramatically. She remembered the first time they'd all gathered on her terrace together and the instant attraction she had felt toward Nat—how clueless she had been.

It had been two months since she had found Nat's letter in her mail box, scribbled in almost illegible hand writing, but the emotions behind it were more than clear. As a declaration of love and intent, it sure had hit home. They hadn't looked back since. Nat had spent every single night at Isabella's. When Isabella left for work, Nat headed down to her apartment to write, but she was there every evening and every weekend.

They had spent Christmas and New Year's Eve together and had booked a trip to Phuket together with Maddie and Alex for Chinese New Year.

Maybe Isabella had been afraid to see it, but once they had taken the last hurdle, their affair had advanced just as rapidly as her best friend's. Maybe she *should* ask Nat and make it official. She was fifty now. What was she waiting for?

NAT

Nat sat slouched in her favourite arm chair in Isabella's living room. It overlooked the window and the million twinkling lights of the Hong Kong night. Isabella didn't know that Nat often came here during the day when she was out. Just to sit and think and make some notes. She didn't tell her because— she didn't really know why. Maybe because she had forced herself to forget what the natural stages of a relationship felt like. Was it normal to want to be in someone's house even when they weren't there? To want to be around their things and be surrounded by their essence? Nat didn't have a clue so she didn't talk about it.

After Maddie and Alex had left, Isabella had gone quiet. She lay stretched out on the sofa, her legs crossed at the ankles, staring at the ceiling.

"Have you got the midlife blues?" Nat asked in a soft voice. "And more importantly, is there anything I can do about it?"

Isabella turned on her side, supporting her head on a bent arm. "You can come closer."

Nat jumped out of the chair and sank down on the carpet next to Isabella. Isabella raked her fingers through Nat's gelled hair.

"You looked very handsome today."

"Who?" Nat pointed a finger at herself. "Moi? In this old

thing?" She'd had the tuxedo tailor made. They usually didn't come with a plunging neck line.

Isabella's hand snuck down to Nat's neck. "Yes." Her fingers squeezed the sensitive spot at the base of Nat's neck. "You."

Nat let her head fall back on Isabella's hand. "Hey, guess what?"

"What?" The sound of Isabella's voice drifted lazily over Nat's head.

"I quite like the thought of being with a fifty-year-old cougar." It was Nat's way of expressing her love.

"An age difference of less than fifteen years hardly makes me a cougar. You really should do better research."

"You know me, Doc. I like to wing it." Isabella's hand had snuck beneath the collar of Nat's top and her nails scratched lightly over the skin of her back.

"Do you want to move in with me?" Isabella's hand stopped and Nat felt her muscles tense. Did she hear that right? She sat motionless for a few seconds, before turning to face Isabella.

"I understand if you think it's too soon. I know you value your independence. You can always keep your place as an office…" Isabella's words came quick and clipped.

Nat rose from her spot on the carpet and kneeled in front of Isabella. "Do you mean you are inviting me to live in a penthouse three times the size of my flat, with a roof terrace, a dish washer and a sexy cougar doctor as accessories?" Adrenalin rushed through her blood. She masked her growing excitement behind a crooked grin. "I'll need a second to think about that." She closed her eyes for a moment. "The answer is yes."

A wide smile took over Isabella's face, a sight so glorious Nat had to swallow the beginning of a tear away. She pushed herself up and straddled Isabella in the sofa.

"Does this mean you want to keep me, Doc?"

"I've thought about it long and hard for about ten

minutes." Isabella curled her arms around Nat's neck and drew her in. "You're a keeper."

"Can I turn the furthest bedroom, the one where you store all your shoes, into my office? All that beautiful light is so wasted on them." Nat had no intention of keeping her flat. It would only remind her of Alex and how she didn't live there anymore.

"Are you saying my shoes deserve darkness?"

"Most certainly not, but will your shoes write my next book?"

Isabella's lips found Nat's mouth. "The room is yours."

Nat hadn't shared a house romantically with someone since Claire. A mere couple of months ago the thought of it would have sent her reeling, escaping into the night, but now, everything was different. Now, she wanted to ring her landlord and end the lease. Find a moving company that could pack up her stuff tomorrow. She couldn't wait to move in with Isabella and call her flat home.

"We must celebrate." Nat's knee already dug between Isabella's legs.

"What did you have in mind?" Isabella's voice softly caressed Nat's ear.

"Have you ever banged someone in a custom-made tuxedo before?"

ABOUT THE AUTHOR

Harper Bliss is the author of the novels *Seasons of Love*, *Release the Stars*, *Once in a Lifetime* and *At the Water's Edge*, the *High Rise* series, the *French Kissing* serial and several other lesbian erotica and romance titles. She is the co-founder of Ladylit Publishing, an independent press focusing on lesbian fiction. Harper lives on an outlying island in Hong Kong with her wife and, regrettably, zero pets. She enjoys talking about herself and her writing process (but mostly herself) on her weekly YouTube broadcast Bliss & Tell.

Harper loves hearing from readers and if you'd like to drop her a note you can do so via harperbliss@gmail.com

Website: www.harperbliss.com
Facebook: facebook.com/HarperBliss
YouTube: youtube.com/c/HarperBliss

Printed in Great Britain
by Amazon